For my da

1. My Sweetest Friend

Manhattan, New York

I had been in love with Terence Bonfant since I was four years old. By the age of 15 I have to admit, even though he had already announced that he was gay, I was still a little bit in love with him. When you bear this in mind it wasn't a surprise that I was the first to see him up there. On the edge of the Bonfant's rooftop, teetering. It had become a habit over the years to glance out of my bedroom window to see what was going on in the grand townhouse that stood directly opposite ours.

That evening, before I spotted him up there, I had been happy as a clam as I practiced the Kung Fu moves Mum had taught me. I punched and kicked imaginary bad guys with a new precision and power. I was delighted, utterly delighted, because I was close. I knew it. Mum knew it. Dad knew it. My sister knew it.

It was time.

That night there were no lights on in the Bonfant's five-storey house. The place looked dead apart from a light on the rooftop garden. There he was. His chocolate coloured hair shone under the Manhattan lights. What on earth was he doing? At first I thought he was just being his usual dramatic self but as I looked closer I saw that he was peering down and he definitely, yes definitely, looked too close to the edge. My heart flew into my mouth.

I pulled on a pair of trainers, ran to the wardrobe, grabbed a fluffy purple sweatshirt and pulled it over my plaid pyjamas. I curled my long brown hair into a bun on top of my head and shot a glance at Terence, out there like a lemming on a cliff edge, all alone. Whatever he was up to I knew I had to get him down. Could this be my moment? What did Mum always say? *Who we are springs forth from what we do.* It was time for me to *do* something. Right then, in that moment – I was pleased, actually *pleased*. If Terence needed me then I, his best friend in the world, would be there for him.

It was just me and my younger sister Kelci in the house because Mum and Dad, as usual, were on a nighttime mission and it was my job to look after her. I sped over to her room – aware that my parents would kill me if they knew I was about to leave her alone. I darted into her room and crept amongst the gigantic piles of comics and clothes on the floor to get to her bedside. She was asleep under the covers with tufts of dusty blonde hair sticking out onto the pillow. She was 13, and looked angelic whilst she was sleeping. Another pile of comics teetered on her bedside cabinet looking like they were about to fall on her head and her glasses lay folded on the top.

'I'm going to leave you just this once,' I whispered, steadying the books with my hand. 'I'll be back as quickly as I can.'

Seconds later I was hurtling across the street and flinging myself at the door of the Bonfants. I knocked hard and yelled like a madwoman through the letterbox.

Give me the strength of a Bear.

Yet the door would not move and no one came. My heart pounded in my ears. I found a rock underneath the sculpted bushes dotted around the front garden, grabbed it then clambered onto the sill of the sitting room window. I drew back my right arm, rock in hand and pounded it through the window. It smashed and I leant in, undid the lock, pulled the window open and climbed through. I raced through the house and up to the roof. There he was. His face, usually so soft and lovely, was pale and sad, lit from below and giving him an eerie glow. Something terrible had happened. That much I knew straight away. All the life had been sucked out of him. But how? My heart ached to see him like this. His puppy dog eyes, with lashes so thick and long they brushed the tops of his cheeks, were empty. It was like he wasn't there anymore, but where was he? My sweetest friend.

He stood on the outer ledge of the roof with nothing – absolutely nothing – between him and the ground below, with his hands clinging to the garden railing, his knuckles sickly white. He wore a faded t-shirt with the faint outline of Elmo's exuberant red face on it, his sleepover t-shirt, making him look about 12 again. He almost never wore t-shirts anymore, only the velvet jackets and cravats we picked out for him in vintage shops. New York shone glorious behind him. The whole scene made me feel queasy. I stood there, still as a mouse whilst his eyes darted around, until finally his gaze met mine.

'Nina!'

His eyes began to fill with shining tears.

'No, no, no, no.'

7

His hands clasped the bar and he swayed back and forth and all I could think of was the massive drop below.

'What are you doing here?' he said, his voice slurred. 'You shouldn't be here. You can't see me like this … not you.'

I gulped. I wanted to scream at him to get down but I knew that wouldn't work. All I could do was try to appear calm.

'I saw you from my bedroom window, Terence,' I said softly. 'You know I like to spy on you.'

But he didn't smile. Not like he usually would. Neither did he poke fun at me or accuse me of stalking him. He just looked so … lost. It made my heart sit like lead in my chest. I just wanted him to come to me, his usual self, drop into my arms so I could ruffle his hair and we could go downstairs for a hot chocolate and curl up on the sofa together.

'Why don't you come over into the garden and tell me what's going on?'

He didn't look at me. Instead, his eyes rolled in his head.

'I can't do that.'

The wind blew around him, rippling his t-shirt against his chest. I saw a bottle of Scotch sat next to him on the ledge.

'Are you drinking whisky? You could've invited me,' I said, still trying to sound normal.

I gave a nervous laugh, hoping, praying, that he might break out into the smile I knew and loved so well, the same smile that had welcomed me to this street seven years ago – the one he reserved only for me when the rest of the world scowled and pointed out my long, curved nose or imitated my British accent. But that lop-sided, adorable grin made no appearance. He didn't even look at me.

'It's the only thing that makes it stop.'

'Makes what stop?'

His eyes met mine for a second with a crazed look.

'I can't tell you that, Nina,' he replied. 'I can hear them. Can't you hear them?'

'Hear who?'

It felt like the world was beginning to spin around me. I took a deep breath and thought to myself that if only I could concentrate hard enough perhaps I might, just might, be able to hear his thoughts. I focused on him with every fibre.

'Terence, come back over the railing.'

'I don't know what's happening to me. I can hear them! Can't you hear them?'

He lifted one hand from the railing and reached for his hair, scrunching it between his fingers, moaning, leaving only one hand holding the railing. I lurched forward, unable to stop myself.

'Terence, oh god!'

He turned his head to face me, eyes wide.

'Don't come any closer.'

The remaining hand loosened on the bar and his whole body wobbled as he shook his head. He was like a puppet hanging loose on its strings. I stopped moving entirely and stood as still as I could, my chest ready to burst.

'Ok, Ok,' I said, trying to hide the panic. 'I'm here. I'm right here.'

'Just stay back ok?'

His voice was slurred. I watched his feet shuffle further back towards the edge, leaving less and less space between him and the abyss below. I wanted to cry out. His right hand clutched at the railing. Tears fell down his face, like he was a little boy again. I let my eyes scan the area. There was about ten feet between us. It wasn't a clear path from me to him because there were chairs and potted plants all around. I needed to get to him, without him noticing ... one step at a time.

'All right. You don't have to come down but tell me what's going on.'

'You wouldn't understand,' he said, mournful.

'Try me.'

His dark eyelashes were wet and sticky. As soon as I saw him lower them I crept forward one small step, keeping my eyes on him the whole time. He pursed his lips and I remembered how those lips had tasted the one and only time I had kissed them. Sweet and salty all at the same time. And soft, so soft. That kiss had been a game to him, but to me it was the most treasured moment of my whole life.

'It's just...'

He broke down in sobs.

'Everything is just...'

'It's me,' I said tenderly. 'You can trust me.'

He looked at me again.

'It's all too much. I don't know what's real anymore. Dad says I'm making it all up, in my head...'

His words petered out.

'Your Dad?'

His eyes closed again and I took another small step closer.

'When I told Mum and Dad. About being gay.'

I couldn't help but cringe inwardly. When Terence had told *me* he was gay I had thought, right up until the last moment, that he was about to declare his undying love – to me! My cheeks burned at the memory.

'My Dad. He's disgusted by me.'

'Your Dad? He wouldn't say something like that…'

'He didn't have to say it. It's just… what he thinks. I'm a disgrace, I'm not his son any more.'

He swung his head back keeping his hands clamped to the railing. His feet shuffled even closer to the edge. It made my heart stop.

'He doesn't think that. Your parents love you, Terence.'

His parents were the nicest people in the world and good friends with mine.

'No,' he said. 'No they don't. Not now. I couldn't believe it either. But it's true.'

He raised his hand to his hair again, scrunching his eyes closed. I lifted my foot a step further, over the top of a plant pot. He opened his eyes suddenly and I thought he had seen me, until his voice came out softly.

'I can't help who I am, can I Nina?'

The puppy dog eyes returned for a moment as the lights caught the curve of his jaw.

'I love who you are.'

I couldn't stop the tears rolling from my eyes. His head lolled downwards.

'Well, you shouldn't.'

My heart cracked open.

'But I do. I always have.'

I didn't know if he had even heard me. That was not how I had planned to tell him my real feelings. He turned his head away from me and looked over his shoulder. I took another step forward. I was closer now, too far to reach out but closer. It felt as though a new strength was building inside me.

It's going to happen.

'It's different for you,' he said. 'Your family is perfect. There's nothing to deal with, not like this.'

I wished with all my heart that I could tell Terence the truth of my life, what my family deal with every day. But I had never been able to share that with him. No normal people knew the truth about that.

'You don't know how it feels. You don't know how alone I am.'

'You're right,' I said, 'I don't know how it feels.'

I wish I could disappear, fast, reappear by his side, grab him, pull him down…

He frowned suddenly then his voice came out almost as a scream.

'*What?*'

'Huh?'

'Did you say something?'

'No.'

'Oh no,' he said, grabbing for the bottle. 'It's happening again.'

He guzzled the whisky.

'*What's* happening again?'

He gasped.

'I'm going insane.'

'Please, Terence. Just come down.'

He lolled his head to the side and I remembered how playful, how innocent we were as children.

'I can't… face it… anymore.'

He took one hand from the railing and a horrible sense of doom came upon me.

'Terence, no…'

My mind scrambled. Should I leap forwards? Try to grab him?

'We can talk with your parents, make sure you get help, I'll help you. I promise.'

He brought his eyes back to mine with a distant stare. His shoulders sank and his voice came out a whisper. He looked empty, utterly alone, all the life, all the laughter – gone.

'I can hear them. Can't you hear them?'

'I don't think I can,' I said, as I edged forward another step.

This time he saw me.

'*Don't* come any further.'

That's when he took both hands off the railing. My chest almost burst. All I could do was look at him.

'I'm so sorry,' he said, eyes brimming with tears. 'It's just easier for me, this way. You weren't supposed to be here. I'm so sorry.'

'Terence, please, don't….'

He leant back and let himself fall backwards.

'Oh God. No. Please!'

I heard my own voice but it didn't sound like me – it was more like some terror-stricken creature that itself was about to die. All I could do was run to the edge with my arms outstretched and a scream tangled in my throat. I tried to find him but all I found was a blustery void. Moments later, a nauseating crack. I couldn't breath. I leaned over the railing. I looked down. What I saw made my heart fly apart into a thousand pieces. Terence Bonfant, my best friend, down there on that pavement – like that. It made me sick, so sick – and not just in that moment. What I saw that night makes me sick to this very day.

2. The Peach Ones

It is exactly one year since Terence jumped from the rooftop, and my heart has never stopped aching since. Not once. Maybe sometimes, on the outside, I look like my old self but, deep inside, I will never be the same. Ever. The pain stays with me, a dark cloud that casts a long shadow. It's *always* there, even when the rest of the world laughs and trips along as though nothing ever happened. It's there as I stand at my window, staring at the never-changing spot where he jumped. It's there when I put my make-up on, when I take a shower, when I walk down the street, like a miserable companion that never goes away.

Sometimes the pain gets less and there will be whole stretches of time where it is not so stabbing, not so all consuming, but it always comes back. Whenever I realise he will never *ever* knock on my front door again with some crazy piece of clothing he wants to try on for me. He will never drape his arm around my shoulders and tell me a juicy piece of gossip as we stroll along the sidewalk. He will never make me giggle, braid my hair, tell me a story, describe to me in unbelievable detail a delicious bagel he just ate, or bring me a handful of green M & M's that he's saved for me, because he knows they're my favourite. There's just nothing I can do, when it dawns on me that my best friend won't ever wrap his scarf around me when it's so cold I can't face the wind blasting down our street. Or hold my hand in the snow as our boots crunch through the white powder. Or sneak into a movie with me on a Saturday afternoon, just so I can wish he would lean over and kiss me. It's always that moment when I realise, once again, that he is gone and he's never coming back.

I have replayed that night in my head thousands of times, remembering every detail, going over every word, every look that passed between us, trying to figure out *why*, trying to see what I could have done differently. Sometimes, I can't help but wonder if I should have jumped over that ledge too and in a way, it feels like part of me did. It's the same part of me that is just as lost as Terence was. In the end, it always comes out the same. Even though I was all he had, I could not help my best friend in his darkest hour.

Today I am with the one person, apart from my family, who didn't crucify me for being there that night. Mason Williams, my boyfriend of two months.

'Which do you prefer, baby?' he says, pointing towards the shoes that are on display like the crown jewels in this ridiculously expensive shop. 'The cream ones or the peach ones?'

He knows exactly what day it is and I'm pretty sure this is his attempt to cheer me up. Sweet really. If only shoes could do it. Which ones would Terence prefer?

'Peach,' I say.

Terence always said I looked good in pastels. I run my finger across the leather noticing how the purple of my nail contrasts with the pale, orangey tones of the shoe. If Terence were here we would spend ages browsing, trying to act like we were old enough to buy stuff in a shop like this.

'Sounds good,' says Mason, turning to the beautiful shop assistant who hovers in the corner like a gazelle hiding in a forest.

'We'll try a pair of these peach ones.'

She looks him up and down, frowning a little. He flashes her a smile and looks at her like 'don't-you-know-who-I-am'? He's been doing that a lot lately, ever since he posted some videos on the internet of him singing and they got a few thousand hits. However, the girl clearly does not know him from Adam but so far I haven't had the heart to tell him that there are *a lot* of people living in Manhattan and the chances of a stranger having seen one of his videos is pretty slim.

'We'll try the peach ones,' he says again, raising his eyebrows.

She turns on her heel and disappears into the back of the shop. He turns back towards me and flicks his hair to the side, as is his custom. I didn't start going out with him because of his online stardom, or because of his hair. I started going out with him because he stood up for me, when no one else would. It happened two months ago, early on a Sunday evening when I was at Charlotte's, the frozen yoghurt place where all the kids from the neighborhood go, sketching outfits in my notebook. I was alone as usual. I spent most of my time outside the house alone, on account of my newfound position as a social pariah, that is unless I was with my sister, in which case that would make two social pariahs – the only difference is that my sister *chose* to be one, and I never did.

And so I sat that day, nibbling on my mango and kiwi yoghurt, covered in strawberry sauce, minding my own business, until Jenna Kutz, one of the girls from East Park, the private girl's school I go to, came over – a girl I *used* to know and say hi to in the hallways. It took her all of ten seconds to accuse me of 'killing her friend Terence.' I almost spat out the contents of my mouth when I heard that. *Her friend?* Terence had never so much as mentioned her in all the years I had known him. It amazes me how many 'best friends' Terence suddenly had after he was gone. It wasn't long before a couple more girls joined in, hemming me in to my booth, making it impossible for me to leave.

Just when I thought I might drown in my own embarrassment, Mason showed up out of nowhere, and told the girls to shut up and leave. Just like that, in front of everyone. And because he's Mason Williams, and he's one of the most well liked guys at the boy's private school, Magnus Heights, they did. In fact, they skulked off and have never spoken to me since. I still don't know why he did that. He was in the same year as Terence, but they never really knew each other, and he didn't know me either. But he did what he did that day, and I'm thankful for it. Much to my astonishment, he stayed to buy me another frozen yoghurt and ever since then, we've dated.

'I can't wait to see you in those shoes,' he says.

'Yes, they are pretty.'

'Oh my god your British accent is so gorgeous. Damn. Every time you speak it makes me want to kiss you, girl.'

I feel my cheeks warm. He's always saying this kind of thing. These American boys are so forward, not like the British boys I remember from childhood who showed they fancied you by either ignoring you or picking on you.

'My English rose.'

I look at him and see that there's no denying the fact that he's gorgeous. His skin is smooth like caramel and his cheeks slant in towards full lips. His eyes are dark green and constantly alive. I still can't believe we're dating. He's my first actual boyfriend, much to the displeasure of my entire family. Most mothers would be delighted to have his handsome face brought home by their daughter, but not mine. My mum wishes I was too busy training to think about boys. I know what she wants for me, I know what they *all* want for me – and it isn't this. I sigh heavily at the thought.

'What's up, cutie?' says Mason, brushing my chin with his finger. 'You're not thinking about Terence are you?'

His eyes shimmer with concern. He knows I still have days when I can't get out of bed, when all I can do is lie in the blackness until Mum comes in to open the curtains. I shake my head and give a half smile.

'No, no,' I say. 'I wasn't.'

He tenderly puts a lock of hair behind my ears. The shop assistant reappears holding a luxurious box the colour of faded gold. She opens it in silence as though we are being shown something of religious significance, revealing a pair of high heels cushioned in velvety material.

'Oh my,' I say.

Mason's eyes widen.

'Try them on.'

The shop assistant pulls them out as if handling pieces of fine art and as I step into them I pray to myself, whilst holding onto Mason's arms, that they will fit.

'Ah,' he sighs, as my feet slip into the shoes. 'Beautiful.'

I walk over to one of the mirrored walls. They are impressive shoes, no doubt about that. I flatten down the front of my light tan dress which flares out from my waist and touch the blue rose which sits in my hair. Terence would absolutely love these.

'Perfect,' says Mason. 'We'll take them.'

'You don't have to do that,' I say. 'I mean, really.'

'Yes I do. I want to.'

I smile at him and squeeze his hand. This is the first time anyone apart from my mum has bought me shoes. It feels nice – that is, it feels nice until I realise Terence will never have a pair of beautiful shoes bought for him by a beautiful guy. Knowing how much he would have loved that takes all the joy out of the moment. The store assistant wraps and boxes the shoes and continues to eye us suspiciously, even as she returns Mason's credit card. Once the shoes are in a pretty brown bag, we walk out of the shop onto the street outside.

3. Tea & Cake

Manhattan, New York

A wave of noise and movement hits us as curls of steam roll up from the sidewalk. Mason hands me the bag, beaming. I catch him looking at himself in the reflection of a shop window as he flicks his hair again.

'Your hair is perfect, Mason,' I say, rolling my eyes.

I've never been around the male species much before – just my Dad who would never do such a thing and then Terence… and well, he had lovely hair but he never messed with it like Mason does.

'I know my hair is perfect, princess,' he answers, reaching over with one arm to lightly tap my nose as he places the other arm across my shoulders, hugging me in towards him.

He gives me a cheeky smile, then tries to squeeze my cheeks.

'Enough,' I say.

I bat his hand away from my face, but I find myself unable to resist smiling. He looks at his watch.

'We have Afternoon Tea booked for three,' he says, pulling out his shades and putting them on. 'That's what you wanted isn't it?'

I nod.

'You're the first girl I've dated who wants to drink *tea* with me all the time.'

I raise my eyebrows.

'I'm British!'

'How could I forget?'

'Without tea, I would be swallowed up by all this… *American-ness!*'

I gesture at the skyscrapers towering all around us. Secretly, of course, I wouldn't want to be anywhere *but* here.

'Besides,' I say, 'are you saying you've been out with other girls?'

I know full well he has, I knew that about him before we ever spoke. It doesn't take a genius to realise that Mason Williams has dated *a lot.*

'Yes, but you are the loveliest.'

He lowers his head and kisses me on the cheek. The warmth of his lips sends a glow from my face to my feet. We walk along the crowded street, past the tourists, the businessmen, past a homeless man sat in a doorway with his feet wrapped in bits of garbage bag. I turn to the buildings that are plastered in glowing advertisements, a multitude of faces smiling down. Without warning, a scream fills the air, making my heart miss a beat. I turn my head towards the noise, close by, and see a man wearing a baseball cap, his face partly covered by a bandana, running away from a woman with a handbag clutched in his hands. Mason pulls away from me but immediately, I pull him back, clinging to his jacket.

'What are you doing?' I say.

'Did you see what just happened?'

'Yes!'

People swarm around us. He peers into the crowd. The man with the handbag has already disappeared.

'We shouldn't get involved,' I say.

'Why?'

He's frowning, craning his neck.

'I don't want any trouble,' I say, my voice rising, my fingers wrapping tighter around the edges of his jacket.

I've had enough strife to last a lifetime.

'Please Mason.'

I feel tears stinging the backs of my eyes. He looks at me, questioning. I glance over to the woman. She looks lost and upset and it makes me feel a stab of guilt; I should go over there, say something – she's confused – but I can't… I just can't.

'There's nothing we can do,' I say, in dismay. 'We'll just make it worse. The cops will take care of it.'

I turn my gaze away from the scene.

'There's people with her now,' he says, peering over. 'He got away though. Damn.'

Up until a year ago, I would've jumped at the chance to chase that guy. I would've torn along at his heels, because I considered it my duty to 'protect' the citizens of New York. That's all I ever used to do. I tried to arrest a boy being mean to a dog in the park once. I found seats for old ladies on the bus. But those days are gone, and looking back, it's like I was a completely different person. I grip on to the shopping bag.

'Come on, Mason. Let's go.'

'Tea,' he says.

I nod.

'Yes, tea.'

We reach Mason's car which is a moody looking Mustang. As I slide into the leather seat I think about how my parents would never buy me such a thing, even though they could afford it. Perhaps Dad would, if I asked sweetly enough. But then Mum would veto the whole deal, saying I had to work for it or something. Had to *earn* it. I turn to Mason who looks more like a boy now than ever behind the thick, leather-clad wheel. Then I glance out the window and see that two cops are stood next to the woman. I bite my lip. I hope she's all right.

A little while later we find ourselves at Mrs Smith's Tea Room: my favourite place in the city. It's been here for generation upon generation, run by the same English family, a legend of the Upper East Side. We open the door which creaks as we walk in. Teapots of all shapes and sizes line the walls, small tables are covered with tablecloths and the smell of baking fills the air, reminding me of London.

We are seated by one of the waitresses, a plump girl with rosy cheeks and shoulders you just want to hug. We are on first name terms, Cathy and I, because I come here so much. She sits us next to a table of four girls who I vaguely recognize – they're a few years older than me and I'm pretty sure they went to East Park. They certainly look like it with their French nails and hip little outfits. They sip from flowery teacups and poke at their phones. Mason smiles at them as we sit down and they all smile back, giving little waves. Here are some people who clearly *have* seen his videos, and he is delighted.

'What?' he says, as he sees me frowning. 'I can't help being loved. It comes with the territory.'

I shake my head.

'You're adorable when you're angry,' he says.

I ignore him and dive into the menu, then order Afternoon Tea for both of us. Cathy bustles back with a red teapot with white spots on it and a selection of sandwiches and cakes displayed on a three-tiered cake stand. I scold Mason when he tries to pour the tea before it has brewed and a little while later, cringe as he overfills his cup and starts drinking from the spoon. Terence would never do that. My mum taught Terence and me how to drink tea from an early age. She tried to teach my sister but she said it was 'too girly' and deliberately kept doing it wrong. At 14 years old, my sister only drinks coffee. Despite this, Mum continues to insist that we never forget our British roots, although there's very little risk of that happening in our house.

Instead of listening to my instructions however, Mason keeps trying to cuddle me. Once we have finished I let him lean in close and he puts his arm around my shoulder, snuggling his face into my neck. I can't help but laugh as his hair tickles my skin and I lean my face close to his for a kiss, but I'm stopped short by the sound of a throat being cleared loudly. I look up from the table and see my sister staring down at us.

'*Kelci?*'

Her fair eyebrows are slightly furrowed and she holds her arms across her chest.

'Hello Nina,' she says, flatly. 'Surprise.'

Mason pulls back from me.

'Kelci… hi…' he says.

Her eyes flick to him for a second.

'Oh. Hey Mason.'

She pushes her black glasses up her nose, then runs her hand through her white-blonde bob.

'What are you doing here?' I say.

'I wanted to stand over you and watch you drink tea.'

'Kelci!'

'Our parents want to see you.'

'What? Why?'

'I can't say,' she replies, glancing to Mason again. 'It's private.'

Everything is private in our family. Like everyone else, Mason doesn't know the truth about us. To him we're just another upstanding family: my Dad the Ambassador and my Mum the Ambassador's wife.

'They want to see me right now? It can't wait?'

'Apparently not.'

'I'm busy!'

She stares at the plates, cups and cake on the table.

'Saving the world, one cup of tea at a time?'

I scowl.

'Not everything has to be about saving the world.'

She raises one eyebrow. Mason looks confused. I kind of smile at him, apologetically. *God, why can't they just leave me alone?*

'How did you know I would be here?' I say.

'Well, it was either this place…'

She gives an unimpressed glance around the café.

'Or Macys. I got lucky.'

She shrugs, and her voice is monotone, but with a distinctly American twang, not like mine which remains as British as it gets. Kelci was eight when we moved here and she likes it 'because the comic shops are better.'

'I do go to other places, you know,' I say.

'Right,' she replies, sighing. 'If you say so. Are you going to come back with me or what?'

She wears a scuzzy t-shirt which is large and pink and says 'I AM A BIG DEAL #1', plus a mangled pair of jeans with gaping holes at the knees. *Sometimes it is beyond belief that we are actually related.* And there's something different about her hair, the fringe looks much shorter than it did this morning, it sits too high on her forehead, and it's suspiciously lop-sided.

'Did you cut your own hair?'

'No. Babs ate it.'

Babs is Mum's cat.

'You *did* cut it,' I say, dismayed. 'Again!'

We agreed she wouldn't do that any more, that she would let me cut it at least, even if a trip to the hairdressers was too much to ask. The fringe has been hacked so harshly it does *nothing* to accent her beautiful baby blue eyes. Believe it or not, once upon a time Kelci was the most adorable child in the world. She was sweet and smiley and blonde and cuddly. I used to try and dress her up like a doll, in fact sometimes I worry that's why she grew up to be such a public eyesore. I just don't understand why anyone would *want* to look so weird. She continues to stare at me.

'My hair is my own personal statement of emancipation.'

'*What?*'

Mason and I exchange a bemused look.

'It's not even straight,' I say.

She rolls her eyes.

'Nina, you have a flower on your head right now. Do not talk to me about how I look.'

I sigh, but her voice softens.

'Look, Mum and Dad really do want to see you.'

'It's not a good time…'

She drops to her knees, crouching at the arm of my chair.

'Sis, they need you – I need you. I wouldn't have come here if it weren't important.'

'I thought you came to watch me drink tea?' I say, sullen.

'I do that every day anyway. Please come back with me. I'm willing to be completely heartfelt if I have to be.'

'You? Heartfelt? Not in the last four years at least.'

'Come on, Nina.'

I feel her hand on my arm.

'Kelci…'

She gives me her begging kitten look, complete with fluttering eyes and pouty lips.

'Please, pretty please… Pretty, pretty, pretty please…'

She's doing the silly voice she used to do as a kid whenever she wanted something. It's cute, even if she isn't quite the rosy-cheeked ball of charm anymore. I turn back to the table and look at the empty teapot and the half bitten bits of cake on otherwise empty plates, then I let out another long sigh.

'This better be good.'

'It is,' she says, breaking out into her first smile since she got here. 'I promise.'

'Fine,' I say, turning to Mason. 'I guess I should go.'

He still looks puzzled, but sits relaxed with his arms up along the chairs next to him. Sometimes I wish I could just tell him the truth. But how? What would I say? Look Mason… This might sound odd but… There are people, in this world, right now, who possess the inner powers of animals. Yes, animals! They manifest their gifts in their teens and go to secret Academies to train. Pretty weird, right? Right! Oh, and my whole family possesses those powers. All of them except me. My Mum can fight like a Tiger – literally. And my Dad can swim like a Fish – underwater, for hours at a time.

'Shall I come with you?' he says. 'Maybe there's something I can do to help?'

I shake my head silently, and bite my bottom lip. Those with the powers, I would tell him, have a name for themselves. Anitars. And once they're trained they devote themselves to making the world a better place. I stare at Mason's face and wonder, if I told him, right this minute, would he think that I was completely mad? But my heart sinks as I realise, once again, that the hard, cold fact of the matter is – I can't tell him any of it. Ever.

'Sorry about this, Mason,' I say.

'If you have to go, you have to go,' he replies.

He reaches out to touch Kelci's shoulder across the table.

'You guys call me if you need me.'

She looks at his hand as though it's a massive spider.

'Let's split,' she says turning to me, speaking through pursed lips.

I hug him, kiss him on the cheek then follow Kelci out the door.

4. Big Almond Eyes

Gregory Residence, New York

Kelci has been tight-lipped all the way home despite my pleas for information, giving me no clue as to what to expect as I enter the sitting room through the double doors. As soon as I'm inside my heart flips. Right in the middle of the room stands a tall woman dressed head to toe in brown leather. She's got dark exotic skin and she's definitely the sort of woman you could legitimately call 'handsome'. The cascading chestnut hair crowns the whole look. Her big almond eyes are watching me. My parents are also here, standing close by the grand piano. The whole scenario has me feeling hunted. My parents are hanging back with apprehensive but hopeful looks. Dad's got his arm around Mum, like he's not-so-subtly trying to hold her in check. Mum holds her cat in her arms, sinking her fingers into the thick, tiger print fur. Babs is a Red Cat, the companions of many Tigers, or so I'm told.

'Hi, darling,' my parents say in unison.

Kelci takes my hand, squeezes it and gives me a look, as if to say – listen to what the woman has to say – before going over to stand next to our parents, leaving me alone in the middle of the room being stared at by this woman in leather. *What the hell does she want?*

Her eyebrows rise.

'That will come, Miss Gregory. But let me introduce myself first.'

What will come? Her accent is thick, foreign. I can't place it.

'I am Persian,' she says.

Is she reading my mind? My palms are getting sweaty. Does this mean what I think it might? She narrows those eyes making the black lashes meet for a moment, then she steps forward holding her hand out towards me. It's like I have no choice but to take it, yet - believe me - I would much rather be running back out the door, *back to Mason, back to drinking tea.* She frowns a little. *Ok, shut up, shut off your mind – don't think. Do not think.*

'It is a great feat to clear one's mind entirely of every thought. Some people devote their entire lives to it,' she says, shaking my hand. 'My name is Artemiz, pleased to meet you, Miss Gregory.'

I let out a massive sigh. Her hand is warm and strong. I get the feeling she could crush my hand if she wanted to and she *is* reading my mind. I glance towards my parents and Kelci who look like they're cheering me on from the sidelines. Why do they have to do that? They know damn fine how I'm bound to feel about this, but they've trapped me into it regardless. Babs leaps from Mum's arms, lands like a miniature tiger, then sticks her bushy tail in the air and walks out the room.

'Look everyone, I think I know where this is headed and I really just … don't want anything to do with it. Let's not waste our time here.'

Artemiz ignores me.

'I am here as a representative of Muldoon Academy.'

This really makes my heart flip. The words I had longed to hear every day of my life up until exactly a year ago today. There's no denying it. *This woman is an Anitar. She is a Horse. And she is here for me.*

'So you understand perfectly,' she says, bowing her head.

The one thing I wanted, before Terence died, was to manifest my own one of the Twelve Animals. To become an Anitar. Just like this woman. Just like my parents, just like my sister. God knows I had been trying every day for years before that. We both had, my sister and I. All we'd wanted was to be like them. But that was then, and this is now.

'We want you for the Manifestation Program,' she says.

Mum, Dad and Kelci look like it's Christmas morning and they're watching me open my presents.

'You've got to be joking. Guys, please!'

This is just too much. Muldoon. The Anitar Academy where Mum and Dad first met. The finest in the world and not to mention the place Kelci is going when she turns sixteen. My parents' eyes shine like their dreams are coming true. Despite it all, I do love them so much and seeing the hope in Kelci's eyes, for a moment I feel like I'm letting everybody down. Again.

———

33

'You won't let anybody down,' says Artemiz.

I turn to her abruptly.

'You have to stop doing that.'

'I did the same program,' says Mum, as though unable to stop herself. 'That's how I manifested!'

As if I didn't know already. Dad gives one of his calm smiles and tightens his grip around Mum's shoulders. Mum is a Tiger, of course. Even knowing nothing of Anitars, you would be forgiven for noticing that there is a definite shade of tiger in my mother. There's the auburn hair that rises up from her face, always thick and full. The green-yellow eyes that shine fiercely. The slender body, the sleek movements. It's not hard to imagine her fighting like a tiger. She's not afraid of anything and, like the other Tigers, so she told us, she brings her emotions under control using Kung Fu every day. As my Dad frequently says: 'Tigers are fire-crackers.'

'Mum, you accidentally broke your friend's arm during a play fight before you did that program, it was *obvious* you were going to manifest.'

'You still have a chance, Nina.'

'I didn't manifest when I needed it, so I'm definitely not going to manifest on some program.'

I drop my shoulders, feeling ensnared, willing this conversation to be over. *Everyone please just leave me alone.*

'Just like me,' she says to my Dad. 'Stubborn and hot headed. I wouldn't be surprised if she's a Tiger, after all.'

Mum's been saying this since I was a little girl.

'I'm *not* like you.'

'Yes you are, Nina. And you're an Anitar, through and through.'

Why does she push me? Even now?

'I am *not* an Anitar. I never was. And I'm not now.'

Livid tears form in my eyes.

'Alright, alright,' says Artemiz, holding her hand out behind her towards Mum. 'You have a point Nina, there's a very low chance you would manifest with your track record so don't get too excited.'

'I'm not getting excited! You can read my mind can't you? I am literally not excited at all.'

'But you do have some potential, even if it is hazy. A Horse can not waste her time on no-hopers.'

But that is exactly what I am.

She is peering at me, as though trying to reassure herself she is right. She can recognise *potential* powers in others but from what I hear it often comes to nothing, even if the person does one of these Manifestation Programs and if they don't manifest – well, they're sent home with their memories wiped of the entire thing. And by guess who? A Horse. I shudder. *I would never be a Horse.*

'The Program will help you find yourself,' says Artemiz.

'I know what I want be. I want to be a stylist, or maybe a fashion designer and I want to live a perfectly normal life that doesn't lead me into near death situations every five minutes.'

I raise my chin to add emphasis.

'I don't care who knows it. I'm willing to be judged for my choices.'

Mum lets out one of her exasperated sighs. I pout my lips.

35

'Nina,' says Kelci. 'We would be at Muldoon together.'

I get a sinking feeling in my stomach. That's all either of us had ever wanted, once.

'We wouldn't be together necessarily. I'm sorry I just... Can't pretend.'

Can't pretend I would make it because I wouldn't. You already manifested, I didn't. End of story. Artemiz tilts her head.

'Won't you just try?' says Kelci.

'I don't want to be an Anitar, I don't want to live my life in secret.'

Artemiz is frowning, still studying my face. Kelci lets out a sigh. *Mind – shut up! Shut up, shut up, shut up. Just look at the clock. Think of nothing. Stare at the clock.* My family watches me like I'm going crazy. Artemiz looks almost sorry for me and walks up, putting out an arm that seems almost protective.

'Nina, my darling,' says my Mum. 'We only want what is best for you.'

'I know,' I say. 'But *I* am the only one who knows what's best for me.'

'This really is something so special,' she says. 'Your Father and I... We just love you so much.'

'So you need to let me do what I want with my life.'

'There was a time when you wanted to manifest. Remember how I taught you Kung Fu?'

She pulls away from Dad.

'Yes I remember. But that time's gone now.'

'Nina, my love, you can't let what happened with Terence ruin all your chances. You didn't do anything wrong.'

'Tell that to everyone at East Park.'

'I know how close you two were and how horrible the whole thing was, but you still have so much potential.'

Mum looks despairing as usual. Artemiz puts herself directly between us.

'Let me speak to Nina alone,' she says. 'It would be best.'

'I really don't want to speak,' I say, folding my arms across my chest.

'You have *no idea* what you are giving up,' says my Mum.

I huff.

'Nina, show me to your bedroom please,' says Artemiz.

I purse my lips and reluctantly head in the direction of my room. I hear Mum's voice as we leave.

'All I'm saying is, the whole thing was *not* her fault.'

Artemiz moves around my 'weirdly neat' (according to Kelci) bedroom, looking dramatic against the pastel colours and creams. She's really quite scary, not least because I've never actually met an Anitar from outside the family. She takes my dressing table chair, swings it around and sits down so her legs are wrapped round the back. I perch on the bed.

'Would you like to know what I think Nina?'

No, definitely not.

'It is not this desire to lead some sort of "average life" you claim that pushes you forward.'

'Very insightful, however…'

'You didn't kill that boy that night but you are letting him kill you. Slowly. By accepting mediocrity. What is this normality anyway? There is no such thing. It's a lie put there by people to keep you small. Mediocrity is the enemy of greatness and let me tell you Nina, *Muldoon* is greatness.'

Terence is killing me … what? All I can do is watch her, open-mouthed, as she rises to her feet again and resumes the pacing. Her voice gets louder and she spins around to face me.

'Forget all this "I can't do this, I can't do that". We don't have time.'

'Please, that's enough!'

I feel tears coming again.

'You are not a victim so why would I treat you like one?'

I reach for a tissue on my bedside table and blow my nose.

'You're not very sensitive are you?' I say. 'Considering you know what I'm thinking. My innermost thoughts.'

'Oh I'm sorry, you expect me to pussyfoot around you? I'm not a kitten, I don't have paws. I'm a horse. I gallop.'

I sniffle. *Does she think she's actually a horse?* She glares at me.

'The point is I'm not here to tell you what you want to hear. I'm here to tell you the truth.'

I scrunch the tissue up in my hand and throw it at the wastepaper basket, watching as it misses and lands on the carpet. I speak quietly.

'I am not going on some pointless program.'

'Believe me, for you this program is not pointless.'

'I already tried to manifest. And I failed.'

I did nothing when he needed me.

Her expression softens. She reaches over to my desk and pulls the papers on it towards her.

'Comic strips. Who drew these?'

'I did. Ages ago. Kelci came up with the story, and I drew them.'

We used to love dreaming up the adventures of Anitars and making comics about them, even though neither of us had much of a clue what actually goes on.

'Nice,' says Artemiz with a knowing smile. 'The superhero saves the day…'

'Of course.'

'Only it doesn't always work like that.'

Her dark eyes burn.

'How do you mean?'

'Winning always comes after losing. Sometimes after losing many, many times.'

'Oh.'

'No war has ever been won without the loss of a battle.'

'Terence wasn't a battle, if that's what you're trying to say. He was my friend and he died and I can never bring him back. I'm not *in a* war. All the Anitar stuff, the taking down evil stuff – it's not my thing. It's just not *me*. I don't want that life and I don't want everything that comes with it.'

Artemiz raises her eyebrows.

'I can't just be what everyone else wants me to be,' I continue. 'As soon as I realised I didn't want to be an Anitar anymore, that was it – my family were disappointed in me. But you shouldn't love someone just because they do what you want. Because they fit into *your* plans and *your* idea of who they should be.'

She walks right up to me.

'I do understand your thoughts, Nina. Thank you for sharing them with me.'

She lowers her face to mine.

'Despite all you say and all you think I sense potential in you. It is my job to give you the choice, to let you know what is possible.'

She's so close now I see the pores on her skin. *Lordy this woman is intense.* She stands up straight, her eyes turning from chestnut brown to black.

'That's what they all think.'

'Besides I've seen what my sister went through when she manifested. It wasn't pretty.'

'It's not supposed to be pretty. All your sister needs is training, which is precisely what Muldoon Academy is there for. Let me tell you, a fully apprenticed and trained Rabbit is a fierce and wonderful thing to behold. Their perceptions can extend to hundreds of miles, they are wild fighters, fabulous escape artists, I've never seen *anyone* catch a Rabbit. But it takes time and hard work to get there.'

I cross my arms stubbornly. *Nothing you say will make me think differently.*

'My mind is made up. I don't want it.'

Her voice drops.

'Very well.'

Silence hangs in the air. I grab a cushion and hold it against my chest.

'You are as aware as you can be of what you are refusing?'

'I am.'

'We cannot force you to take part.'

'No.'

She strides across the room and reaches for the handle, giving me one last look.

'As you wish, Miss Gregory.'

With that, she opens the door and leaves.

5. Happy Birthday, Kelci

Two weeks later, Grand Old New Yorker Hotel

———

The visit from Artemiz was awful. I wish she had never turned up with her long legs and leather suit. It has been so awkward in the house since then, with Mum looking at me like I'm an idiot, Dad looking at me like I'm a dying puppy and Kelci looking at me like she can't even understand who I am anymore. She wanted me to say yes. Of course she did, she wants everything to be like it used to be. She thinks I've 'changed' and that I didn't try hard enough to manifest and that all my new plans are stupid and pointless. She can't stand Mason either, obviously. He's not 'one of us' and worse still, he's popular. But I'm not 'one of us' either, and I'm not the only one that has changed. I'm not sure exactly when Kelci began acting like a surly adult trapped in a teenage body but she did, and sometimes I just plain miss the soft-hearted girl that I know must still exist underneath the sulky face and awful clothes. If it were up to her we would still be on our manifestation rampages together: two powerless fools trying to manifest at all costs. Except there's only one powerless fool left now.

Back then the two of us would go to the most ridiculous lengths. We would hold our breaths under water until we went blue, trying to see if we were Fish, or try to lift benches, hoping we were Bears or attempt, somehow, to disappear into walls like Chameleons, or - craziest of all - spit at each other to check for the venom of a Snake. We ran, hid, fought, crept, hunted. When I jumped out of a tree in the park and broke my wrist it was Kelci who bundled me into a taxi and took me to hospital. And then there was the endless fantasising about which Animal we could be. Hours spent discussing the scant knowledge we had about the Twelve Animals. Listing them off in unison, over and over: *Fish, Bear, Chameleon, Snake, Tiger, Horse, Eagle,*

Frog, Snow Leopard, Deer, Rabbit, Fox. We would spend ages creating our comic strips too. As if any of that stuff would actually work.

We always remained perfectly powerless at the end of each session. Until Kelci manifested that is. But that was nothing to do with any of our efforts. That was just random and terrifying. It happened in the middle of the street as we were walking home with Mum one afternoon, not long after Terence died. She was eating an enormous ice-cream at the time, chocolate and vanilla, and I'll never forget the way she suddenly stood stock still and dropped it to the ground. She bolted forward in a blur, stopping some distance away and looking back at us in total shock. Her hair turned from dusty blonde, to the white blonde it is now. Her skin became softer, dewy and her eyes turned a brighter blue. She stamped her foot and the pavement cracked and the earth started to shake in waves. As people around us began shouting 'earthquake' we ran to her and led her away before anyone realised *she* had caused the tremor. She struggled against us and held her hands over her ears the whole way home. Apparently it doesn't often happen all at once – or at such a young age without a Manifestation Program – but for Kelci that was it. In an instant she was a Rabbit.

———————

Tonight we are here at the Grand Old New Yorker Hotel for Kelci's fifteenth birthday party. She said she didn't want a party of course, but I insisted. I can lose myself, even if just for a while, when I do something creative like designing outfits or planning an event. Besides, *I* take care of birthdays in our family and now she's 15 I finally get to do it properly. My heart swells as I look around at the candles lighting up the tables, the sweet little banners I put up on the walls, and I think of how much Terence should be here. He'd be teasing Kelci most likely, as he always did, calling her 'little miss sunshine' until she snapped at him with one of her insults. She always saved the best ones for him. The two of them bickered more than she and I do, but they loved each other all the same.

A peek out of one of the windows reveals Central Park glittering below. It isn't a big crowd, but it's enough. I used to know a lot more people than this but none of them would come now, so it's basically a smattering of kids Kelci knows from school and a few of our parents' friends. I run my hands down my dress, which is violet, entirely covered in sequins, and has purple slashes running across it. I bought it in a vintage costume shop and I love it. Kelci showed up in a grey t-shirt with a comic book hero emblazoned across the front, even though I bought her the cutest plaid dress to wear tonight. The t-shirt hangs loose over her pale arms. Her hair sits straight and neat at her chin and she has glittery scarlet eyeliner across her eyes. That's something, at least.

My eyes are drawn to Mason. He cradles a glass in his hand and looks super handsome in his cream shirt which makes his skin look good-enough-to-eat honey brown. It's so cute how he smiles and casually lifts his thick eyebrows as he talks to my Dad, who wears the shirt and jacket I picked out for him. It makes my heart skip to see them together. I'm grateful to Dad, for talking to him. This is the first time I've brought Mason to anything like this and I wasn't sure how my parents would react. But Dad is a proper gentleman. You'd have to be a full-blown homicidal maniac for my father to ignore you at a party. He always gives everyone the benefit of the doubt, even those he has to deal with on his missions, or at least I think he does, from the snippets I pick up in conversation. Mum reckons he's too forgiving.

My eyes flit, to find my mother in the crowd and I see her, standing in the corner, haughty and glamorous, holding a bubbling flute of champagne, which I know she will barely sip all night because Anitars rarely drink, it dulls their powers. Her flaming hair is piled onto her head and shining rubies hang from her ears. As I look at her there – beautiful and fierce – I really do wonder how no one else can tell she has the inner Tiger, it seems so glaringly obvious once you know.

She talks to another woman, smiling and nodding but I see her eyes flicking over to Dad and Mason. I know what she's thinking. That boy Mason is not an Anitar, he's leading my daughter astray, distracting her from her 'real' calling. My mother is not subtle. She thinks he's part of the reason I don't want to manifest, but she's wrong about that. I push down the familiar knot of frustration and remind myself that tonight is Kelci's night, despite the fact that she doesn't actually want to be here. The least I can do is make sure she has some semblance of a good time. I scan the room and see her over at the back, away from everyone else, holding a glass of orange juice. I walk across and I swear there's a glimmer of relief in her eyes as I reach her.

'Happy Birthday, sis,' I say.

'How amazing,' she drawls, unamused. 'This is just what I wanted. A party.'

'Come on, Kels, just enjoy it. The beautiful tables, the décor, the people, it's all for you. Your special night. 15 years old, my little sister!'

She looks at me as though I just presented her with a dead cat.

'What?' I say.

She remains silent.

'I would have preferred a ladybird cake,' she says, eventually, a sly smile forming on her lips.

She means the cake I made for her tenth birthday – a ladybird, of sorts. It took me a whole day in the kitchen, and it turned out a bright red splodge with black marks on it, a total mess. She loved that cake. I wish she could love anything I do for her now even half as much.

'That cake was a pinnacle moment,' I say, but as I'm talking, I notice that her half-smile is fading and I see a shade of worry darkening her eyes, just for a moment.

'What is it?' I say.

She frowns.

'It's nothing.'

'Tell me, Kelci. What's wrong?'

She turns her back to the crowd, awkwardly, then speaks in hushed tones from the corner of her mouth.

'I just, I don't know. I don't *feel* right.'

'Oh?'

'I have that feeling again, here.'

She places her hand on her stomach.

'Ok…'

This kind of thing has happened before, since she manifested. Rabbits have this enormous sense of danger and they perceive things, even before they've happened. But before Rabbits are trained, it's out of control. The slightest thing can set them off. There were times, at the beginning, where she would get so worried about nothing, that I would sit with her all night, just so she could get some sleep.

'Nothing bad is going to happen,' I say. 'I've spent way too much time organising this party for that.'

She pushes her glasses up her nose.

'Suppose.'

I feel a warm hand on my back and turn to see Mason at my side, his hand sliding up around my bare shoulders. His soft lips nibble at my ear playfully, and I have to stop myself from gasping as the tingling travels from my head to my toes. Kelci folds her arms and stares at him in disgust, but before she has a chance to ruin the moment any further, the kitchen doors burst open and an enormous cake is lifted along by two waitresses. Five layers of vanilla sponge, loaded with strawberries and thick cream, covered in a dusting of icing sugar with 15 shining, pink candles on top. Exactly as I had planned. People gather round and I beam with delight, as Mason's hand drops to the small of my back. *I never knew the delights of feeling a guy's hand resting right there.* Mum and Dad appear, stood close. The waitresses carefully lay the cake on the table and I give Kelci a nudge towards it. She looks appalled, shaking her head stubbornly – she hates being the centre of attention.

'Go blow out the candles, sis,' I whisper.

Everyone looks at her expectantly. She purses her lips at me, and her eyes flash pink for half a second, then she creeps forward and stands in front of the cake. Everyone sings 'Happy Birthday' to her and, as the candles light up her face, I can't help thinking how, despite the unimpressed expression, she *is* still the cutest girl in the world – with her button nose and soft cheeks and an innocence she tries so hard to hide. The clapping begins and she reluctantly bends forward and blows out the candles, not forgetting to give me a sour look once she is done.

There's a flurry of cake eating but it isn't long before Kelci pinches my arm.

'Can we *please* go home?'

Her eyes are wide.

'It's too early for that, Kels,' I say, twirling in front of her. 'This party is just getting started… Here, have a cheese stick.'

She stares at the cheese stick I'm holding out to her.

'Please. Nina.'

I wave it in front of her face.

'I'm not even kidding,' she says. 'We have to get out of here.'

I drop the cheese stick to the table. Something in her voice has me listening. There's a look in her eyes that I can't ignore – she's scared.

'Alright, sis,' I say. 'Stay calm. Remember? Breathe.'

'Oh god, stop,' she says, looking at me like I'm a mad woman. 'Let's just go.'

We say our goodbyes and it's hard to pull myself away from Mason, knowing that he will stay at the party without me. But Kelci makes her impatience so visible it isn't long before we are spilling out onto the sidewalk. I keep my eyes out for a taxi. The street is quiet, the sky is dark.

'Do you feel better now?' I say, tempted to put my arm around her shoulder.

'I guess, I –'

The loud sound of tires screeching stops her from continuing. I frown. Right there in front of us is a blacked out van. Kelci grabs my arm and I feel her nails dig into my skin. I look at her and see fear turning to terror. The doors of the vehicle open and four men jump out onto the pavement. They're dressed head to toe in grey uniforms, wearing helmets and their faces are covered by grey masks leaving just their eyes visible. My breathing stops. Kelci pulls me along. I run but I am slowing her down. I know she could be gone by now, she's Rabbit fast.

'Let go of me, just go!'

I try to shake her off my arm but she has her hand clamped there. She will not just *go*. I put every last ounce of power into my legs. The men are right behind us. I feel a sharp blow to my side and fall to the pavement. My shoulder hits first then my head, things go out of focus and in again. I look up and see the four men holding on to Kelci.

'No!'

She kicks out with her right leg and one of the men is catapulted backwards, at speed, into the side of a vehicle, creating a body-sized dent in the door. She stamps her left foot and the ground begins to shake. The windows of the nearby buildings rattle and the parked cars vibrate. I clamber to my feet. The men struggle to keep hold of her as she continues to thump her feet on the ground, causing the entire street to judder. I dive forward onto one of the men and punch him as hard as I can in the back of the neck. He turns around and flings me away. I land, back first, on the ground. Pain shoots up my spine and I can't move. I see one of the men prod a long, thin weapon against Kelci's neck. She suddenly goes quiet and everything fades to still as she lies there completely limp.

I cry out as her glasses slide down her face and fall to the ground. Just before they move away I see a symbol on the chest of one of their jackets. A purple flower. Sprouting from a layer of small green leaves. I see her face, eyes closed, head lolling. I fight hard to keep my eyes open. One of the men points to me.

'What about that one?'

'Leave her. Not needed.'

'Kelci,' I whisper.

I see a blurry vision of her glasses on the ground. My eyelids close.

'Please. She can't see anything without…'

Within moments the blackness comes.

6. Breathe

One day since Kelci was taken, Gregory Residence

I open my eyes and take in a massive gulp of air. *Where am I?* My sight is blurred. My head hurts, my back hurts. I can't focus. Panic washes over me. I gasp:

'Where's Kelci?'

I hear my own voice but it's like someone else speaks. My eyes focus in and out, in and out. The lilac walls, the feel of the covers on me. Swaying. Everything is swaying. Then, two strong arms, and a voice I know.

'Nina, darling, you're home.'

'Dad!'

I can't catch my breath. *I can't breathe.*

'Ok, slow down. Look at me.'

His face appears in front of me. I suck in air, then:

'Where's Kelci?'

I'm shouting.

'Nina. Look at me. Focus on my eyes.'

Everything spins. *I can't see him. I'm lost.* His voice comes again, commanding this time.

'Focus on my eyes.'

I drag my eyes onto his. Violet blue. Familiar. Fading blonde hair.

'That's it. Stay focused on me. Breathe.'

My heart fights to get out of my chest.

'Dad!'

I heave air into my lungs. Then out again. In, out. In, out. In, out. I see his eyes, but still… I can't find myself.

'Where am I?'

My arms fly out, grasping, until I find the sheet beneath me. I grab on, my fingers balling into fists. Dad places his hands on my shoulders, gently.

'You're home, Nina. You're home, with me.'

I catch sight of the lightshade hanging from the ceiling behind his head, glowing papery purple. The sketches and little pictures on the walls, the mood boards. The rows of fashion magazines on the shelf, all in perfect date order. The tiny camera I take out on the streets with me. My bedroom. He holds his gaze steady, right in front of me. I keep forcing air into my lungs, then let it out again, it's all I can do. I don't know how long it takes for my breath to settle, but as soon as it does I try to think. I let go of the sheets then clasp onto Dad, unable to stop my nails digging into the muscles of his arms.

'How did I get here?'

He loosens his grip on me.

'We found you.'

'But no Kelci?'

'No Kelci.'

There's despair in his voice. I can hear it. He's trying to hide it, he doesn't want me to hurt, he can't *stand* to see me hurting, but it's there. I see it in his eyes too – just like it was after Terence died. He didn't know what to do then, but this time, it's worse. *His baby girl is gone, and it's my fault.* I almost choke on the thought.

'Where is she?'

He shakes his head.

'We don't know.'

Another wave of panic rises.

'There was nothing I could do…'

'Shhh,' he says, tucking my hair behind my ears, just like he did when I was a little girl at bedtime.

'Nina, sweetheart, take as long as you need to rest. We can talk when you feel better.'

The bedding is covered in sweat. I reach for my hair. It feels like a bird's nest, all matted at the back.

'How long have I been here?'

His eyes turn from violet blue to aqua.

'A day.'

I throw my head back, groaning.

'And you don't know where she is?'

'No, we don't. Rest, and you may be able to fill us in on what happened.'

I take in a deep breath. I see Babs sat on my windowsill, her bright yellow eyes watching me, her paws perfectly still on the edge. I turn to the bedside and see Kelci's glasses laid there.

'Oh.'

Horror fills me.

'Dad, Kelci's glasses – they're here. She's blind as a bat without them!'

I'm shouting again. And losing my breath. I can't imagine… The terror… Those men… A look of misery creeps across Dad's face. The door of my room creaks open and Mum's head appears around the side. She is makeup-less, and her hair lies flat and sad at the sides of her face. There are grey circles underneath her eyes and her skin has turned ashen, making her look much older. It scares me, I've *never* seen her like this before. She creeps up to me and perches herself on the bed, at the other side to Dad, taking hold of my hand. Babs leaps from the windowsill and climbs onto her lap, purring loudly.

'Are you all right Nina, sweetheart?'

I watch her long fingers, familiar, stroking my hand. The rose-gold band around her wedding finger. Her hands are shaking, ever so slightly. I've never seen them shake before – I didn't know they *could*. It makes me feel sick. She shoots a look towards Dad – it's a look I've seen many times before, it speaks of dread that maybe I won't survive. *She thinks I'm crumbling, like before. Too weak to take the pain.*

'I'm ok,' I say, but I can't help wincing.

My back feels like it has been smashed by a hammer.

'What is it?' she says.

'Just my back. And my head.'

Another look passes between them.

'Sol should be here soon,' Mum says to Dad, who nods.

'Who's Sol?' I say.

'He's going to help you feel better.'

I frown, but it's the least of my worries.

'Do you know where she is?'

Mum's eyes are red and raw. Her voice comes out hollow.

'We don't know.'

I let out another groan.

'Nina, darling, tell us what happened.'

Dad's arms wrap around me.

'She's not ready,' he says. 'She's just woken up.'

Mum frowns at him.

'She can talk, she can do it.'

I wonder if they are going to have one of their arguments, where Dad wants to shield his little girl from the horrors of the world, whilst Mum wants to throw her tiger cub right into them, to 'prepare her for life'. But I think all of us know that this is not the time.

'I'm ready,' I say.

I try to pull myself up the bed but I cry out as stabbing pains travel the length of my spine. Dad frowns, shooting a look of

---

frustration at Mum. *He thinks she's pushing me too hard. But this time, she should.*

'Nina, stay still,' he says.

'I'm ok. You need to know this.'

I grit my teeth against the pain and make myself talk.

'We came out of the party, after we said goodbye to you,' I say. 'I was looking for a taxi…'

I tell them what I can remember: the van, the men, the struggle. How Kelci could have got away if it weren't for me. Mum takes in a quivery breath. By now, tears are streaming down my face.

'There was nothing I could do. They just… They had weapons…'

Sounds familiar. Nothing I could do. That same black feeling I had when Terence died is back, except this time the feeling has fingers, long ones, and they are choking me. I sob into Dad's shoulder until there is nothing left. I feel a hand stroking my head. It's Mum, and I think she might be crying too. She's only ever cried in front of me twice before. Once when we left London to come here. And once when Whispy, her overweight old Red Cat, had to be put down at the vets. I hear her blow her nose. Then, her voice.

'Was there anything else, about these men?'

I swallow hard. I feel like there's something more I should tell them… I rack my brains, trying to remember. But there's nothing.

'I don't know, I don't think so … it all happened so fast.'

She nods and wipes her eyes with a tissue.

'We've heard about a few disappearances…'

'Huh?'

'Just in the last few months, Anitars have gone missing in different parts of the world… We don't know why, or who's behind it.'

They knew about this?

'Kelci's an Ambassador's daughter. Maybe they took her for ransom.'

They both look doubtful.

'We haven't had any ransom calls,' says Dad. 'And you are the Ambassador's daughter too, remember?'

That makes me feel like a deflating balloon. He's right. But I keep going.

'Have we called the police? The FBI? We should have them out searching.'

My head buzzes.

'You know we can't do that,' says Mum, clenching the tissue in her hand.

'Of course we can do that! She's a fifteen year old girl. We need everyone in New York to know about it, so we can find her.'

Dad reaches for my arms again.

'Come on Nina, calm down.'

'But Dad you can see how we need to call the FBI, right?'

I give him an appealing look.

'I love you sweetheart, but in this case calling them wouldn't be the right thing to do. We have the resources we need to find her.'

And we all know that the British Ambassador cannot go public with something like this. Especially not one who is secretly a Fish, and an amazing one at that.

'Dad, you still haven't found her and it's been a day. What resources?'

'We have people we trust in the FBI, and the police.'

'You do?'

'Very few, but yes.'

'I thought no one knew about Anitars?'

'There aren't many. Whenever there are more than a trusted handful, all Anitars are in danger.'

I raise my eyebrows.

'Which ones know in the FBI?'

'You know we can't tell you that Nina, darling,' he says.

Holding it all back from me, keeping me out.

'Because I'm not an Anitar. Right?'

He sighs, and so does Mum.

'We have to find her. Now,' I say.

Unless I manifest, unless I train, I can't know anything. I've hated this fact for a long time. It got to the point where I just didn't *want* to know any more, but right now I *need* to know. Who could have taken her? *What is actually going on?*

'I'm calling the police.'

They exchange a look of alarm.

'Nina,' Mum says. 'You know that would put all Anitars in danger.'

'I don't give a damn about *all Anitars*! It's my sister I care about – and you should too.'

The old exasperation flashes across her face, like I am some fool who just *doesn't get it*. But actually, *she doesn't get it*. I may not be an

Anitar, but Kelci is out there, and she needs me, whether I have powers or not.

'Nina, you would be putting your sister in more danger that way,' she says.

I let out a long breath from between gritted teeth. Become an Anitar, they said. Manifest, they said. Get some awesome powers, they said.

'And you honestly wonder why I don't want anything to do with all this?'

Neither of them answer. Babs jumps from Mum's lap, landing with her tail upright, onto the fluffy carpet. Mum rises from the bed and starts backing towards the door.

'I love you,' she says, sadly. 'But I have to go. I must get back and help with the search.'

I strain to sit up, but it hurts too much to move.

'Wait, *I* want to help with the search, she's my sister.'

'I'll keep you updated. I'm sorry. I have to go.'

She darts out the door and I turn to Dad.

'Just know that we are doing everything we can,' he says, squeezing my arm. 'Believe me.'

I give a deep sigh.

'What's the use of all these powers, if we can't protect our family?' I say.

He sits back from me.

'Be patient, Nina. Be patient.'

I fold my arms across my chest as I realise that there's no use arguing. All I know is that I can't let Kelci be out there, alone. *Not when it's my fault.* There's just no way I can 'be patient', knowing she's in the hands of those brutes. Not for one minute.

7. Empty Hole In My Heart

One day since Kelci was taken, Gregory Residence

The man Mum had mentioned, Sol, turned up after she left. He was short and handsome with round, fawny eyes and soft tanned hands. I know how soft they were because he used them to completely heal my back. And my head. Being around him drenched my whole body in a feeling of calm that I knew wasn't coming from me. I felt more energised than ever, which is incredible considering all the pain I was in. Under any other circumstances I wouldn't have been able to stop myself being excited to meet a Deer for the first time. And to actually be healed by one, a fully trained one as well. But right now everything has lost its colour. There's no excitement to be had, not with this empty hole in my heart.

Dad went out to join the search, giving me a cool kiss on the head before he left and I was in the house alone. I went straight to Kelci's bedroom. I don't really know why. It's jam-packed full of her stuff but it felt eerily empty, her bed still unmade. Weird t-shirts of hers with their ridiculous captions lay across the floor, her absurd Batman slippers strewn behind the door, the sparkly pink eyeshadow she wore to the party left open on her desk. Posters of her favourite superheroes lined the walls. Shelves full of comics and books and little toys of her favourite characters, all her obsessions. I stared at the piles of comic strips we had made together. I gave up drawing them after Terence died, it seemed stupid to dream about my future superhero self after that, but I don't think Kelci ever understood why I stopped, and she resented me for it. I clutched her glasses in my hand and found the case for them and slipped them inside. At the party she knew something was wrong. *Why couldn't I listen?*

After that I came out here. To the roof of our house, where the wide, outdoor pool is and Mum's collection of bonsai trees. This is where Kelci and I tried to manifest, hundreds and hundreds of times. It's also where Terence and I used to hang out, gazing out over our city. The first thing I did was jump into the glistening pool with my clothes on and try to breathe underwater, just like Dad does. Then I came over here, to the heavy iron bench that sits in the middle of the rooftop and tried with all my might to lift it. I let out a cry of despair as it refused to budge. So now I'm freezing cold with strands of hair sticking to my face, but it doesn't matter because I *must* manifest. What other choice do I have? They won't call the police. This won't be done any way, other than the Anitar way. I reach for the bench again and try to lift it until my muscles are on fire and I can bear it no longer.

My whole body hurts, I squeeze my eyes shut, I see the men in grey... *Who the hell were they?* I see Kelci's terrified face. *Where is she? All alone?* Rabbits aren't built to be alone too long. Droplets of rain begin to fall and I'm shivering so hard my teeth chatter. I crumple up into a ball, pulling my knees up to my chest as the rain continues. I hear the door of the roof garden open and lift my sodden head to see who it is. The long limbs gliding along are unmistakable. Frowning and beautiful, her eyes are searching.

'Miss Gregory.'

'Artemiz.'

She strides over and looks down at me. Without a word she lifts me from where I sit and guides me from the rooftop. I'm too cold, too weak to resist and I don't even bother to ask why she is here. She guides me all the way back to my bedroom, finds a towel in my closet, hands it to me and tells me to get dry and changed, then leaves the room. As soon as I'm done she enters my room again and I sit on the edge of my bed like the first time she was here and I try to control my breathing, try to steady the thoughts in my head. *She'll be listening.* She takes the towel and stands next to me, drying my hair and dabbing my face. It surprises me how gentle her movements are.

'Why are you here?' I say.

'I know what happened to your sister.'

'Do you know where she is?'

'No. I don't.'

'Why come here then?'

'I am here to invite you – for the *final* time – to join the Muldoon Academy Manifestation Program.'

I look at her with disbelieving eyes.

'You've got to be joking Artemiz. I'm not going to go all that way now. I have to be here in New York with my parents, trying to find her. Don't you understand?'

'I do. I understand perfectly.'

'Well then.'

'You want to find your sister. Muldoon Academy is the centre of the Anitar world and anything that is worth knowing is right there. I make no promises but I do know that you *want* to manifest now.'

I don't want to. I have to.

'Very well,' she nods.

'This doesn't make me like the idea of being an Anitar any more than before. In fact I hate it *more* now. Look what's happened to Kelci…'

The chestnut of her eyes turns to a glowing red-brown.

'Don't wait around here in New York for something to happen. This program will speed things up considerably.'

'How much?'

'You only have 21 days, whether you manifest or not.'

'21 days! Anything could have happened to her by then.'

It's a stab in the chest as I say the words.

'It's something. What will you do here instead?'

I could do my own investigation.

'You could.'

She stands up then moves towards the door.

'If that's what you want to do, I can't stop you.'

She reaches for the handle.

'Wait, where are you going?'

'I don't beg Nina. I give opportunity. That is all.'

I sigh. My options are terrible. I think of Kelci. I think of the men who took her. I think of Mason, my parents, all of it. What am I supposed to do? If I stay here, they will leave me out in the cold and I'll know nothing. Perhaps, at Muldoon there will be answers.

'All right,' I say.

Artemiz turns around.

'Yes?'

'You already know what I'm thinking.'

'I like to hear Trainees say it out loud.'

I roll my eyes.

'I will go on the Manifestation Program.'

Her eyes flicker.

'I am very pleased to hear that.'

———

Everything is packed and sits neatly in my matching set of floral suitcases which comprise two enormous ones, three average ones and four smaller ones for the bits and pieces that would not fit into the larger bags. I cling on to Kelci's glasses case. Dad carries the bags to the front door where Artemiz stands waiting beside a black jaguar with blacked out windows. She raises the shades she wears when she sees my bags. I turn to my parents who stand on the doorstep, with Babs prowling at Mum's feet. They hug me tight but there's no triumph, no excitement. How could there be? When things are like this? Mum grabs my shoulders and levels her eyes at me, the mustard-yellow of her irises blazing. She makes me promise that I will send their love to someone called 'Lady Muldoon'. Dad wraps his arms around me and I nestle my cheek into his chest, as he whispers into my hair to *please, stay safe*. I peel myself away and we all agree that one way or another, we will find our Kelci.

As I walk down the steps, sadness chokes my throat. Am I losing them too? Artemiz guides me and I climb into the plush seats and I notice that there's a black screen between us and the driver. The car rolls along and I take a look back as we turn the corner, seeing my parents stood there watching the car. Just like that, only the two of them left. With one turn of a corner, they're gone and I feel completely alone. I stare out the window and think of Mason, of how I gave him a lame story about visiting my old aunt in London; how I wouldn't be able to contact him because she would need me every minute of the day, because she's ill, with some terrible disease. I told him Kelci was already with this sick old aunt of ours. I hated lying to him.

I sink into my seat, missing him already, missing Mum and Dad, missing Kelci, missing Terence. Is this how it is now? We zip along for ages until finally, we reach a long stretch of flat ground somewhere outside the city. The car comes to a stop and Artemiz nods to me to get out. When I do, I see an airplane in front of us which is small, but with long wings. We're going to fly across the Atlantic in this thing? The driver steps out and reveals himself as an enormous dark haired man who nods and looks at me with tiny brown eyes. He shakes my hand and introduces himself in an Irish accent, saying his name is Kenny Collins. Then he proceeds to lift all my bags from the car and tuck them into the plane's storage. As I watch him moving the bags all in one go, which even my Dad had struggled with, I realise that this man must be a Bear. I try not to stare at him. *A real life Bear.* He could lift that bench on my rooftop. He could fling it across Manhattan if he wanted to.

The interior of the plane is all soft beige leather, with a glamorous retro feel to it. There are six small cabin windows on either side and above each window there is a round gold symbol. I recognise two of them, the Fish and the Tiger, they are the same symbols that are tattooed on my parent's upper backs, just below their necks. Each of the gold symbols has a different animal curled inside the circle, twelve altogether. This would have been the stuff of dreams to Kelci and me back in the day, but now…

Minutes later we're airborne. I watch the city disappear below and wonder when I will see it again. Do I have to say goodbye to *everything* I love? Artemiz sits opposite me with her shades on, making it impossible to tell where those Persian eyes are directed. There really is no privacy with this lady around. One of her eyebrows rises above the glasses. *Shut up mind, shut up!* It looks like she may possibly be smiling, but it's hard to be sure. I look around the plane again and can't help wondering how many times she's taken this trip and with how many people?

'This is the life of the Horse,' she says, turning to me. 'I travel the world and find those who may one day be the most powerful Anitars on Earth.'

'Right,' I say. 'Cool.'

A while later I drift off into a fretful sleep and some hours pass before I open my eyes again and see Artemiz pointing to the window. I rub my eyes then look out. There, surrounded by the rolling blue sea, is an island. It is a jagged oval in shape, with two great mountain ranges that curve along the sides, rising up like a pair of enormous sleeping dragons, encasing a wide valley in the middle. Nestled within the valley

I see a series of old looking buildings, all the same light beige. The largest buildings form a circle – I count them, 12 in total. Then there is one more building, even larger, that sits in front of the circle with a long driveway, surrounded by trees leading up to it.

Along one side of the complex there's a forest, which spreads out for at least a few miles. To the other side there's a great lake, which shimmers in the sunlight. The island is a world of greens, browns, greys, purples, and white where snow lies at the top of the mountains. It seems to me like I've never seen these shades of colours before, so muted, so *natural*. All of a sudden I feel a long, long way from home. My heart pounds as the plane dips its little nose and we glide over to the right, away from the buildings. I look at Artemiz, questioning.

'We need to land.'

She points to a long expanse of ground to the side of the lake and the plane noses down towards it. Once we are at a standstill I descend the steps with Artemiz close behind me, followed by Kenny Collins. I stand there shielding my eyes from the sun. I see the ancient looking buildings across the lake. Artemiz turns to me and now it is unmistakable. A smile is forming on her face.

'Miss Gregory,' she says, 'welcome to Muldoon Academy.'

8. Hello, Everybody

Two days since Kelci was taken, Muldoon Academy, Muldoon Island

After I have stood and gaped at Muldoon Academy for some time, Artemiz takes me by the elbow. Kenny Collins appears behind us, loaded up with my selection of floral bags dangling from his hulking frame. We begin to walk around the lake towards the buildings and immediately I realise that the peach high heels Mason bought for me were a bad choice of footwear. I cry out as mud sticks to them, actual mud. Meanwhile, Artemiz ignores me and pushes us forward at an uncomfortable speed.

As we move along the side of the lake, I cannot help but be amazed at the beauty and grandeur of the place. I'm used to looking up at skyscrapers in Manhattan but even that hasn't prepared me for the sheer height of the mountains here. After a good trek which basically ruins my shoes, we end up on the driveway, heading towards the main entrance, a gigantic door surrounded by ornate stonework, but Artemiz steers me away from that door, towards the right side of the building. My stomach churns with apprehension and I fiddle with the lacy collar of my dress then adjust the bow at the back. I pull out my lipstick from my handbag and apply a dab to my lips. It is the exact same colour as the peach shoes, which unfortunately are now brown.

I'm really quite nervous by the time I'm tottering down some steps that lead to a small door at the side of the building. I almost have to duck my head to get through and I feel surprised by the pokiness, and the dinginess, of the place. Kenny has to enter sideways and wiggle his way through with the bags. We walk down a corridor lined with sandy stones that look like they have been here for thousands of years until we reach a windowless room set up with a wooden table manned by a small, disheveled woman dressed head to toe in dark green who sits there, staring directly at me.

'Nina Gregory?' she screeches. 'You're late.'

I chuckle politely.

'Oh,' I say, trying my best to be good-natured. 'Well I don't think so – you see we just arrived on the plane from New York, we were –'

'Audrey, please,' says Artemiz placing her hands on the table and looking down at the woman. 'We are not going to go through this again. She's not late, she wasn't even aware of what time she was supposed to be here.'

The woman gives a raspy sigh, flits her eyes to Artemiz and points a long, bony finger towards the bags in Kenny's hands.

'Only one bag allowed for Trainees,' she says. 'One bag. It says right here in the Trainee Introduction Notes. And one *small* bag at that.'

I gasp.

'You've got to be joking. I was never told about that.'

She gives me an irritated look and we proceed to have a whole conversation about how I need everything in those bags and her insisting that all but one of my smaller bags is put away until the end of the program. *Stop*, I tell myself. *Think of Kelci.* Only the thought of her prevents me from taking the bags from Kenny and dragging them out the building. It is only the thought of her that drives me to choose one of the bags – the one with the make-up and toiletries in it – and to allow Kenny to stalk off down the corridor with the rest of them to god knows where.

'What on earth am I supposed to wear?' I almost scream. 'All my outfits are in those bags.'

The woman smiles at me, showing four or five long, protruding teeth at the front of her mouth. Her eyes are aged yet lively. She fiddles with the large bloodstone ring that sits on her right middle finger. I can't figure out which of the Twelve Anitars this woman is. There isn't such a thing as Rats. Artemiz lets out a stifled laugh.

'Audrey is a Snake,' she says.

'Yes, and don't you forget it young 'un!'

She points her finger at my face.

'I've been here since before you were born. In fact I remember your mother. Stella Smythe she was back then. What a feisty little number that girl was! Married that lovely Luke Gregory and now… You.'

She eyes me up and down.

'Yes. *Me*,' I say.

'No need for cheek, little lady.'

I feel the right hand of Artemiz on my shoulder.

'Let's get on with this shall we? She should be at induction right now.'

Audrey shakes her head, puffing, and looks down at her clipboard.

'Fine. Down to business. What you will wear,' she says. 'Is this.'

She reaches underneath her desk and whips out a pile of grim looking navy blue clothing and slaps it down. Said clothes are made of thick, uncomfortable looking material, the likes of which have never touched my skin before. I reluctantly pull out the garment on top and am dismayed to see it unfold into a long sleeved top with two depressing looking pockets on the chest. The trousers are even worse, shudderingly manly in style. To top it all off Audrey reaches under her desk again and bangs down a dark pair of trainers. I try to explain that I can't be seen dead in such a drab ensemble but Artemiz is already leading me out of the room. The last I see, Audrey has a toothy grin spreading across her face.

———

Artemiz takes us down a flight of stairs that are so steep I constantly feel like I am going to fall. We then walk along cramped corridors with small lights fixed to the walls. The whole place has a distinct dungeon-like feel to it. I cling to my one bag as if it is my last possession in this world, which by the looks of things isn't too far off the mark. We're well below ground now. Oh dear. This is playing havoc with my claustrophobia, so I take deep breaths. Finally we end up at another door, old and battered. Artemiz whispers to me that this is where I will sleep and I hear a booming voice coming from inside. Just as I am about to ask Artemiz where I should get the refreshments she opens the door, which creaks loudly, and she forcefully guides me into the room.

She's so forceful in fact, it makes me sort of teeter on my heels as I enter. The room has low ceilings and seems to be a continuation of the dungeon theme. It feels like people may have died in here at some point. I clutch the navy blue clothes under my arm. I stand there as a small crowd of people, all about my age, turn to face me. I sense Artemiz leaving, closing the door on her way out. They all stare at me. About thirty of them. I look down at my orange, pink and white dress and suddenly feel very *bright* in this dim room. I hide my gulp. I clasp my clammy hands. I look around the room to see rows of tiny bunk beds. Ugh.

'Hello, everybody,' I say, my voice much louder than I would've wished.

There's a kind of intense air in the room and the group nods in return then shuffles apart to reveal a woman standing in their midst. She is swathed in mounds of rich velvet, a luxurious purple colour with an enormous amethyst around her neck. She has silver hair styled back from her majestic face. A large wolf-like dog sits at her heels, its sloping nose turned up towards her, its massive grey tail coiled around its feet. The woman's hands are wrinkled but graceful and covered in gold rings. Her brown eyes look straight in my direction, and at the exact same moment, so do the silver eyes of the dog.

'Ah,' she says. 'Miss Nina Gregory I believe, a little late but I suppose we shall forgive you. I am Lady Muldoon, the Principal of Muldoon Academy and the last living member of the Muldoon Family.'

The woman Mum wanted me to send her love to. She gestures to the dog, touching it lightly between the ears.

'This is Shadow, my guardian. Many Deer have such guardians, to provide protection when necessary. And these fine young people are your team for the next 21 days.'

Everyone is still staring at me.

'Pleased to meet you,' I say.

I cough politely, covering my mouth with my hand.

'This will be your bunk,' says Lady Muldoon, pointing to a top bed in the middle of the right hand row.

Despite the staring faces I feel it would be best to set things straight right away.

'Yes, about that,' I say. 'I was wondering if it might be possible for me to arrange a room above ground? I really can't stand being underground, I'm claustrophobic actually – I'm sure you understand. My parents, well my Dad, I'm sure won't mind if there's any extra cost, he knows how I feel about being underground.'

I see a guy, just to my left, roll his eyes. *Is he rolling them at me?* I throw him a look but he steadies those eyes and turns back to Lady Muldoon. Dark eyes, with thick black lashes. Lady Muldoon steps forward and ends up close to me surprisingly fast.

'Your parents, my dear, stayed in these same dorms exactly twenty-five years ago. You wouldn't think so, but I remember it like yesterday. Your mother slept in that very bunk, right there by the door.

There are no rooms for Trainees above ground, only Apprentices. We find that a few weeks down here provides just the distraction-free environment necessary for what we hope to accomplish.'

I can hardly picture my mother in a place like this.

'They could just be a bit bigger, couldn't they?'

Lady Muldoon's expression turns indignant. She widens her eyes and puckers her lips. Mum and Dad didn't mention any of this. Of course they didn't. I can't get over the fact that it has been the *same beds* for the last twenty-five years… Lady Muldoon sweeps away from me, her nose held high in the air, Shadow sloping gracefully at her side, his grey coat shining. The group's gaze follows her as she goes.

Meanwhile I am left to place my bag on the ground in silence and edge towards the group. A girl, strikingly pretty with delicate, elfin features and a wide, mischievous grin, makes space for me to stand next to her. I shuffle my way in. She has short, messy hair which spikes out all over the place, dyed blonde with dark roots. She looks younger than me, quite a bit younger – perhaps more like Kelci's age. Her skin is radiant, the colour of buttercream. She turns to me suddenly, and I feel like she's caught me staring at her. She looks at me through her wide-spaced eyes, and before I have a chance to react, she winks at me. I'm not sure what to do until she sticks out her hand and whispers:

'I'm Lucy.'

I reach for her hand, which is cool to the touch.

'I'm Nina. Pleased to meet you, Lucy.'

With that, she whips her hand away and turns back to Lady Muldoon, bouncing on her toes like an excited pixie. I try to concentrate on Lady Muldoon's uppity voice. She tells us how privileged we should all feel to be here and how this program is the best in the world. She tells us how this is proven to be the fastest, most efficient route to manifestation. My ears perk up when I hear this and I squeeze forward, raising my hand.

'How long does it usually take?' I say.

'How long does *what* usually take?' replies Lady Muldoon, her eyes widening again.

'Manifestation. Only, I've got to be quick about it.'

'Really? Shall we all just stop right now and concentrate on getting you through, Nina?'

I hear a muffled laugh from somewhere in the crowd.

'If you want.'

Her eyebrows shoot up.

'It's just, I have to find my sister,' I say. 'She's been kidnapped and I have to get her back. Pretty much now.'

'I am aware of what has happened to your sister, Kelci Gregory. However, I would suggest that we discuss that later.'

'You know about Kelci? All right. So you know how serious it is. We need to all be on the same page right away – I have to go and find her as soon as I can.'

I give an appealing glance to the whole group but it seems to be met by blank stares. Lady Muldoon's expression turns to thunder. Her voice rises.

'From this moment onwards and for the next three weeks – *no less* – the only "page" you will be on is mine.'

She gives me a withering look.

'Oh.'

She swivels away from me. As I am letting out a breath through my nose I notice the same guy who rolled his eyes, raising an eyebrow. Is that on my account? All these facial manoeuvres? I force myself to turn away from him to look at Lady Muldoon who continues to tell us about carefully worked out challenges and tests and how fantastic it all is. I shuffle uncomfortably in my muddy heels. She is keen to tell us that those of us who manifest will spend three days at the end of the program in the House of their Animal, receiving specialised, intensive training.

She also says that out of those who do manifest *two* will be chosen to stay on at Muldoon to become Apprentices for a five-year duration. The remainder of those who manifest will go to another one of the Academies that are on each of the seven continents, aside from Antarctica. Mine would probably be in Canada, the North American one, not that I have any intention whatsoever of going on to become an Apprentice. Lady Muldoon continues and it is made abundantly clear that only the very best are given this opportunity and that we all ought to be extremely grateful for the chance.

My gaze wanders back to the guy. He looks like he is about to go into battle or something. Looking at his face from this angle reminds me of one of those Grecian statues, all sculpted lines and curves, with dark hair and smooth skin. I pull my attention back to Lady Muldoon who goes on to remind us that should we fail to manifest, we will be sent home with our memories of the entire thing erased. Great. As she tells us we can manifest at any moment during the next three weeks, I become increasingly desperate to ask her if she knows where my sister could be. I don't care what anyone says. *Why else am I here?*

I begin to raise my hand again but before it rises more than a few inches I feel Lucy's hand pushing it gently back downwards. I frown at her.

'Later,' she mouths quietly.

She's smiling at me and the moment has passed. I suppose this isn't the best time. Finally Lady Muldoon wraps up her speech by belabouring the point that 'teamwork is key' and telling us that 'our adventure starts here.' I sigh as a ripple of anticipation buzzes around the group. Not one person seems to realise that my sister's safety is way more important than any of this could ever be.

'Boys,' bellows Lady Muldoon. 'Return to your dorm. You all have exactly eleven minutes before dinner. Before that time you need to be fully unpacked. Do not be late.'

'Eleven minutes?'

Lady Muldoon shoots me another pointed look, then leaves the room.

'How can I unpack and be ready for dinner within that sort of time scale?' I mutter to myself.

The group scatters and I sidle over to the pitiful object that is my new bed.

'This place looks like a prison,' I say, shaking my head.

'Believe me,' says a voice behind me, smooth and sultry. 'This is a holiday camp compared to prison.'

I whip my head around. There stands a girl who looks like a beauty queen on her day off – luscious red hair, plump pink lips and large hazel eyes that are staring right at me.

'Oh,' I say. 'And you would know?'

'Let's just say I'm grateful for the opportunity to be here. But clearly not everyone feels that way.'

Her words flow like velvet. She places her hands on her slender hips. There's a silence that I can't help but fill.

'And you are?'

'My name – *Miss Nina Gregory*,' she says, doing a passable impression of Lady Muldoon, 'is Heather Jackson.'

There's an edge to her voice that you'd have to be a complete idiot to miss. She curls a strand of hair with her right middle finger and I notice there's a delicate tattoo on it, a leafy coil that travels right up to her knuckle. She looks me up and down.

'Your dress,' she says, raising her right eyebrow. 'Interesting choice.'

'Yes, my dress,' I say, struggling to stay calm.

I look her up and down in return, but there's no denying it. She's gorgeous. And she's the kind of gorgeous you can't help looking at. Some of the other girls are watching her too. It just sort of draws you in.

'T-shirt and shorts,' I say. 'Both of which are two sizes too small. Also an interesting choice!'

She crosses her arms over her chest. She wears a pair of red socks too, pulled right up to her knees.

'Good luck in the program,' she says. 'Miss Nina.'

With that she flings her hair over her shoulder and walks off, hips sashaying as she goes.

9. This Is Ridiculous

Two days since Kelci was taken, Trainee Canteen

I am the last person to enter the canteen, which is crammed full of Trainees all bumbling along with their trays of food, sitting down, chatting. I'm not sure if it's my imagination but the room seems to hush a little when I enter. After I get myself a pile of mince and potatoes from the food counter I look around the room and catch sight of the guy who rolled his eyes at me. He's hard to miss. He sits sandwiched between two girls, one of whom is the impish girl, Lucy, who chats wildly and the other one is Heather who leans in ever so slightly towards him. Lucy catches sight of me and waves enthusiastically, making the other two turn their heads in my direction. I politely return the wave.

I look around the room but it is so full I don't see anywhere to sit. I hope the three of them have taken their eyes off me as I look for a place to sit. Every table is full. I hold onto my plastic blue tray, gripping tighter as heads begin to turn towards me. *There are no chairs left.* My heart sinks. I feel like a shining beacon stood here in my muddy high heels. More heads are turning and my cheeks are getting hot… But then, I hear a deep, booming voice from somewhere within the crowd.

'Hey. There's a seat here.'

There's a hand waving. A big hand, attached to a big body. An enormous body, to be frank. It's a guy, about the same age as me, possibly a little older, with a mop of long blonde hair that grows to just below his wide jaw. He has thick eyebrows and kindly eyes that crease at the sides and I'm glad to see those eyes because without them it seems like the size of him would just be *too much*. He gestures to the chair opposite him. I gulp, and begin to move towards it. As I get closer, squeezing through and holding the tray above people's heads, I see that he is too huge for the plastic chair he sits on. I finally get to the empty spot, put my tray on the table and sit down, smoothing down my outfit.

'Thank you,' I say, reaching my hand out towards him. 'I'm Nina. Pleased to meet you.'

He looks at my hand for a moment, then grabs it, swamping it completely in his.

'I'm Ben,' he says. 'Ben Hult.'

I hear an accent as he speaks, European… As soon as my hand drops away, I feel it picked up by another, much smaller one.

'He's Swedish. And I'm James Johnson.'

Ben nods his head.

'This is my friend.'

'Hi there,' I say.

James is sat next to Ben and he looks so small in comparison it's slightly startling. A huge grin lights up his face, he shakes my hand with vigour and holds onto it a little too long, until I have to pull it away as gracefully as I can. He has ebony skin, lively brown eyes and black hair that sits tight against his head. He wears a shiny black bomber jacket over a white t-shirt, whilst Ben wears a bulky knitted jumper with elaborate patterns on it. I nod, amused by this odd pair. I arrange my knife, fork, glass and plate nice and neatly and place the napkin across my knees. I can't help but notice the piles of food sprawled in front of Ben. There's so much of it you can't see the plate. Then about ten slices of bread covered in butter, two bowls of soup, an orange, an apple, a banana and an enormous slice of sponge pudding, swimming in custard.

'My compadre here,' says James, leaning towards me, 'likes food. And when I say he likes food, I mean he *likes* food.'

He sits back then punches Ben against his arm, but it's like his fist is hitting a brick wall.

'Wow,' he says, staring at his fist, then turning to me. 'Look at the size of this guy. Do you know how much energy a body like this needs?'

'I have no idea,' I say, nibbling at my fork.

Ben gives a sidelong look towards James.

'It's true,' says Ben, giving a smile that reveals a dimple in his left cheek. 'I eat like a donkey.'

James turns his head towards him.

'You mean, you eat like a horse.'

Ben's expression turns to a mixture of disgusted and insulted.

'Eat like a horse?' he says, pursing his lips. 'Never.'

James frowns.

'Were you guys friends before you came here?' I say, changing the subject.

'No. We just met,' says James. 'But it's a done deal. Sometimes you just know, right?'

'Sure,' I say.

'I need all the friends I can get around here,' he says. 'I have no clue what's going on. I mean, do you? Because I *do not*. Some lady walks into my home and tells my uncle Steve she wants me for some scholarship program and he's like, what's in it for me? And she tells him, you can get rid of your nephew for three weeks, at least. When she said that he was like, yeah, yeah, I'll do it. And I was like, *what? Is she reading his mind?* Uncle Steve has been trying to get rid of me for years. This was Christmas come early for him, but he never said a word about it to her. Then she tells me, when we're on our own, that I've got potential for some crazy powers. So I'm like YES. Finally. Thank you! Somebody out there is listening.'

He bangs the palm of his hand on the table and shakes his head.

'And now I'm here with my new Nordic friend, and all these people and I'm like, I'm home baby! Because I'm not going back there. *I'm staying.* I'm doing this. No matter what.'

He frowns a little. I'm guessing James is from a family who aren't Anitars.

'Hey,' he says, hushing his voice and leaning in towards us. 'You guys got any idea what Animal you'll manifest? I'm thinking Tiger for myself. Or Snow Leopard. It has to be one of the wild cats, you know? Fierce, fighting, that kind of thing. I mean, look at me.'

He makes his hands look like paws and gives a 'roar!' I can't help but burst into laughter, and neither can Ben.

'Seriously though?' he says.

'I'm here with one thing in mind,' I say. 'To find my sister. She's missing and this is the place with all the information, apparently…'

I notice that the seat next to me must've emptied because suddenly some guy is pulling the chair back and falling into it.

'Nina Gregory,' he says. 'Am I right?'

'Yes, that's right. And you are?'

He's slim with dark eyes, shaved light brown hair and a little scar running across his left eyebrow.

'Dominic Federov,' he says. 'You've probably heard the name Federov before, most likely because of my brother, Tony Federov.'

I look at him blankly.

'Tony is the greatest living Chameleon in the world. He trained here.'

I have no idea who he's talking about, and I can only presume that this shows in my face.

'Your parents must have told you about Tony. *I* know about the Gregory's…'

'I'm sorry, I don't know much about other Anitars.'

He looks ruffled by this.

'Too busy shopping?'

'Excuse me?' I say.

'I'm just surprised you don't know who I am. But you'll learn I suppose. You're not what I would've expected from a Gregory. Your parents are legends. But still, we can talk.'

'Oh. I'm sorry I'm not what you expected.'

85

Is this guy for real?

'That's why we're on the Manifestation Program. To improve, so I wouldn't worry about it.'

I stare at him, disbelieving.

'Listen, we should make the effort to get along. Our parents would expect us to.'

He flashes a critical look towards Ben and James.

'Would you like me to save you from little and large here? I have no idea who either of them are.'

'This is Ben, and James,' I say, glancing towards them. 'And no, I don't need saving. I'm quite happy where I am.'

A dark look flashes across his features and he says nothing for a few moments.

'So you actually are what you look like?' he says, eventually. 'One of those idiot high school girls?'

'Hey, hey,' says James. 'It's dangerous talking to the ladies that way, don't you know that?'

'This *lady* is clearly not dangerous. Are your parents disappointed by how you turned out?'

My blood boils, but before I have a chance to say anything Ben's face changes from mild-mannered to enraged in less than a second and he hits his fist on the table, causing the cutlery to fly upwards and an almighty clatter to clang out as his plates and bowls hit against each other.

'Enough,' he says. 'You take a trip.'

Dominic scrunches up his face.

'What? I take a trip?'

'Hike,' says James loudly, leaning forward. 'He means, *take a hike.*'

Dominic stands up, looking at us down his nose.

'Happily. She's not worth wasting my time on. She's all yours, fellas.'

With that, he walks away, leaving me staring at the back of his head as he disappears out of the canteen.

———

I wake up from a fitful slumber spent trying not to fall off my rock hard bed. The lights are on, bright, and a commanding voice is telling me to get up. I look at the clock on the wall. 5am. My body is a dead weight. The room sways before my eyes – jet lag I presume. This is ridiculous. Why get up now? As I pull myself up onto my elbows I stare at the pile of navy blue clothes at the end of my bed, like an unwelcome present on Christmas morning. I hear moans and groans from the other girls as they flop off their beds, onto the cold floor. Lady Muldoon is booming us along like some kind of nightmare. I lay my head back on the pillow and without warning a head pops up at the side of the bed. Lucy. She grins at me as she deliberately messes up her hair so it flies out at all angles.

'We're bunk buddies!'

I grunt at her. She darts off and trips over her towel, landing flat on her hands, before bouncing back up and assuring me that she's ok. Just watching her makes me feel exhausted. With great effort, I go to the communal bathroom and splash my face with cold water. I drag myself into the blue ensemble and stand in front of one of the long mirrors, appalled at the sight. I look like a convict. I comb my hair and curl it into a bun on top of my head, trying to make the best of a bad job. As I apply a coat of lipstick Lady Muldoon appears and tells me to 'get along'. I huff and puff all the way to the canteen which is full of the same navy blue uniforms. We *all* look like prisoners.

I help myself to two boiled eggs and some toast covered in butter, then join Ben and James who beckon me over to join them again. They sit in their matching blue overalls, Ben munching through bacon, eggs, sausage, tomatoes, mushrooms and hash browns whilst James explains to us the virtues of peanut butter, maple syrup and pancakes, preferably the way his Grandma makes them. I sip on my hot mug of tea but there's not enough time to drink the whole thing before we are hauled outside and marched across the front of the grounds. The sun has barely risen and everything looks hazy and beautiful. Lucy runs up alongside me and pinches my arm as she moves on ahead. Eventually we reach an enormous assault course. There are walls and frames and nets and pools of muddy water. This cannot be good. *I'm not made for this kind of thing.*

Lady Muldoon sweeps to the front, Shadow darting along behind her, explaining that our first day will consist of a physical assessment 'to see where we are at.' I haven't exercised in a long time; over a year, pretty much. I used to, with Kelci, when we tried to manifest, but lately I've walked while shopping and that's about it. Lady Muldoon says we should see these first few days as an opportunity to prepare for our first 'challenge'. I swallow hard, surely *this* is our first challenge?

Too soon, it begins. I'm clambering under a rope net, staring at the backsides of my fellow Trainees rushing away from me. I'm down on my stomach, trying to pull myself through the net when Dominic crawls alongside me.

'Looking good, sweetheart,' he says, 'Just be careful not to break a nail, they look expensive.'

He takes off into the distance at great speed. *How the hell does he move so fast?* It takes a surprisingly short amount of time for me to be left behind by the majority of the group. Only myself, James and a sullen-faced girl called Linda are left under the net. James' seems to expend a lot energy trying to throw the net off himself, but he still gets out before me. He jogs on, gasping for air and muttering 'man, I need to start working out.' After jumping over various obstacles and winding my way around others I find myself slap bang in front of a huge, upside down-V-shaped wall. My spirits sink at the sight of it. *I can't do it…* but I clamber up somehow, though by the time I'm at the top I realise that I'm now well and truly last. From this vantage point I can see that half the group are already at the finish line, standing there staring at me. I can even see the outline of that eye-rolling boy with one hand on his hip, the other hand shielding his eyes from the sun, watching me. *For God's sake.*

I swing myself over, clinging on for dear life and wish there was some other way, any other way, to get down the other side. Unfortunately I can't think of anything so I sort of slide my way down, with no control and bruising all manner of body parts as I do so. I see

Linda up ahead wading through a pit of mud. I've got no choice but to do the same and I soon feel the wetness soak into my trousers. James is at the finish line, bent over holding his hands to his chest. I look at the back of Linda's head and try to speed up – *catch her for goodness sake, don't come last* – but within a few steps I realise I've made a mistake. My feet have nothing to grip on and I'm out of control. I see one flash of the group before I fall head first into the mud. For a second it feels like I'm drowning. I pull myself up. It's slimy and cold and brown. My ears are filled with the sound of giggles and snorts.

As I am grappling to stand up I see a muscly form looming towards me. Because of the mud in my eyes I can't see who it is but I soon feel two enormous arms scooping me up. As I'm being carried out of the pit I manage to get enough dirt off my face to see that the person I am being rescued by is Ben. We get to the finish line and he places me gently on the floor in front of Lady Muldoon, then stands back – like I'm a present he has brought for his master. I sit on the ground, sodden. The laughter's louder now. Lady Muldoon stares at me like I'm the creature from the black lagoon, which I can only presume is not too far off the mark. Shadow trots over to me and nudges my leg, looking at me, questioning. There's nothing else for it. I plaster back my hair from my face, stand up, ineffectually brush myself down and say:

'That went well, didn't it?'

10. Lavender & Hot Chocolate

Three days since Kelci was taken, Lady Muldoon's Study

The rest of the day did not get any better. There was rock climbing, archery, swimming, running, all of which left me utterly exhausted. By now, with night fallen, I've become a ghost of my former self. I just saw my face in the mirror and I hardly recognised the red-faced, frizzy haired person looking back at me. I almost laughed when I thought of what Mason would say if he saw me, but no laughter came, not even a smile. Worst of all is the fact that I am no nearer to finding Kelci. Not one bit closer. Here, in this place, I feel further away from her than ever. I have to do something. *Right now.*

That's why I'm here, knocking on the door of Lady Muldoon's study as we approach midnight. I persuaded Artemiz to guide me up here, after she supervised us for the last part of the day. Somehow deep down below the cool demeanour, I get the feeling Artemiz really does want to help me – I can't help thinking she wouldn't let anyone else do this, but then I did beg and plead and hover around her like a fly, until she said yes. It's the first time I've ventured above ground and even though I've only seen one corridor, things look very different up here. It is plush and warm and there are beautiful lights along the walls, silver bands entwined over bunches of crystals glowing all colours of the rainbow.

As Artemiz disappears I hear a muffled voice coming from within the room. I push the door open slowly and immediately my nostrils are hit with the smell of lavender and chocolate and old books. Lady Muldoon sits behind a huge oak desk that looks like it is growing out of the floorboards. Her eyebrows rise like two arches when she sees me. Shadow is curled up on a thick purple rug in front of the roaring fire. He turns his head towards me for a moment, then rests his nose back down on his paws.

'Hello, Lady Muldoon,' I say.

I feel like I should curtsy or something and I think it's because she looks so regal sat there, holding a silver pen in her hand, a great spray of purple feathers and flowers next to her. There's a painting of a stag too, looking out of a dark forest, just behind her. I can't help staring at it, and the shelves of books and the nooks and crannies in the walls containing amethysts and candles. In front of her sits a steaming mug.

'Nina Gregory,' she says. 'Would you like some hot chocolate, my dear?'

That was unexpected…

'Yes,' I say. 'I would love one. Thank you.'

She rises from her desk, gathering the swathes of her robe as she goes.

'Of course, you know you are not supposed to be here?' she says.

'Artemiz said I could come up, just this once…'

'Oh did she now?' she says, giving me her incredulous look once again. 'I shall have a word with Artemiz in the morning.'

'It was me, Lady Muldoon,' I say. 'I pestered her.'

'Very well.'

She pours the contents of a ceramic jug into another mug.

'Do take a seat, now that you're here.'

She gestures towards the carved wooden seat in front of her desk, with swirling half circles for arms. I sink into the plump lilac cushion and moments later, she places a thick, stony mug into my hands, before floating back behind her desk. I cradle the mug, then take a sip. It is like drinking pure, melted chocolate, thick and rich, like velvet in my mouth. There's a taste of lavender in there, and a little bit of spice. It is the most delicious thing I have ever tasted. Lady Muldoon smiles.

'It is rather good, isn't it?'

I am staring at the contents of the cup. She sits herself back down at the desk and leans forward.

'Now. Might I ask what all this is about?'

I look up, then take a deep breath.

'As you know, Lady Muldoon, I need to find my sister. She was supposed to be an Apprentice here next year, when she turns 16, and she disappeared right in front of me and there was nothing I could do and that's why I'm here. Because Artemiz said I should try to manifest and that if there's anything worth knowing, it will be here. I need your help. I can't just do nothing.'

She takes a sip from her own mug.

'I see,' she says. 'What is it you intend to do?'

'Well, I was hoping you could help me, to find her… Somehow.'

She stays quiet for a moment, then continues.

'I know all about your sister, Kelci. I sent for her myself when I found out she manifested. It is terrible, absolutely terrible what has happened…'

'So you will help me?'

Her eyes widen.

'Nina, I am helping you.'

'But I mean, to find her. As soon as possible.'

She lets out a breath through her long nose.

'There is more to this than you know, I'm afraid. All I will say is, I assure you that we are doing all we can to find Kelci. If your parents have any news, of course, I will relay it to you straight away.'

I place my mug on the table.

'But whilst we are sitting here, drinking hot chocolate, my sister is out there, in the hands of god knows who.'

'I understand, but the best thing you can do right now, is excel in your training.'

'It's a waste of time.'

I won't manifest anyway.

'There are others in the same situation as your sister and believe me when I say that everything in our power is being done to find them.'

'But *what* is being done?'

'Nina.'

Her nostrils flare slightly.

'Concentrate on what you need to do right now.'

I sit back in my chair. She's giving me nothing. All she wants me to do is manifest, but I don't even think I can and I don't even know if I *want* to. If I could just get some information about the people who took her, where she is… I might not even need any powers, and everything that goes along with it. I can still have a life, my dreams, Mason…

'I can't concentrate.'

She gives me a stern look.

'Yes, you can. And you really ought to. And if you would like to find your sister, you *will*.'

She stands up, and swoops over to the fireside, pointing to a framed picture on the wall, a class photo. She beckons me over.

'Come.'

I rise from the chair and step over Shadow who nuzzles his nose into Lady Muldoon's ankle. Her voice softens.

'See those two there, on the back row. That's your parents. Luke Gregory and Stella Smythe. Two of the best Apprentices of that year.'

I peer at the picture and see that, yes, that's my Dad, with a thick head of blonde hair, wearing a blue jacket with enormous lapels on it and next to him is Mum, young and beautiful, beaming a big smile. I feel a pang of sadness to think of the last time I saw them, looking so drawn and desperate.

'I did so want them to stay at Muldoon, to teach – they would have made great Trainers in their Houses, but they wanted to go out in the world and start a family. To have you.'

I sigh. I wonder if Dominic is right. Are they disappointed in me?

'Let me ask you something, Nina. Today, at the assault course, did you believe you had a chance of finishing anything but last?'

'I don't know, I mean, Linda was pretty slow, but no, not really. It's just not really *me*, all this clambering about.'

She raises her eyebrows again.

'So you expect to release your sister from the clutches of her kidnappers without any, and I quote, "clambering about" because "it's just not really me"?'

I stare at her open-mouthed.

'I mean, well…'

I can't think of anything to say to that.

'Would you like my honest opinion?'

'I guess.'

She turns to me and smiles gently.

'All you need to do, is believe.'

I let out a half laugh, half moan.

'Believe in what?'

And with a mysterious kind of look, she says: 'Only *you* can decide that.'

11. Punch From The Hips

Four days since Kelci was taken, Trainee Hall

At 5am this morning, when the wake up call came around once again, I was still going through the conversation with Lady Muldoon in my head, over and over. How, as she said, would I release my sister from her kidnappers? How *would* I do that? They were *armed*, they were huge, even Kelci with her abilities couldn't get the better of them. Even if I do find out right now where she is, am I going to go there empty-handed and alone? There's no one to help me. Except my parents, who are thousands of miles away. All I know is that *something* is going to have to change. But then, the moment I start to think that, a feeling of dread takes over… What if I start trying to manifest again, just like I did in the past, and still, I can't do it? *What if nothing happens?*

Right now, we are all lined up on benches in the 'Trainee Hall', which is basically a massive gym. There's a big mat and we are kitted out in navy blue tracksuits. I look down at my blue trainers in dismay. Lady Muldoon sweeps past and informs us that today we will 'engage in some one-on-one combat', something about checking our ability to balance attack and defence. Shadow sits perfectly still at the edge of the mat, a noble look on his face. My heart drops as she waves a little whistle in the air and tells us the only rules are to cease fighting if we hear it, and to raise one hand if we want to stop. I sit sandwiched between James and Ben. The first name called out is Heather Jackson. As she shimmies up to the mat James' mouth falls open.

'That is one hot cupcake right there,' he says, his eyes like saucers. 'Damn.'

I roll my eyes and cross my arms over my chest.

'You can't call her a cupcake, she's a *person*,' I grumble.

But somehow I don't think Heather could care less if someone refers to her as a cupcake. She has customized the outfit to her advantage. She's discarded the tracksuit top and tied the blue t-shirt in at the waist which makes her chest appear all the more curvy and her waist all the slimmer, revealing a flash of bare skin which is smooth and tanned. She wears red lipstick, making her lips appear lush as freshly washed cherries. As she ties her big curls up into a ponytail Lady Muldoon calls out the next name. Nina Gregory. For a split second I sit looking for this this person... then my heart drops like a lead balloon as I realise that she means me. There's not much I can do apart from rise warily from the bench, with Ben and James whispering well wishes. Heather has her hands on her hips by the time I get to the mat and she squints her eyes, scrolling me up and down. I couldn't help but notice that yesterday, this girl met every challenge with ease, finishing in the top three sometimes.

Am I supposed to fight her? She looks ready and willing enough, turning towards me with a sly grin on her face. I feel the eyes of the whole group on us. I have to act fast. All I can think of are those Kung Fu lessons. The stuff Mum used to go on about. What was it? Tiger hands? I rack my brains, trying to remember but there is little time to formulate a plan before I hear the whistle peep and I am in the first fight of my life. Heather's eyebrows furrow and she raises her chin. Then she kicks me in the chest, with one astonishingly quick move. I am thrown back by its power, the wind knocked out of me. I gasp for air. This is definitely not *her* first fight.

I have to remember the moves. What was it? Punch from the hips? Use my hips? Something! I lunge forward, with a right-armed punch that has nothing to do with my hips but it does land on her shoulder. She looks down at the spot where I hit her for a second, whilst I stagger backwards. Then she turns to me once again. A look flashes across her face and then she sort of swirls, and kicks me again, swift and accurate. It hurts. I cry out. She does the swirl again and before I know it she has punched me in the stomach with an uppercut that has me flapping on the floor like a fish thrown out of water. *Could it be over that quick?* Through a daze I hear the sound of laughter. I lie there writhing. The whistle is blown. Heather looks down at me for a few seconds, her red nails on her hips again.

'It's no fun when it's that easy,' she purrs.

I consider kicking her in the shins but her shapely legs disappear before I can move. Shadow's face appears, his wet nose within inches of my own, his long, white whiskers brushing across my cheek. He places a paw on my chest and all I can do is lie here, unresponsive. Then Lady Muldoon hangs over me and enquires if I need to go to the infirmary, but after a minute, the dizziness and sense of impending doom passes and I haul myself up from the ground, hold my stomach and limp back to the benches where the others sit. James and Ben give me sympathetic smiles. I flop down next to them. Ben pats me gently on the shoulder. All I can do is shake my head. *Where has my dignity gone?*

This just highlights, in no uncertain terms, that Lady Muldoon was right. I don't stand a chance of rescuing Kelci, not like this. *I would make the situation worse.* All Heather had to do was kick me a couple of times… The next two called up are Rodriguez, a big-chinned, dark-complexioned guy and Galina, a Russian girl with a heart-shaped face and very long fingers. After a bout of tussling, Galina wins by trapping Rodriguez in an uncomfortable looking headlock. For the next fight, James is called first. He stands up immediately, runs a hand over his hair and begins puffing his cheeks in and out, so rapidly I worry he might hyperventilate.

'I got this, I got this,' he says, frowning at the ground.

'You do, you got this,' I say.

He darts over to the mat then bounces on the balls of his feet, like boxers do and raises his fists in front of his face and throws air punches. Lady Muldoon calls the second name, 'Alisdair McDowell'. The eye-rolling guy. Alisdair. I never met anyone with that name before. He looks confident, ready. Heather leans forward.

'Go, Alisdair,' she croons.

Please!

The whistle blows and the fight begins. James does a good job of jumping around and dodging the first punches, however it isn't long before Alisdair floors him with one painful looking jab to the cheek. The whistle goes again, then all you can hear is James moaning on the mat. Alisdair leans down and tries to help him back to his feet, but James flaps his arms about. It takes a while but Alisdair persists, and eventually manages to help James up, as he holds his cheek, grumbling. Alisdair holds out his hand and, eventually, it is taken and the two of them shake hands then return to the benches.

The next names are called. Ben Hult and Dominic Federov. I gulp. The two of them didn't get off to a great start; on account of me.

Ben hulks his impressive frame to the mat as Dominic strides up, lithe-limbed. Yes, Dominic is smaller, well *everyone* is smaller than Ben, but there's something creepy about the guy. Maybe it's the way his nose slants down towards his delicate lips, or his unnerving stare. Lady Muldoon gives a shrill blast on the whistle and the two of them glare at each other for a few seconds. I find myself edging forwards on the bench, willing Ben to do well. He makes the first move, diving forwards, but Dominic is light on his feet and he sidesteps the swipe.

'Who is this guy?' says Dominic, turning towards us for a second. 'Does anyone actually know who this guy is?'

I groan as he turns back.

'Who are you?' he says.

Ben lunges forward again but Dominic jabs with his right hand and hits Ben in the face, so fast you can hardly see it happen. Ben's grunt echoes around the hall as he sways on his feet.

'Damn!' cries James, jumping up.

Dominic laughs.

'This little guy knows you.'

James hops up and down, looking like he wants to join the fight himself.

'Sit down,' says Lady Muldoon, glaring.

I stand up, and pull James back to the bench as he spits threats and insults.

'He can handle it,' I say, hoping I'm right.

Ben regains his balance then launches again but Dominic slips away, then darts around his back, hits him on the other side of his face. James and I groan.

'I've been getting ready for this all my life,' says Dominic. 'What have you been doing?'

Ben's face grows a shade darker. He lets out a low growl and stamps forward, shoving at Dominic who falls back a few steps. A murmur rises up from the benches.

'Yes!' says James.

But Dominic quickly finds his balance and resumes his dance. He jabs again, hitting Ben in the neck, then darts away, comes back and tries again but is blocked by Ben's enormous arm. Ben swipes with his other arm and Dominic bends down to avoid it. I can see that Ben is trying to keep his opponent in his sights but it is hard for him, and tiring. Sweat is forming in beads on his forehead whilst Dominic looks fresh. The whole group gets louder and louder as the fight goes on, not to mention James who is practically screaming. Lady Muldoon watches intently from the sidelines, holding tight on to her whistle.

'Your size is not your strength,' says Dominic. 'It's your weakness.'

I can't help shouting out.

'Don't listen to him, Ben! Come on.'

'Yeah, come on,' goads Dominic, trying to imitate my voice. 'Your cheerleader wants you to block me out...'

Ben lurches again, faster this time, but Dominic drops to the ground and rolls away, only to jump back onto his feet and punch Ben in the jaw, hard. There's a collective gasp.

'But a guy like you can't help but listen to a guy like me.'

I throw my head back in despair. Ben's hands clasp his jaw. He let's out a deep snarling noise.

'What a waste of all that power,' says Dominic, shaking his head.

Ben steps back and for one moment I think he's about to raise his arm and surrender, but then he lets go of his jaw. He takes another step back and crouches with one knee to the ground. His eyes don't leave Dominic. My heart thumps in my chest *What is he doing?*

'Quiet!' he roars, his voice resounding across the hall.

He slams his hand down and there's a deep thwack, followed by a crumbling sound. He's smashed through the mat and left a great dent in the floor! The entire room goes silent. Another few seconds pass, and Dominic stares at him. Then Ben throws himself forward, so hard and so fast there's a loud 'smack' as they meet. A look of shock lights up Dominic's face as he finds himself pelted to the ground. He places his hands either side of him, then fury fills his face. He doesn't say anything else. All you can see is his eyes, turning from brown to blood red. I gasp, and so does everyone else. *His eyes are glowing like hot embers.* He pushes himself up onto his feet. Then, so quickly I can barely see it happening, he spits at Ben. I can't see what he spits, I can just hear the cry as it hits Ben's chest, burning and sizzling through his tracksuit top.

'He's manifesting!' cries James.

'No!' I say, dismayed.

Not him. Ben seems to have been sent completely over the edge. He lunges towards Dominic, full force, and I wince as he meets him head on and Dominic is lifted from the ground, flying through the air like a rag doll. I can hardly watch as he is thrown *way* down the length of the gym, then lands with a thud. Dominic wriggles about on the floor as Ben stands before us, chest heaving. I swear he is growing, actually growing. I catch my breath.

'Ben's manifesting too,' I whisper.

James and I look at each other in stunned silence. Dominic scrambles to his feet and runs to the mat, visibly seething. Lady Muldoon blows the whistle, but Dominic ignores it and looks as though he is about to spit more venom. Lady Muldoon strides over to him and places her hand on his chest.

'This is the end,' she says. 'No more.'

He backs down, breathless. She turns to us, Dominic on her left, eyes radiating, and Ben on her right, his top burnt away to reveal his bare chest beneath, which is astonishingly sun-kissed and sculpted.

'And so we have our first manifestations of the program,' she says. 'A Bear and a Snake.'

The silence continues for a few more moments, then the whole place erupts into applause. As I stand up, clapping, I can't help wondering... Could that ever happen to me?

12. A History Lesson

Four days since Kelci was taken, Trainee Quarters

It is time for our first theory lesson. In order to attend this theory lesson, we need to venture up into the main Academy building. As soon as we are told this, by a man named Professor Dunedin, a ripple of excitement runs through the group. We follow the professor up a steep, wide set of stairs that are made of smooth, cool stone. He looks a bit like a young Granddad in his brown and green cardigan. He's a Frog, my first real life Frog. I try to imagine him jumping from skyscraper to skyscraper like in our comic strips but it's impossible to imagine with that cardigan and the wiry glasses clinging to his nose. When he talks I get the feeling this might be his first attempt at teaching. He speaks softly, with a slightly nervous edge and it seems like he doesn't quite know what to do with his hands; he constantly puts them in his pockets or runs them through his sandy hair, which flops over his face.

Eventually we reach a landing which is bare apart from a large door made of swirls of intertwining wood. The professor pushes the door open and we funnel through, a mass of navy blue overalls. Once through the door, with Ben and James next to me, what we see catches our breaths in our mouths. We find ourselves in a corridor that is so big it is more like a long hall, filled with Apprentices dashing this way and that. The ceiling is high and arched and there are bright paintings up there – eagles twisting through the sky, rabbits standing watch, foxes creeping, bears beating their chests, a snow leopard; all the animals. There are archways carved out of the opposite wall too, 12 of them, each containing a circular window made from stained glass – each window a different combination of colours – lime green merges to yellow, pink turns to grey then white, black fades to orange. The colours of the different Houses? We all stand there, gaping. I look closer and see that etched in the windows are the outlines of the same symbols I saw in the plane, the same symbols tattooed on my parents' backs – one of each animal curled inside the circles.

'Welcome to Theory,' says Professor Dunedin, hands behind his back. 'Where Apprentices, regardless of House, come to study.'

Bodies swoop past us and all we seem able to do is stand here, amidst the whirlwind. There's so much colour, so much light, so much life up here. Who knew?

'Apprentices are usually between the ages 14 to 19, sometimes younger and sometimes older. For Theory, the younger ones wear the uniforms, in their House colours.'

He points to a group of doe-eyed girls wearing dark purple blazers and pleated skirts with silver lines running along the edges. They all have long, shiny hair and move gracefully.

'Deer,' he says.

They whisper to each and look at Alisdair as they approach, but he doesn't seem to notice.

'Hello, Professor Dunedin,' they all chime in perfect unison as they float past.

'Hello, ladies,' he replies, nodding awkwardly.

He turns back to us.

'The older ones wear the jackets.'

He points to a tall guy wearing a lightweight black jacket and black trousers, with fiery orange lines along the arms and a bag across his shoulders.

'A Tiger,' I say to Ben and James. 'Black and orange. Like my mum.'

'That's right,' says Professor Dunedin, looking at me. 'A Tiger.'

He smiles, the corners of his eyes creasing kindly. Suddenly, a guy bumps into my arm. He turns around to apologise as he stomps along holding a leather-bound notebook. He wears a black tie and his eyes are so dark they look black too.

'A Bear,' says James. 'Am I right?'

'I'd say so,' I reply.

'One of yours,' he says, nudging Ben.

A boy and girl with golden hair that ends with sea-blue tips, glance at us whilst deep in conversation.

'Oooh! Fish!' says Lucy, bursting with excitement.

'You got it,' says the professor.

Just like Dad. I want to stay here. I think we all do. But Professor Dunedin guides us along the marble floor made multi-coloured by the light shining through the windows, as Apprentices dive into their classrooms. I hear accents from all over the world – Africa, Europe, South America, the Far East.

'Apprentices study espionage, strategy, world politics, Anitar History, mission technique,' he explains, as we move along amongst it all. 'And more.'

Without warning, two figures swoop over our heads, flying in the space below the arched ceiling, holding books across their chests and wearing brown uniforms edged with gold. We stop in our tracks to stare at them.

'Eagles,' says the professor.

I watch them soar over everyone, two guys. A red-haired boy with a spattering of freckles across his nose and cheeks, and a slim boy, long-necked and graceful. They both land lightly on the floor and I see the red-haired guy's wide-set eyes, shining gold, and the thickness of his hair. He bows his head to the other boy as they part to enter two different doors.

'This entire floor is devoted to Theory.'

A crowd of boys and girls bound along together, their heads all in a huddle.

'Rabbits!' says Rodriguez.

My heart soars and aches all at the same time. They have exactly the same white-blonde hair as Kelci. *She should be here.* We pass a wide set of doors with the word 'Operations' etched into the wood panel above.

'What's in there?' says Lucy.

The Professor coughs into his fist, frowning a little.

'We won't be going up there today. What goes on here isn't all strictly Academy business. In fact we won't be going up there any day during the Manifestation Program, Operations is strictly out of bounds to Trainees.'

Lucy listens with fascination and my ears prick up too. What did Artemiz say? *Muldoon Academy is the centre of the Anitar world and anything that is worth knowing is right there.* Could there be something that might help me find Kelci through those doors? Lucy gives me a look; it's clear she's wondering the exact same thing. But before I have a chance to dwell on it, Professor Dunedin leads us through another, smaller one of the ornate doors and we find ourselves in a classroom with the same arched windows as the rest of the Academy, as though they have been carved out of the thick walls, with their organic, swirling patterns. He picks up a remote control from the desk and announces that today, we will receive our introduction to Anitar History. He turns out the lights and presses a button on the remote. A picture appears on a large screen at the front – the Professor with a group of guys who all look similar to him, smiling at the camera, everyone putting their thumbs up.

'Oops,' he says, fumbling for a button. 'Wrong slide!'

He gives an awkward laugh and there are titters across the room, then he bounds over to the projector and fiddles with it until the image of a woman appears. It is a painting, hundreds of years old. She is regal looking with a long nose and beautiful brown eyes.

'Who's that?' says Heather, twisting a strand of hair around her finger.

'That is the original Lady Muldoon.'

'Ooooh,' she coos. 'Interesting.'

She gives a toothy smile to the professor and he almost jumps back. *She's flirting with him.* And he can't handle it. He flusters for a moment and hovers away from her. She keeps smiling and looks like she regularly makes a sport of terrorising gawky teachers.

'The current Lady Muldoon's great, great – many times great – grandmother,' he continues, edging further away. 'She founded Muldoon Academy in the 16th Century.'

I sit forward in my chair. I notice Lucy at the front, looking enthralled. She sits next to Alisdair and whispers something in his ear. He turns to her and smiles, affectionately. I haven't seen him smile before. It completely transforms his face.

'The original Lady Muldoon was called Agatha. She was a Deer, but at that time she didn't know of anyone else with powers like hers.'

I rest my chin on my hands.

'The story goes that she found out she could heal when her horse broke its leg. Ordinarily it would have been put down, but Agatha saved it.'

'Oh,' says Heather.

'Later, Agatha's Mother became ill. Agatha healed her and the doctor who witnessed it pronounced her a witch. She was now in great danger, so Agatha and her family fled. They moved to this very island and began work on the buildings we find ourselves in now – so that their precious daughter, Agatha could grow up in safety.'

The first Anitars had it bad; it's been sacrifice right from the start. A girl called Stacey in the front row, with an orange bob and small eyes, shoots her hand up in the air.

'Professor Dunedin, were Agatha's parents Anitars? Do you have to come from an Anitar family to manifest?'

The Professor joins his hands together and looks thoughtful.

'No. According to the few documents we have from that time, Agatha's parents were not Anitars. It was just her to begin with in this family line. You don't have to come from an Anitar family to manifest.'

'My parents weren't Anitars,' says James. 'At least I don't think they were. And Grandma isn't one. Unless she's keeping it secret, and when I say secret, I mean *very* secret. Uncle Steve has no superpowers. *No way.* Uncle Steve's got nothing.'

He shakes his head violently. The professor rearranges his cardigan.

'The potential for manifestation lies in many,' he says. 'Some say in *everyone.*'

There's a collective gasp.

'But the overwhelming majority of people do not come anywhere near to manifesting, although in theory, they could.'

I see Alisdair lean in to whisper into Lucy's ear. The professor clicks to another image of Agatha, but this time sat next to a man wearing a white, ruffled-necked outfit, with her hand on his lap.

'One day she received a letter from this man,' he says, pointing to the image. 'Federic Almanov. He heard about her 'witchcraft' and explained that he had similar abilities. They shared their knowledge and ended up marrying.'

I raise my eyebrows.

'Damn,' says James.

'He was a Frog, as it happens.'

He looks proud of that fact.

'Together they found others like them and brought them here, to provide sanctuary and learning. And the rest, as they say, is history!'

He laughs at his own joke, but the rest of the room remains quiet.

'It was right here that the Anitars' principles were formed. And it was clear even then that Anitar powers blossom from goodness.'

Goodness? What's that supposed to mean?

'It has always been our purpose to rid the world of evil.'

An image of Adolf Hitler flicks into view.

'We do the things that no one else can or dares do. We've had a silent hand in ending the careers of some of the most vicious people of the last few hundred years. Serial killers, corrupt dictators, drug barons.'

The images keep flicking from one grim looking individual to the next.

'We've delivered killers straight into the hands of authorities without anyone knowing who did it – what we do *never* reaches the history books.'

I am stunned.

'Whenever too many people know about us, it has only ended in disaster.'

I remember what Dad said after Kelci was taken, that a few people *did* know about us.

'We have been hunted, abused and killed throughout history. That's why we must operate in complete secrecy.'

There's a chill in the room.

'You may be surprised to learn which well-known individuals are Anitars; the list includes some of the most influential people in the world. Many have trained in this very Academy. Politicians, sportsmen, business moguls. From those positions they can influence many lives. Yet there are just as many who lead the everyday lives of schoolteachers, charity workers, chefs, train drivers, doctors.'

I can't help but wonder if I've ever met another Anitar and didn't know it.

'And then there are those who never return to the world but remain at the Academy, after their Apprenticeship, to lead a life devoted to the highest level of missions. We call these Anitars, Paladins. They don't marry or have children, their life is dedicated to being the very best of their kind.'

Artemiz springs to mind. Is she a Paladin?

'If, and when, any of you manifest, before you officially become an Anitar you will be asked to make The Promises. It will be your choice entirely to make them, or not.'

He presses a button on his remote and a bright screen comes up with these words:

'I promise that, from this day forward, I will devote my life to the goal of all Anitars: to rid this world of evil so that good people may thrive. I promise to help others, but in doing so, I will seek no glory. I will develop my abilities to the highest levels I can reach and I will assist my fellow Anitars when they are in need. I refuse to allow the powers I possess to be used to further any one of the political agendas and allegiances of mankind and I promise to keep the Anitar way of life confidential at all costs. These promises I keep until my last breath.'

The room is quiet. I feel a spark of pride that my parents do this stuff, that they trained here. I wonder what disasters they have averted, what lives they've saved? I remember how I felt that pride years ago, even before I knew this place existed, when I dreamt of my parents as superheroes, saving the world. I remember the girl I was then. The lionhearted fourteen-year-old with a dream. I wonder where that girl is now.

13. Snow-covered Mountain

Fifth day since Kelci was taken, somewhere above Muldoon Island

I can't see a thing. I have a blind-fold on, as does every other member of the group. I am weighed down by a massive backpack strapped to my shoulders. Today we are kitted out in heavy boots and boiler suits with tight little hoods that cling to our heads. However, my attire is the least of my concerns right now. From what I can tell I am in an airplane – I know only because of the sound of the engine and the distinct feeling of having taken off from the ground. We were already blindfolded before being led out of the Academy.

This is the first of the special challenges Lady Muldoon has talked about, and the whole thing has me on edge. She told us, this morning, prior to the blindfolding that in the first challenge we will be pitted against each other in two teams. The selection of the teams was random and I took note that I am on the same team as Heather, Alisdair, Rodriguez, Stacey and about 10 more Trainees. Anitars must act in secrecy, she said. And any Anitar worth his or her salt always knows their way home, no matter where they are in the world. All I can say is, my sense of direction is terrible. The teams will start in two different locations: Team One, my team, must get back to Muldoon and Team Two must find Team One before they're able to do so – if they are able to catch any member of our team with a shot of the paint guns they have been provided us with, then they win.

It didn't sound like a good idea when she outlined it and I certainly don't think it's a good idea now, as I cling to the hull of this aircraft. I can only hope we land soon. I hear the rumble of the engine and shouting around me. I hear the booming voice of a man instructing us to line up, but I can't see the line! I feel a strong set of arms pulling me from the side of the plane. The arms guide my gloved hands to what I can only presume is someone else's back. I guess I'm now in line. An almighty blast hits us, out of nowhere. It's so loud everything else is blocked out. I feel a rush of cold air on my face. Panic sets in. What has gone wrong? I feel myself being pulled along by the arms again – *towards* the air. I struggle and cry out. Seconds later I feel the person in front of me disappear.

'No!'

I am right in the midst of – what feels like – a hurricane. My blindfold is removed. A guy stands in front of me, red hair blowing straight up from his forehead, freckles sprayed across his nose. The same guy we saw swooping along the Theory corridor yesterday. Another guy and girl are behind me, adjusting my backpack. I feel as though my face is blue. Before me is a gaping hole showing the earth far below it. I fear that it is all over. The girl thrusts an orange handle, attached to my backpack, into my grip. She smiles, yes, smiles at me! I look at the red haired boy and gulp. He starts yelling.

'Count to 40, when you get to 40, pull on this handle. It will open your parachute.'

'What! No! I can't....'

My heart does actually stop.

'Find the others when you get down there. Don't forget to pull this. If you don't we'll have to come and get you.'

'Get me? What?'

I can only presume my face is now green. The guy winks at me and says:

'Enjoy it.'

With that he proceeds to shove me out of the plane. I let out a scream, which comes from the very depths of my soul, but the wind moves so fast it can't be heard. Time freezes. I am star shaped and falling. *Count. Must count.* 1, 2, 3, 4. The wind stretches my face. I'm hurtling faster. I cling on to the handle and when I get to 40 I pull it – hard. I'm winded as it blows up behind me. The straps of the parachute ride up my back and I thank god it works. The ground spreads out below me, a great patchwork with the mountains and forest, and a river that looks like a black snake. There's nothing else for me to do but take in the beauty of it all. I feel a yearning somewhere deep inside myself, a feeling of sudden calm. Which is strange, considering my utter panic of moments ago.

I see a spaced out line of airborne people in front of me like ants dangling from balloons. I'm moving slower now but the ground is getting closer. There are bunches of trees materialising beneath me. I presume landing on one of these is not a good option. I look back and see another line of floating ants behind me. My parachute billows above and I'm past the trees now. There's a snow-covered mountain. I peer down – by now there is no more line in front of me – instead there are three dark splodges on the side of the mountain that I presume are members of my group. I drop towards the mountain, but there's very little time to ponder how to land as it speeds towards me. Without further ado, I land in a heap. The parachute flaps at my side. Embedded in the snow, I lift my head up and peer out. There's someone there, moving towards me.

'Hello?' I cry. 'Who is it?'

The figure appears before me. Alisdair.

'Oh,' I say. 'Hi.'

This is the first time we've spoken. And I'm wedged waist-high in snow.

'Hi there,' he says. 'Let me help you.'

'I'm fine, I'm fine,' I reply, struggling to move my legs.

He puts his hand out towards me and I take it. As he hauls me out, three more navy blue bodies catapult into the side of the mountain, one after the other. With his help I manage to wriggle out of my hole and sprawl gracelessly on the snow.

'Are you ok?' he says as I lie face up.

I nod.

'I'm fine, really. Yes, I'm great.'

'Here, let me help you up,' he replies.

He gives me his arm which I use to lever myself upright.

'Good,' he says, as I regain my balance.

'Thanks,' I reply.

As I brush down the wads of snow on my suit I see Heather nearby, her parachute laid out beside her, staring at us. Alisdair jogs over to help the rest of the team get to their feet. Then, after a fair amount of scrabbling around from everyone, he speaks up.

'Guys,' he says.

His cheeks glow, his eyelashes are thick and dark. He looks alive. *Ridiculously alive.* He's revelling in this. He's tackled every piece of training with relative ease and skill, but this is something else. It looks as though he's been waiting to be catapulted onto the side of a mountain all his life.

'We need to find cover, quickly. We're way too exposed here.'

Small clouds of breath billow as he speaks, which lends a certain drama to his words. Everyone else looks dazed and confused, apart from Heather who strides over and positions herself right next to him. Without further ado he leads us down the mountain, moving fast. Eventually the whole group is on his heels and we march down to the trees. It's cold – the kind of cold that gets into your bones and stays there. Once we have some cover we gather together and try to figure out which skills we have to help us get home. We realise we have virtually none, apart from what Alisdair seems to have to offer. It feels like, somehow, he just knows what he's doing. Where does his confidence come from? The rest of the group immediately request him as leader.

'If that's what it takes to win, I'll do it,' he says.

Our hero. I let out a large breath, which condenses into a billowing cloud. My hands are beginning to throb. There are more discussions about directions and locations. Alisdair instructs us to travel South West. I can only presume this is based on some sort of instinct of his because there's no other reason why we should do so. He assigns us all the task of keeping our eyes peeled for the other group. We plunge further into the forest. He moves with speed and gives out steely looks when we don't all move as quickly as he does. When Rodriguez and Stacey lag behind, he doesn't look impressed.

'We need to move. Now,' he says.

I get the feeling he just wants to run off into forest on his own and leave us all behind. But he won't win the challenge if he does that. At one point he throws a glance in my direction. I frown at him and he just sort of broods, or at least I think he does. He's impossible to read. We bustle through the forest until we find a river, which we then follow all the way into a deep valley. We plunge through snow, mud, water, and ice. I slip and slide all over the place, and I'm not the only one struggling with the conditions. I wish Ben was here to grab on to, he's unbelievably steady on his feet. So is Alisdair. He doesn't seem to put a step wrong the whole way. We eventually enter another forest with more ferny type trees and I hear Heather shout Alisdair's name. *She's obsessed with him.* But then I hear her saying he's 'gone'.

Apprehension ripples through the group, but we keep moving. Moments pass and he's nowhere to be seen. We can't call out, in case Team Two hears us, so we look around in every direction. Nothing. Where is he? Seconds tick by like minutes, then suddenly he appears in front of us, so fast I didn't see him coming. He looks exhilarated and his hair now has great white streaks running through the blackness!

'I think I just discovered some abilities,' he says.

He's a blur of motion… appearing again at the other side of the group. We've all come to a standstill, watching him. Suddenly I realise. *He's a Snow Leopard.* His eyes have changed colour. They glow ice blue. He's taller, wider in the shoulders, his features are sharper. *Definitely a Snow Leopard.* Mum always said that Snow Leopards get talked about the most, but they are the least seen – so rare, even she only ever knew one, personally. She always had a dreamy look about her when she talked about them, which made me wonder about her Snow Leopard friend. Who was he? But she never did tell me that. She did tell me that they are one of the most powerful Anitars, that they like to work alone, and that most of them are male. And now, we have one here right in front of us. Heather has her eyes locked on him, in fact every girl in the group is looking at him misty-eyed, but he's breathing hard, his eyes darting around the forest, on full alert, and he doesn't seem to notice a thing.

14. Chalk & Cheese

Five days since Kelci was taken, Muldoon Island

The sky is getting dark. After hours more trekking we find a clearing and set up camp. We agree that each of us will take a shift on night watch. Mine is 3.30am until we rise at 5am. I'm shaken awake at half past three and I sit up in my sleeping bag and breathe in the freezing air. I watch the other lying bundles and stare at the fire. With Alisdair's leadership there's a feeling that we've done well; there's been no sign of the other group, and I suspect we've put some distance between us.

It is quiet, so quiet and still, just the flickering flames and the trees above, swaying, back and forth, back and forth. Out of the silence… I hear Terence's voice. We're in our favourite toyshop in New York and he's calling me to join him on this giant keyboard on the floor. Plink, plonk, plink, plonk. We think it's hilarious. But then, in a flash, we're on his rooftop again.

'I can hear them. Can't you hear them?' he says, desperately.

'No. Hear who? *Who can't I hear?*'

I run to him, there on that ledge, try to grab him… but he's gone. I hear the crack, again. Then Mason is standing in front of me, stroking my hair, so gently. He smiles at me and lowers his head towards my lips. I tell him I miss him, that no one understands me like he does… He tells me that it will be all right, that we belong together. Then I feel something against my chest. His hand? No … I wake up, startled, heart racing. Sunlight is peeking through the trees. *Wait, what?* Dread sinks in. Within seconds, the members of Team One are sitting up and turning their eyes towards me. I gulp. I'm sure I can't have been asleep for long. Heather is the first to point at my chest.

'She's been hit.'

Alisdair is releasing himself from his sleeping bag, his face a stony grimace.

'I was, I mean… I don't know what happened,' I say.

He strides over and looks at my chest too. I look down and see that I am covered in bright red paint. I groan.

'We've *all* lost now,' says Heather, standing over me. 'Thanks.'

'All you had to do was stay awake,' growls Alisdair.

I feel the heat of his anger.

'I know!' I say. 'Look, I'm sorry. I can't have dozed off for more than a second.'

'Whatever, it's enough to lose the entire challenge,' says Heather. 'Little Miss Nina, too much of a *princess* to stay awake.'

'It was only a second!' I cry.

'What are we supposed to say?' she says, creeping towards me. 'That's ok, sweetheart. You fell asleep, could happen to anyone? But you're not in New York now, are you? There's no Mummy and Daddy to bail you out, no walk-in closets, no posh friends or schools or whatever it is you did all day before you came here. It's just you. And us. And the program.'

I stare at her, my eyes filling with tears.

'You might not care if you win this challenge, or manifest, or get a place at Muldoon,' she continues. 'But some of us do. Some of us care more than you could ever imagine. For reasons that you could never understand because you're too busy thinking of yourself. All the time.'

She turns her back on me, prowling away, leaving Alisdair and the rest of the group looking at me in grim disappointment. One guy throws his flask to the ground and it smashes into a rock then bounces into the river.

'Why are you here?' says Alisdair.

I try to hold back the tears but they burst onto my cheeks.

'I want to find my sister,' I reply. 'That's all I want to do.'

He turns from me as I wipe the wetness from my face. *He can't stand me. Heather can't stand me. They think I shouldn't be here …*

And maybe they're right.

————

The next day all we hear about is how utterly delighted everyone at Muldoon Academy is to have a newly manifested Snow Leopard. There hasn't been one for seven years, apparently. There are around hundred times more Rabbits than Snow Leopards, we are eagerly informed – so that just shows how few there are. I spend the day trying hard not to visibly roll my eyes. The next night the dreams continue. I awake to the sound of my own cries, with every inch of me plastered in sweat, tangled in bed sheets. I turn my head, unsure of where I am and I see the sleeping humps of the other girls in my dorm. Mason was there again, strumming on his guitar, his sweet lips smiling at me. But then I heard screaming – Kelci. She was in the arms of those men, struggling and writhing. My heart pounds. The room is dark. I'm breathing hard, clinging to the sides of my plank-like bed. I hear a little whisper.

'Hey. It's your bunk buddy here. Are you ok?'

Lucy.

'Just a bad dream,' I reply.

Her head pops up at the side of my bed and I can just about see her dark eyes and unkempt hair.

'Was it a nightmare? I get them all the time, I always wake up just before I'm about to die.'

She grins widely. I nod, then sigh, then let my head fall back on the pillow.

'Can I join you?' she says.

Before I have a chance to answer, she's gripping the side of my bed.

'There's not much room,' I say, actually wishing I could lie here alone, in silence.

I pull my knees up and she's already clambering in. She slips on her way up, landing in a heap on the floor. I lean out of bed and she grabs onto my arms and I help to haul her up. She scrabbles about noisily until finally she is crossing her skinny legs and settling in. She wears a t-shirt with a cartoon hedgehog on it, pyjama bottoms and thick bed socks gathered at the ankles. There's something about this girl, the way she talks and acts, which makes me feel like something strange might be about to happen. She whispers again.

'I've got a confession to make. It's really bad.'

'Oh yeah?'

She stares at me.

'I shot you. With the paintball gun.'

'That was you?'

'What can I say? I'm a great shot. I told them that, I said, anyone I aim at is going to get it. And you were so close, the first one I saw. I felt bad it was you but I did it. I'm sorry.'

She doesn't look like the kind of girl who'd be a dead shot. The slim shoulders and heart-shaped lips... I can barely imagine her holding a gun, but I shrug anyway.

'If it wasn't you, it would've been someone else.'

'So you forgive me?'

'Sure.'

Her eyes light up and she presses her hands together.

'Thank you! I only found out later that you were the one on watch, which obviously makes you look *really bad.*'

'Thanks, yeah.'

She winces.

'You're the last person I want to get into trouble.'

'Remember not to shoot me in the chest in future then!'

She bites her lip, but I can't help smiling.

'I won't,' she says. 'I promise. I actually do promise. Because I want to be on your side. I decided that when I saw you splattered in red paint. I like you.'

I stare at her, a little shocked. *Why?* I want to say, but I don't.

'Are you ok?' she says. 'I mean, really ok?'

'You don't want to ask me that…'

'Yes I do, I'm very inquisitive. My brother says too inquisitive but I don't care. I heard you up here, crying out. You can tell me. I'm not as crazy as I look. Well, not quite!'

She giggles. Should I open up to this girl? Trust her? She seems to be the only friendly face on the horizon at the moment, especially after what happened today. Even just one day away from Ben and James is too long around here… I suppose they've become my companions… Which is funny because at home, I would never even meet a pair of guys like that.

'I need to find my sister,' I say. 'She's been kidnapped but I'm here, and she isn't. I need to manifest, but I can't. Oh and everyone hates me.'

She wriggles under the end of my covers.

'*I* don't hate you.'

I frown.

'If you don't hate me,' I say. 'Then plenty of other people do. Alisdair hates me.'

'Alisdair? No!'

'Oh yes. I lost us the challenge. He can't stand me. You guys are friends, I know, but I hope for your sake you don't do anything wrong because he's not forgiving. Not one bit.'

'I know. He *can* be like that… He's not always the best, you know… with people. But believe me, he doesn't hate you, he doesn't *hate* anyone. He doesn't even know you. Alisdair… What can I say? He's not much of a team player…'

'He *thinks* he knows me. He's the most arrogant…'

'Hey, hey,' she says, leaning forward and holding on to her socks. 'He ain't heavy, he's my brother.'

'What?'

'He's my brother. You didn't know?'

My eyes widen.

'No. Your brother? Literally?'

She smiles.

'Yes. Literally. Related by blood. Same parents. Bona fide family and all that.'

She grins.

'Oh.'

I look at her through the darkness and realise that there *is* a shade of resemblance between the two of them, especially in the eyes. And that would explain the fact that he talks to her because he hardly talks to anyone else; except Heather of course, but she makes it impossible for him to avoid her. But I would never in a million years have guessed they were brother and sister. They are just so *different*. Like chalk and cheese. But then that's exactly what Mum and Dad always say about Kelci and me. Chalk and cheese.

'He probably can't understand why anyone would not be *desperate* to become an Anitar. This life is everything to him. It's all he wants. And you can hardly blame him.'

I sit forward.

'Oh?'

'We're alone, he and I, you see. Dad died before I was born, and when Mum passed away too, it was just the two of us from then on. I was four and Alisdair was seven. We've had so many foster families I can't even remember them all. Daddy was the Anitar, a Fox. The best around. We know because Mum told us stories about him every single day when she was alive. She met him when she came over from China and she stayed because of him. She always wondered if we would manifest too, like him. Just before she died she made Alisdair promise that he would look after me and that's what he's done, and still does, to this day.'

I fold the pillow under my arms and bring it in to my chest.

'Alisdair will never be able to think of anything else that could be more important. He remembers Daddy, and he loves him, so much. It makes him kind of *focused*, he doesn't need friends like the rest of us but then he's always been like that. I wasn't surprised at all that he's a Snow Leopard. I just knew he would be.'

'And you agree? That there's nothing more important than this?'

She nods.

'I don't know what an ordinary life is. In here I can be anything… I can belong to something. I just know I have an animal in me fighting to get out!'

She bounces up and down a little. *She believes, without question, that it's going to happen. Just like I did.* I can't help but hope it comes true for her.

'I was thinking,' she goes on. 'About your sister. Maybe I could help you. Wouldn't that be fun?'

Fun? I'm not sure what to say to that. I could use a hand but it sounds like this girl has enough to deal with.

'We should find out what's behind those doors marked 'Operations'. There's got to be something interesting in there, right?'

I murmur agreement but I won't commit to anything. *I* should go up there but I can not risk getting caught because from what Professor Dunedin said, I would not get the chance *ever* again if I did, not to mention the fact that I would lose the trust of Lady Muldoon, the person who knows the most, and I would probably lose my place on the program too. I lie my head back and stare at the ceiling for a while, then I prop myself up on my elbow and for the next hour at least Lucy stays exactly where she is, on my bed, whispering about her hopes and dreams and her life with her brother. I don't even know when she finally gets into her own bed, because I drift off to sleep without seeing her go.

15. A Glimpse

Six days since Kelci was taken, Trainee Canteen

Today something different is going to happen. Artemiz just strode into the canteen and announced that we are going on an 'Apprentice Tour'; this sparks a buzz of excitement that spreads through the whole team. We wolf down our breakfasts and soon enough are heading out of the main building towards the enormous circular enclosure surrounded by the 12 Houses. The sun is bright, the air is clear and I walk directly behind Artemiz, with Ben and James to my right. I keep my eyes on a set of thin, delicate arrows sitting in a quiver that is strapped to Artemiz's back. Their tips sprout brown and dark red feathers. A wooden bow with two deep curves either side sits on a diagonal slant and I stare at the intricate, carved design – the head of a horse with hair sweeping down along the arms of the bow.

As we reach the enclosure, she turns to us, wearing a full body suit, which is made from faded, chestnut brown leather with a low-slung belt at her hips. The symbol of the Horse's head curled into a small circle sits on the right side of her chest and her hair is pulled back, flowing like a mane down her neck. We all stare at her. She looks utterly beautiful, with the buildings rising up behind her, and the mountains behind them. We, on the other hand, look like a bunch of escaped prisoners. All we were given to wear was a pair of navy blue combats, a t-shirt, a monstrous pair of boots and a small, extremely functional looking rucksack. I valiantly try to make the best of a bad job and take a moment to style my bun up neater and pull a few strands out at the sides of my face. I try to stand up tall like Artemiz does. *How does she get her back so straight?* Her huge, almond-shaped eyes – framed with thick black curves of eyeliner – meet mine.

'Chest, out. Chin, up,' she says. 'Proud like a horse. Now. Today, you will see Muldoon Academy for the first, and possibly last, time. This is an opportunity most people will never have. Just remember, you could be a Muldoon Apprentice too.'

I feel apprehensive and excited and sad all at the same time. I spent half my life wondering what this place was like. And now I'm about to have the glimpse… but Kelci should be here, she should be seeing this. Evidently James is nervous as well, he's jumpy and his eyes are shooting off in all directions, plus he keeps biting on his bottom lip and he's barely stopped talking since breakfast. Ben looks positively serene in comparison, arms folded across his mountainous chest, jaw set, his blonde locks shining under the sun. As Artemiz leads us over to the first House I feel a hand on my back.

'Hey, can I hang out with you guys?' says Lucy.

'Sure,' I answer.

I can't help glancing to see if Alisdair, *her brother*, is with her, but he isn't. He's right at the back, his eyes so bright I can see them glowing from here – but he is watching us, that's for sure. Lucy slips in between Ben and me, sticking out her hand towards him.

'We haven't met, not properly, I'm Lucy, Nina's bunk buddy.'

'It's great to meet you,' says Ben, enveloping her hand in his.

She looks up at him, like a chick in a nest. James darts behind Ben's back and nudges in beside Lucy, so that she is sandwiched between the two of them. He introduces himself and shakes her hand, a little too hard and a little too long, like he did with me but Lucy doesn't seem to mind, in fact she's beaming, and she doesn't even bother to take her hand away. They fall into step with each other and move ahead a little, leaving Ben and me behind. James starts telling her about his Grandma and that he's sure he's a Tiger and she giggles when he does his growl, teeth gnashing. The two of them are almost exactly the same height.

'Remember Trainees,' says Artemiz. 'This is just a glimpse. There will be far more to come *if* you manifest.'

I nod solemnly and clench my fists, looking at the towering structure in front of us. It is the same sandy colour as the rest of the buildings, a collection of tall spires sprouting from the ground, covered in archways and rounded windows and spiralling stonework. There's a bridge, which looks like it grows out of the side, linking this House to the next. Like all the doors of the Houses, it is enormous and there is a huge chameleon, carved out of wood, crawling up it, with protruding eyes at the side of its head and scaly skin – painted hot pink with sunset orange and yellow marks all over it. Artemiz places her hand on the door, then says:

'Welcome to The House of Chameleons.'

We soon find ourselves in a grand room with hanging lights and elaborate sculptures all along the sides of the room. Weirdly, there are blue-violet laser beams running from the left side of the room to the right that are moving continuously, forming a shifting grid across the room. When James expresses his surprise Artemiz gives him a look which is enough to silence him and after that we stand there quietly, until five figures appear out of the walls, all wearing playful grins. They acknowledge our presence with nods but Artemiz guides us further away from them. Clearly, we are not supposed to talk to each other. They wear head to toe black, with gloves, but each one has bright hair: rose-pink, raspberry-red, grass-green. As they gather together where the laser field begins, Artemiz leans in and tells us in hushed tones that Chameleon's can disappear against any surface, so long as they are stood against it, touching it with their body.

My eyes travel – beyond the lasers – to a golden orb sat on a plinth. One boy, with hair that is navy-blue but slowly changing to green, moves forward and places himself at the start. He faces the lasers, closes his eyes and says:

'Nowhere is beyond our reach.'

The motto of the Chameleons, Artemiz tells us. The lasers look too thick, too close together and too fast moving for anyone to ever have a hope of getting that orb. He begins by lightly stepping in and over the first beam then bending his back gracefully underneath the next one, somersaulting over a third.

'Chameleons would be the world's greatest thieves if they didn't have such honorable intentions,' says Artemiz.

I keep my eyes on the boy as he controls every inch of his body, gliding past the lasers as they almost graze his face. The boy sprints along, deftly climbs on to a statue and jumps down without a sound, then lies down, allows a few of the beams to cross inches from his chest then jumps back up onto his feet. He gives one small falter right at the end and for a moment I think he may touch the last laser but he steadies himself, makes it through to the end, turns to face us, gives a wave then runs towards the orb. The Chameleons start cheering, and as we are swept us out of the room, so do we.

Next, Artemiz leads us through the Houses of Snakes, much to Dominic's satisfaction, who spends the whole time wearing a smug expression, acting like he already knows everything there is to know about his fellow Snake. It is he that announces loudly their motto:

Forever ready.

However, not one of the Snake Apprentices so much as look at him, they don't look at any of us. From the moment we walk in, greeted by a coiling snake painted on the wall that stares at us with bloodstone eyes, it is all dark and moody and they practice their ancient fighting style in near total blackness, in temperatures that make me sweat, practicing thermal imaging which basically means they can see in the dark, which is creepy, because we can barely see them, we can just hear the swoosh of their dark green clothes as they move.

I am relieved when we pass along to the House of Foxes because the atmosphere is entirely different in here: luxurious and civilised. They all stand around, listening to their Trainer, a silver-haired man in a sharp suit, who looks like he should be the hero in some stylish old movie. They wear fine, tailored outfits and coolly inspect various objects in front of them – necklaces, cameras, purses, sunglasses, bags – concealed weaponry of all kinds. Perfect for close combat, Artemiz explains, which is the only kind of combat a Fox needs because they are more than capable of getting up close to whoever and whatever they choose, on account of their remarkable *persuasive abilities*. This immediately becomes evident when one of them, a handsome Indian guy with thick hair styled back from his face, catches my eye and just looking at him makes me fall in love a little bit, much to my embarrassment. When Artemiz notices, she swiftly guides us out of the building, clearly annoyed that Foxes 'can never be trusted to leave Trainees alone!'

We soon find ourselves at the front of the main building, with the lake spreading out gloriously to one side and the thick forest to the other. High up along the edge of the roof, we see a collection of small blonde girls, in grey and pink tracksuits, blindfolded. 'Perception training,' Artemiz tells us. Learning to rely on all their senses, not just their sight. *Doing what Kelci should be doing.* There are more Rabbits than any other Anitar type, she tells us, and they can be found in all areas of the island, right through the forest, up into the mountains, always on the lookout for danger.

As we move through the huge round courtyard we pass a group of Horses, each with their intricately carved bows, just like Artemiz. They shoot at targets, whilst constantly moving – running, jumping, tumbling, wearing coffee-coloured shirts and trousers with the symbol of the Horse on their chest. They each stop and bow their heads towards Artemiz as she passes and when Lucy exclaims how amazing it would be to hear everyone's thoughts Artemiz is quick to tell her that such a skill may not be as thrilling as it first sounds. It is very hard for Horses, at the outset, because they can hear *everything*, all at once – a kind of insanity that can spin out of control. Without care and guidance some have been driven mad by the voices. For a Horse, she explains, it takes a huge amount of training to block out the noise and tune in to what they want or need to hear.

We move deep into the dark, luscious forest. We keep going until we reach a clearing with a shaft of light that highlights a small group of boys and girls dressed in plum robes trimmed with silver, kneeling amongst the ferns. Young wolf-dogs, just like Shadow, one for each Apprentice, encircle them. Deer. A feeling of calm washes over me. Artemiz puts her finger to her lips and we stay silent, watching. A few glance towards us with blinking brown eyes but nothing seems to take their full attention away from whatever they are focusing on, down there in the undergrowth. One of the girls leans forward towards a long plant that lies dead on the ground. As the group kneels around her, she pushes back a strand of tawny hair, then reaches down to touch the plant softly. She closes her eyes and holds the stem with both hands.

'Restore, renew, revive,' she whispers.

A few moments later the bottom of the stem starts to turn from dusty brown to bright lime-green. Slowly but surely, vitality imbues the length of the stem. The branches turn green too, the brittle leaves spring back to life, and lemon-yellow flowers begin to pop. Soon the entire plant is springing into the fullness of life, blooming and abundant. I can't help but feel a burst of joy. Once the plant is standing tall the girl opens her eyes and the other Deer gently pat her on the back, murmuring congratulations. We watch, in awe, as Artemiz tells us that Deer must be protected, that's why they have their guardians, the dogs, because they cannot heal themselves or be healed by other Deer.

They can easily become weak too, if they practice too much healing at one time. All a Deer wants to do is help others, she says. But they must learn to look after themselves too, otherwise they become useless to everyone, including themselves.

We trek a good distance through the forest, before arriving at another clearing which is decidedly noisier and busier than the last one. We hear the bellowing way before we arrive. It's a group of large, strong-looking Apprentices, so obviously Bears Artemiz doesn't even need to tell us. Some are chopping wood, some are pulling great logs along the ground and hauling them onto piles. As I stare at a mighty looking girl with black hair and rippling muscles, hacking away at a log sending sprays of woodchip into the air, Artemiz tells us that Bears are the most soft-hearted of all the Anitars. When a Bear loves, they really *love*, apparently, which makes everyone turn to Ben whose cheeks turn a shade of pink.

We eventually come out into the valley that lies between the two mountain ranges, heading away from the Academy, towards the coastline, alongside the Emerald River which connects the lake to the mountains and the sea. Artemiz points out a bunch of rocks that look like God has thrown them down from heaven, with the sea lying just beyond – ten of them, different heights but all sharp and fearsome – with wide spaces between each one. Tiger's Claws, she calls them. As we draw closer I see dark dots bouncing from one rock to the next. *One foot wrong and those dots would be dead.* The sound of hollering echoes through the air. As we get closer we see one of them, a boy, shout then catapult himself high into the air, tumble mid-arch, straighten up then pound on to the next rock.

'It's always a party when the Frogs are around,' says Artemiz, before leading us out towards the edge of the island.

The land tapers downwards until the grass turns into sand and we find ourselves on a wide beach with great rocks sitting here and there, white waves crashing onto the shore. In the space between two of the largest rocks there is a group of Apprentices, barefoot on the sand, wearing wrapped white cloth suits, belted at the waist with orange and black stripes down the sides, moving in perfect Kung Fu unison. Not one of them turns towards us as they keep their eyes fixed on the water in front of them, moving from one beautiful pose to the next. They are precise and fierce and graceful all at the same time. I think of when I used to practice Kung Fu every night in front of my mirror. The last time I ever did that was before I tried to help Terence… Before the black clouds came. Back then, I wanted to manifest for me. Not for Mum, not for Kelci. *I wanted it for me.*

We continue along the coastline which takes a steep turn upwards. We pass a bunch of Apprentices in sea-blue swimming gear who run, one by one, to the side of the cliff and without pause glide over the side, spinning, before landing in the water feet first, leaving bubbly white circles behind them. They could be under there for hours, says Artemiz. As we head inland towards the mountain range I can't help wondering if Dad ever jumped from this cliff, into these waters.

It is a long, arduous trek up the side of the mountain but it's worth it when two Eagles swoop by – a dark-skinned boy and a caramel-haired girl – majestic against the backdrop of the entire island. They can fly, of course, Artemiz tells us, but they are also good fighters, and they are able to see things hundreds of miles away, once trained. *The skies belong to us*, is their motto. Those words stick in my mind as we climb higher, in search of the elusive Snow Leopard. I am the first to spot her. A girl, hanging to the side of the rock in a grey outfit with a white furry hood, cropped champagne-coloured hair framing her radiant face. She will most likely become a Paladin, Artemiz tells us. Like the majority of Snow Leopards: no marriage, no children. The girl has the same icy blue eyes as Alisdair, and she is every bit as beautiful as he is too.

16. Ice Hell

Seven days since Kelci was taken, Muldoon Academy

Today was the first day I woke up wide-eyed, with a feeling of anticipation for what the day might hold, and a sense that maybe, just maybe, I can make something good happen. I find myself wearing an all-in-one rubber suit, navy blue. Every one of us wears the same thing, forming what looks like a troupe of divers. We are piled into the back of two massive black trucks with monster wheels. The suit covers our heads so it is hard to tell who is who. I pick out Alisdair from his height and Ben from his width and Heather from the fact that she is stood so close to Alisdair and the fact that she pulls the rubber suit look off like no one else ever could.

I try to focus on what skills I have that might be called upon to help me. What am I good at? I hark back to those days with Kelci, battling our way through our self-made challenges. The trouble is we never focused on any one thing in particular, leaving me, well, not that good at *anything*. Apart from that I've read quite a few books, not as many as Kelci, but I was pretty good at school, apart from Geography, and I do have impeccable taste and I'm great with all things fashion. Ha, as if that's of any use. I look at the rubber-clad bodies around me and am filled with doubt. I try to ignore my palpitating heart.

It takes an hour of jostling and bumping along to reach our destination. The scenery has turned from green to white and unwelcome memories of our first drill come to mind. I tell myself that today I will not be the idiot who falls asleep. I'm still trying to encourage myself as we pile out of the truck onto an enormous flat sheet of ice. I keep my mouth decidedly shut about the Arctic temperatures, while everyone moves from side to side trying to keep warm, like dancing seals.

Artemiz appears in her own version of the all-in-one and we form a line, we're used to forming lines by now. We're good at it. It's harder on ice but our special gripping shoes seem to help. In the hustle and bustle to line up I find myself next to Alisdair. I feel his arm, solid against my shoulder. I remember what Lucy said about him. He doesn't hate anyone, she said. But is that just a younger sister idolising her brother?

'Today is the day you take on the famous 'Ice Hell',' says Artemiz.

I refuse to groan. Alisdair seems unperturbed. I suppose this kind of thing is no problem for a Snow Leopard. He's not even shivering.

'Today is a race which you all need to embark upon as individuals – a race against each other – and you will be judged, amongst other things, on your finishing position.'

'Yes,' I mutter to myself. 'Must get some points.'

Steamy air comes out of Alisdair's mouth. I shift my eyes in his direction. *Is that a smile on his face?*

'What?' I say, under my breath.

He *is* smiling, sort of.

'It's just I don't think I have any points yet.'

'You may even be in the minus numbers,' he whispers.

I glare at him and he looks down at me from the corner of his eye.

'Not all of us can be expected to manifest straight away,' I say.

I'm huffing, but I wish I wasn't.

'You're above all that, anyway,' he says.

'Above what? If anyone's above anything it's you!'

That sounded weird. Calm down. I lower my voice.

'What I mean is, you act like you're above stuff all the time.'

He says nothing.

'Well *I'm* not above anything,' I go on.

He raises his eyebrows.

'Oh yeah?' he says.

'Yes! I might just win this thing, I'm really good with ice and stuff.'

It's a blatant lie. He looks down at me again.

'Interesting,' he says. 'Well, I'll see you on the other side.'

With that Artemiz blows her whistle and we're off. I try not to let my annoyance show. I will channel it; use it to spur me on. I'll show him, I'll show them all that I am not just some wimpy female out of her depth. Immediately I realise that due to that little chat I didn't hear what Artemiz said about the racecourse. She talked about ice... And water... Something about a maze? Just follow the blue bodies, I tell myself. The first thing we whizz into is an extremely high wall of ice, a perfectly carved block of it with bits of rope hanging down. I take a cue from the others who begin grappling their way up.

The first thing I notice is how incredibly *icy* the wall is. I then notice how difficult it is to climb. I bend my neck backwards to take it all in and as I do, Alisdair climbs up the wall next to me, making it look infuriatingly easy. I watch his movements and although they are quick I see that he is finding little indents in the wall upon which to place his feet and hands and so I begin to do the same. I am slow, but I'm doing it. I'm also *not* the last Trainee to scale the wall and get down the other side. I am delighted to leave behind a group still grappling behind me. Yet as I move forward I hear a little voice coming from behind, high-pitched and troubled. I spin round. It's Linda. She's got her leg tangled in the rope and she clings to the wall staring down at the icy ground below. Blue bodies are racing past me, and I see more moving off into the distance.

'I'm stuck,' she says.

'Keep going, Linda,' I call.

'I'm stuck!'

Her face is turning purple. I let out an exasperated sigh and run back to the wall. I throw myself at it and struggle my way up to where she is, clinging on to one of the ropes.

'Here,' I say. 'Hold on to me.'

Her teeth chatter. I try to look reassuring. She takes hold of my hand and I pull her towards me. She clings to me, pulling on my arm, heavily. I see the rope wrapped around her leg and begin to pull at it as she huffs and puffs. It is wedged in tight around her thigh.

'Get it off me,' she says.

I pull once, twice, three times, as hard as I can. It comes loose, thank god, because I can barely hold on to her much longer. I place her hand onto a good bit of ice which she can hold on to. I move with her, step by step, all the way to the bottom of the wall. When we reach the ground she plonks herself down, looks up at me then puts her head in her hands. I'm unsure what to do until Artemiz appears behind me and places her hand on my shoulder.

'I'll take it from here. Continue with the race,' she says.

She bows her head to me then crouches next to Linda. Once I see that Linda is ok, I turn again to the ice in the distance. I see a group of bodies. Alisdair is one of them, and he's looking right at me. Then he disappears, into what I can only imagine is the maze Artemiz talked about. I start moving, as fast as I can on the slippery ice. It takes a while but eventually I plunge into the opening of the maze and am instantly disorientated by the cramped space. Blue and green lights glow from within the ice blocks. I try to tap in to some sort of sense of direction. That's what Alisdair did on the mountain, isn't it?

I turn left and find myself faced with more choices. I turn left again hoping for the best. I keep going and going, but in what direction I am soon not sure. I feel my claustrophobia rising. My throat gets tight. My hands ball into fists. I begin to believe I am the very last person in this maze, I haven't seen another soul in here yet. Where is everyone? It must be massive! The random movements continue for what seems like an age. I am clinging to the walls and sweating by the time I see a slip of light. I follow it, muttering hopeful words to myself. Sure enough it's the exit. *Hallelujah.* I throw myself out into the daylight, wishing I could rest for just a moment. But I see a couple of people way up ahead, running and so I follow them.

After manoeuvring over and around various obstacles I eventually end up in view of a hole in the ice with shadowy water bobbing below the rim. I see someone plunge in, swim across and clamber out the other side. Freezing cold water. *Oh please.* I force myself forward and stand at the edge of the hole. The water really does look menacing, I dread to think what might be lurking under there. I pause, but I shouldn't because it makes me more nervous. By now a few others have reached the pool as well but I am too concerned with the task ahead to see who they are.

I hold my nose and leap forward. I plunge into the cold. Into the freezing pain. I'm immediately bewildered as my ribcage tightens up so much it feels like I can't breathe. *Swim girl. Get to the other side.* But my body isn't listening. *Move!* After some floundering my legs start to kick and I flap like a panicked duck. My muscles are getting weaker. My energy is being sucked into the water. Despair rises. *I can't do it!* I look at the edge of the ice. It's not even that far away but it feels like miles to me right now. I plunge my arms towards the edge but I'm too weak, my arms are failing. I'm slipping from the edge. My chin is under the water, my mouth. My muscles won't work. The voice in my head is getting smaller, desperate. I stop moving altogether.

Suddenly I feel a whoosh next to me, another body. It's Lucy, her face pale and her eyes scrunched up. She pushes me forward, dragging my hands onto the side. She's shaking. I force myself to move. She's trying to push me up the side. She's pushing, pushing. And I'm reaching, reaching. But I feel her arms start to slow, her breath

146

getting shorter. We're both falling back from the side, we're moving slower, slower. We're sinking! There are yelps all around then Alisdair and Heather appear in front of us. I feel Heather's two hands on me, powerful, pulling me to the side. I check where Lucy is and see that Alisdair is doing the same to her. With great gusts of force they pull us out onto the icy bank.

I lie there, freezing cold, teeth vibrating.

'Thank you,' I mutter.

I am so relieved to be out of the water I feel like I could kiss Heather, but she looks down at me with one eyebrow raised.

'You're welcome, honey,' she says, with a sly smile. 'Just try not to drown next time.'

With that she races off, leaving Lucy lying next to me as Alisdair tends to her anxiously.

'I'm fine, Alisdair,' she says, her face an odd shade of blue.

He is scolding her but she won't listen, she's saying she wanted to do it, and he can't stop her… I am so grateful to this impish little person I roll over and put my arm around her back.

'You tried to save me,' I say.

'I tried,' she says, grinning. 'We both nearly sank, but I tried…'

We prop each other up, with Alisdair hovering next to her, then arm in arm, we hobble to the finish line. Once there we fall over, and then somehow, the whole thing seems so ridiculous we burst into giggles, like a pair of five year olds. Everyone stares at us, bemused, including Alisdair. I catch his eye for one brief moment and I can't help wonder how foolish my words at the start of the race must sound to him now.

17. Chess

Seven days since Kelci was taken, Trainee Quarters

It takes ages for everyone to warm up after our icy day and because we are back so late we are permitted to change into our own clothes for the rest of the evening. There were two more manifestations today. Rodriguez, it seems, is a Fish. He dealt with the ice pool much better than I did, clearly. He hardly felt the excruciating cold. Fish can tolerate the lowest of temperatures, I know that because Dad used to swim in the rooftop pool without the heating on in the middle of winter. *I think we can safely say that I am not in any danger of manifesting as a Fish any time soon.* But that thought makes me sad because I always secretly wanted to be able to swim to the bottom of the ocean with my Dad. Then there's an Icelandic girl called Kristin, who always wears her blonde hair in plaits, who manifested as a Horse whilst finding her way through the maze, of all things. It can happen anywhere, we are told. *Just not for me.* Rodriguez's eyes shine aqua and Kristin's did glow chestnut brown for a while, but she looked confused and lost and was eventually led away somewhere by Artemiz. Everyone is manifesting, everyone except me.

I'm still drowning and pulling others down with me. Tonight we are permitted one hour to 'relax' in the games room. We eat a dinner consisting of fish fingers, mashed potatoes and beans, then we

149

are led into a room crammed with a snooker table, a ping-pong table, board games and lots of worn but comfy looking armchairs. I spot a little table in the corner with a chess set on top. Dad taught Kelci and me to play chess as soon as we could understand what the pieces did, telling us it would 'sharpen our minds'. I make a beeline for the table whilst Alisdair, Ben and James pick up the snooker cues. Lucy is already bouncing a ball on a ping-pong bat. I hover near the chess set and pick up one of the pieces. Hand carved wood.

'Hey! Heather wants to play,' says Lucy, suddenly.

'Sorry?'

Can I just pretend not to hear her?

'Heather! She wants to play!'

Apparently not. Lucy is nudging Heather on the shoulder. She wears a baseball t-shirt that must be intended for a child, it's so small, and a tight pair of jeans. Before I can answer Lucy is pushing her over to the chess table and sitting her down, then plonking me in the opposite chair.

'There! You two can have a nice game,' she says, beaming.

Is Lucy aware just how annoying this is? Heather and I glare at her as she darts away, bouncing the ball against her bat. Then we stare at each other for a few seconds. I feel Ben, James and Alisdair watching us from the pool table.

'We don't have to play,' I say.

'You're not being all spoilt again are you?' she says, her voice oozing like molasses. 'Surely not, not after I saved you today?'

'I'm grateful for what you did. I'm just saying, we don't have to play.'

She pouts her lips slightly and leans forward. I see the freckles spattered across her nose, her cheeks, across her collarbone and chest.

'Are you scared I'll win, honey?'

'Not in the slightest,' I reply.

A pair of hoop earrings poke through her hair.

'Come on, play!' hollers Lucy from across the room.

'This isn't punching people,' I say. 'It's not climbing and it's not running. This is chess.'

She rolls her eyes, leaning back in the chair, letting her elbows land on the armrests.

'Oh please. You don't think I'm aware of that? You think you're the only one smart enough to play chess? You don't have to be a stuck up little English girl to play this game. Even girls like me can learn chess if they want to.'

What is it with this chick?

'What do you mean, *girls like you*? Like you're so different to me?'

She narrows her eyes.

'Different to you?' she says. 'We are about as different as two humans can get.'

I give her my best look of outrage, even though I'm not sure exactly how offended I should be by that statement. She shakes her head, slowly.

'Who turns up to a place like this and says the *beds* aren't to their taste?' she says.

'I'm claustrophobic!'

'Yeah well, this opportunity is all I've got. Beds or no beds. When I get home my mother probably won't even realise I've been gone. She's most likely on the couch right now, drinking herself to sleep. Not to mention my step-father. Well, he calls himself that but he's never been anything like a father to me. Where did *you* grow up?'

But before I have the chance to answer she carries on.

'In some big house in Manhattan from what I hear… With famous Anitar parents. I bet you never wanted for *anything*. I bet it was all so easy. I came here hoping I'd seen the back of girls like you, brought up with so much privilege they don't know what they've got. With your perfect lives, your perfect clothes and your perfect families, thinking the world owes you something, just because you were born.'

'I don't think the world owes me anything.'

She thinks all this about me?

'I've not always had it easy,' I say.

I think of Terence, of Kelci.

'You don't even know me,' I go on. 'Do you really think that having Anitar parents equals happiness? That's ridiculous. Besides, look at *you*.'

She lifts her eyebrows.

'Go on,' she says. 'This will be good.'

'You're privileged. You're the most beautiful person I've ever seen!'

I suddenly realise this isn't much of an insult.

'What I mean is… You're so beautiful, people like you just for existing!'

She smirks, quietly, keeping her eyes on me.

'Beauty isn't everything,' she says.

'Yeah well, neither is money.'

'*It is when you don't have any.* Looks don't last forever, honey. My mum was once so beautiful she won so many beauty contests she couldn't tell you how many. But lately she's suicidal on her birthdays, just because she doesn't look like she used to.'

She shudders, as though recalling a horrible memory.

'I'm not going to end up like that.'

All I can do is stare at her, astonished and with that, it seems like the conversation is over. There's nothing left to say apart from:

'Let's play.'

And so we begin. Immediately I am planning a path to her King. That's how Dad taught me. Never take your eye off the piece you need to win, never get sidetracked. I make my first move and Heather returns with hers. The atmosphere between us intensifies and things go very quiet. I make some good moves and she counters them, but really she's just defending herself. *Finally, something I can do around here.* I begin to use a sequence of moves that I often use when playing with Kelci. It practically never fails. I move my knight, poised for attack and Heather squeezes her eyebrows together. She looks at me suddenly and her eyes flash and when I say flash I mean literally – flash – from hazel to bright yellow for a second. *What was that?* She leans back in her chair, takes in an enormous breath and squirms.

'Are you ok?'

She doesn't answer. She sits back up and makes her next move – taking my knight. Didn't see that coming. I make another move, sure that checkmate is just around the corner. Before another second passes she moves again, capturing my queen with her queen. *What?* I need that piece for my sequence. *How did she get so good all of a sudden?* By now she has a strange look on her face, concentrated.

'Heather,' I say raising my voice to catch her attention. 'What's going on?'

Her eyes lock with mine.

'My mind,' she says. 'Something is happening in my mind.'

She's sweating. I play another move but I already know she has me. Three moves later, played so fast I can hardly see her hands, and she has my King defenseless and exposed.

'Checkmate,' she says.

It's undeniable. I wait for the gloating. And the insults. But there's nothing. Instead she looks bewildered. She puts her head in her hands and I hear Ben's voice behind me.

'Is she ok?'

'I don't know,' I say. 'She said it's her mind ...'

We all watch as Heather takes her hands from her head revealing her eyes – shining yellow and her hair – even thicker and more luscious than before. She doesn't speak but she doesn't need to. She's different and we can all see it. *For God's sake. Right in front of me ...*

Heather Jackson is now a Fox.

No matter what I do, I cannot get to sleep this evening. I stare at the ceiling, my mind going round and round and round. Heather manifested, just like that. Right in front of me. I even helped her do it, by playing chess with her! But how did she do it? How did she make it happen? *Did* she make it happen? Or did it just happen *to* her? I can't work it out. But meanwhile, I'm still here, failing at everything … and Kelci is still god knows where. There's been no word from my parents. I can't bear to think about how they must feel right now.

I hold her glasses case in my hand. I brought it to bed with me, a reminder of why I am here. My mind drifts to the time we all went to buy her very first pair of glasses: me, Mum and Kelci. She was only small at the time and wriggly, very wriggly. Every time I tried to hug her or put her on my knee she would squirm off in the opposite direction. But she was cute. So cute. She loved a soft toy she called 'Mi Mi', a grey bunny, of all things. Her hair was both blonde and curly then, not straight like it is now. And she had sweet red lips and a button nose that I liked to poke. Her first pair of glasses were pink and plastic and she looked even more adorable when wearing them. Since then, Kelci was hardly ever without glasses and if she did take them off she acted like a mole. She wouldn't know it was me until I got close. *I miss her. I miss her terribly.*

I close my eyes tight and try to sleep. I need all the energy I can get right now. But there's nothing for it… My mind drifts to Mason. Somehow, here, with these people, doing these things, none of it seems real anymore. Like I've made him up in my mind, a make believe boyfriend, a delicious dream. But when I think of his sweet face and his tanned hands, I miss him too. I miss the simplicity of being with him, that feeling of his lips brushing against mine, the warmth of his breath against my cheek. If only he knew what I was up to right now. He wouldn't believe it.

The future I imagined for us... Can that ever happen? I dreamt, all the time, of us moving in together one day, into a perfect apartment. With an enormous closet... You see those women in New York, sauntering around Central Park with diamonds on their fingers, drinking coffee in elegant cafes. I bet they all have enormous closets... I want to be one of those women... I *wanted* to be one of those women. I don't know anymore. Does it make me spoilt, like Heather said, to want to live like that? Is it wrong? No one here wants to live like that – that's for sure. But does that make it a bad thing? I lie awake for a long time until finally, thankfully, sleep takes over.

18. A Burning Building

Eight days since Kelci was taken, Muldoon Island

I am stood close to a river some distance from the Muldoon campus. I am staring at James's face which is encased in a massive helmet and he's talking loudly at me, wearing a silver suit that is too big for him. It's a challenge day. We all wear silver suits with helmets. In front of us is the blackened shell of a metal building being consumed by the flames of a blazing fire. Strapped to our wrists are huge digital timers set to ten minutes. Licks of fire are coming out of the windows. The flames are so strong they reflect orange and gold onto the helmet screens, meaning I can only just see James' face as he talks.

'I am not going in any burning building. No way! Nuh-huh. Who's going to know if we die in there? My Uncle Steve's never going to know what happened to me, out here on this damn island. Look at those flames! Besides, what is this?'

He tries to look down at the suit but the helmet won't allow his head to turn that far.

'This suit is like some kind of joke. It's like… It's like foil. It's not going to protect us against those flames. We're like a bunch of uncooked turkeys! About to be put in the oven! We're going to get cooked! I've been through some crazy stuff since I got here… I've been drowned, thrown from an airplane, been through mud, ice… But man… I *hate* fire.'

His arms are waving about wildly. I agree with him but I can't get a word in edgewise. I'm just not convinced Lady Muldoon and her team have got it right this time. Ben, who stands close by, has morphed into a shining mountain in the suit. He smiles down at me through the helmet screen. Lady Muldoon starts to speak, but it is hard to hear, because the crackling of the flames is even louder now.

'Today is a test of teamwork. Inside that building there are a number of mannequins. You will be matched in pairs and each couple has ten minutes to enter the building, retrieve one of those mannequins and bring it safely out here.'

Shadow runs between us, sniffing the ground as if searching for something. Lady Muldoon tells us to stay low and avoid the flames. Do not exceed ten minutes, do not get stuck, do not set self on fire. James repeats her words, disbelieving.

'*Do not set self on fire?*' he says, hopping up and down. '*Do not set self on fire?*'

It feels like some sort of joke is being played on me as she then announces that Heather and I are being paired up. I find Heather in the crowd and we exchange a glance. I sense that she is just as dismayed as I am, but she hides it better than I do. She hides everything better than I do. For once, even she cannot make the fire suit attractive. Right now she looks just as shapeless as the rest of us. First up is Ben, alongside a girl called Lily, a German girl with curly hair and thin lips. As they disappear off through the black doorway, James paces up and down, still talking and shaking his head. They are gone for just under ten

158

minutes, then they're back out again, empty handed. James runs to Ben and reaches up to help him with his helmet.

'Dude, are you all right?' he says.

Ben's blonde hair cascades out of the helmet, gathering in front of the black marks on his cheeks.

'I am in the heat of the moment,' he says, shaking his head.

'What?' says James. 'No Ben, in the heat of the moment… You wouldn't say that now, that means… something else.'

Ben knits his eyebrows.

'Something else? Like what?'

'I don't know, like, you did something you shouldn't have because you're so angry, you know? *In the heat of the moment.*'

'But I am not angry,' says Ben.

James gives a long sigh whilst Alisdair and a longhaired Canadian guy, Steve, go next, but ten minutes later they too come out with nothing but frowns and gasps as they pull off their helmets. It's the first time Alisdair has looked out of his depth. The same happens over and over until it gets to the unlikely pairing of Dominic and Linda. Dominic speeds ahead but just before they get to the doorway he turns to Linda and pulls her in by the shoulder. Nice. I'm so nervous I can hear the beat of my own heart and seeing James pace up and down in front of me is only making it worse.

How am I going to hold up in a burning building with Heather Jackson as my only company? After ten minutes Dominic and Linda are past back out. Linda's left arm is on fire. She's moving fast, much faster than I've ever seen her move before. She runs straight into the river, flapping her arm, extinguishing the flames. She pulls herself back

---

159

out then lies there for a few seconds before taking off her helmet and giving a weak thumbs up, whilst Dominic stalks beside her, glaring. This sends James into overdrive, and it only gets worse when Lady Muldoon announces that he and Lucy are up next.

'You can do it, James,' I hear myself saying, despite the fact that I have no confidence I can do it myself.

All of a sudden James stops talking and stands perfectly still. He holds his hands together and looks like he is praying. Without another word he finds Lucy and together, they disappear through the door. I'm surprised he actually went inside after all that. Like the other pairs, they disappear for ten minutes, but once the time has passed, they make no appearance. I start to wonder about them and glance over to Lady Muldoon… She looks at her watch. More seconds pass. Alisdair is the first to speak up.

'I'm going in to find them,' he says.

'No,' says Lady Muldoon, holding up her hand. 'A few more minutes.'

A look of thunder passes Alisdair's face but he does as she says. We all stare at the building, wondering what's going on inside. There's no sound apart from the flames… All eyes are on the door. One minute… Two minutes… Three minutes… Just as Alisdair starts to move towards the building, a head pops up in one of the uppermost windows.

'Hey, hey!' says James. 'Look at me!'

He clambers out on the windowsill. My heart stops. What is he doing?

'Oh my god, don't jump!' I scream, rushing over.

I can't stand it… The thought of him dropping from there… Ben is right behind me but before we get to where he is, an exhilarated whoop fills the air. James jumps clean out of the window. I gasp, covering my mouth with my hands. Lucy is on his back! And they're not dropping straight to the ground, they are soaring through the air in a big arc.

'Lucy!' shouts Alisdair.

They land right in front of us.

'I'm a Frog!' says James, ripping off his helmet. 'Holy moly, I'm a Frog! I'm a Frog!'

Lucy clambers down from his back, beaming at him and holding on to a mannequin.

'Thanks for the ride,' she says, patting him on the back.

Alisdair takes her by the arm. He's scowling but she just pouts at him.

'I'm fine, Alisdair,' she says.

James shouts and curses and leaps up into the air again. I can't help but laugh, first of all from relief and astonishment, but then because manifestation couldn't have happened to a better person. He is bounding all over the place, up and away, landing, then pelting off in the other direction.

'Woah! If Uncle Steve could see me now!'

He looks like a crazed astronaut in the silver suit, defying gravity. Lady Muldoon swoops in front us, looking pleased.

'Our first Frog of the program. James Johnson. Very, *very* well done,' she says.

He keeps on bounding.

'It can take weeks, months, sometimes even years before a Frog can fully control the urge to jump.'

'*Years?*' shouts James, from high in the air.

'I'm afraid so,' says Lady Muldoon. 'But you're in good hands.'

James's face turns to concern mid air, but I've got bigger things to worry about. There's only one group left to tackle the burning building. Heather and me. Lady Muldoon reminds us of this fact and tells us that our time is now. I position myself next to Heather and we set the timers on our watches. We speed towards the building and step inside the doorway. The smoke is thick. *I can't see, I can't breath.* There's nothing else for it but to fall to our hands and knees and begin to crawl. Flames dance all around us. There's a flight of stairs – Heather points towards them and we crawl over. There's a layer of burning flame on the ceiling above them. We climb the stairs on our hands and knees, moving clumsily in the suits. I'm already covered in sweat – so much my hair sticks to my face. We get to the top of the steps and see the landing area with various doorways. We crawl along, searching the rooms. There's a group of mannequins in one room all sitting back to back on chairs in the middle.

We crawl underneath fallen beams of wood that lie diagonally across the doorway. Once we are through, I point at my watch – five minutes left. She nods. We run to the middle of the room and I grab a mannequin. There are flames on every side. We have a mannequin, maybe we can do this. But as I am looking around for the best escape route I hear a loud crack behind me. I turn around to see Heather, laid on the floor, trapped under an enormous beam of wood. She writhes and wriggles under it but there's nothing she can do – it lies across her so heavily she can't get out. She looks up at me from the floor, a pained expression on her face, trying to push the beam off her chest. The flames are growing, closing in on us. It is hot now, so hot.

I drop the mannequin and rush towards her. I get hold of the beam with both hands but it is like lead. *We need Ben, someone strong. I can't do this alone.* But as I see the flames licking all around us I realise that I have to do this alone, there's no time for anything else. I put both hands on one side of the beam and begin to push, as Heather struggles beneath. I pull back then shove with all my might and it does move, even if just slightly. I gesture to Heather, to push with me. We do it again, a shove, both of us. Her face grimaces as the beam moves a little more. We continue like that, for who knows how long, both of us using all our might, sweat pouring down our faces. Eventually the beam rolls off Heather's body enough for me to drag her from under it.

She's weak, so I hook her arm around my shoulder and guide us out of the room. We duck through a doorway, then back down the stairs, slower this time, taking every step together until we finally reach the ground floor. The fire is roaring down here so once again, we get down on our hands and knees, crawling, me holding Heather's arm and guiding her along. Finally, mercifully, we see the door, get to our feet and stumble into the open air. I pull off Heather's helmet, then my own and there we stand together, dazed and exhausted. It takes a while for us to adjust to being outside, but then she looks at me with a slightly sheepish expression on her face.

'Thank you,' she says.

'You're welcome,' I say, 'Just try not to burn alive next time, honey.'

She rolls her eyes, but her features soften and she raises an eyebrow.

'I guess I asked for that,' she says, a smile on her lips.

19. What Just Happened?

For the first time ever Heather smiles at me at breakfast. At first I just stare at her, holding my tray, but once I realise she is definitely smiling at *me*, I half-smile back, wondering what it means. I slide into my chair, opposite Ben who is munching his way through a mountain of food and James who is pouring golden syrup over some spicy sausages on top of butter-covered waffles. I feel a glimmer of hope in my heart this morning. *I helped Heather yesterday, I really helped her.* But before I have a chance to dwell on this sliver of positivity, Dominic, in all his short-haired glory turns up at the end of the table, looking down his nose at me. I groan inwardly. *What does he want?*

'Your poor little sister,' he says. 'Has there been no word? How old is she? 14? 15? Terrible for her to be out there all alone.'

'Go away, Dominic,' I say.

'And a Gregory too,' he goes on. 'It just doesn't seem right. I know if one of us Federov's was kidnapped the entire family would be out searching night and day. But then all us Federov's are Anitars. There's not much *you* can do is there? It just goes to show some people are naturally gifted, and some people, *aren't.*'

Ben looks up from his food, a snarl beginning to rumble in his chest.

'It's all right,' I say, touching his hand across the table. 'I can handle it.'

He burrows his big eyebrows but doesn't say anything. I feel everyone looking at us and listening. Heather, Alisdair, Lucy. They're all there on the opposite table, watching. *I have to try to look brave, show I can fight my own battles.*

'Even one of the great Gregorys couldn't manifest. A warning for us all, I'd say. You can't rely on your family background, you can't rely on anything but yourself. I mean, even these two nobodies manifested and you didn't.'

He gestures towards Ben and James who are both glaring at him wide-eyed.

'Maybe those of us that *did* manifest will be assigned to find your sister. Wouldn't that be ironic? You, sent home with your memory erased. No clue that you've been here all this time. Of course, not *much* happened here as far as you're concerned.'

My chair scrapes against the floor as I stand up slowly. My heart is racing and my cheeks flush as I sense all eyes on me.

'The program isn't done yet,' I say. 'And it won't be *you* who finds my sister.'

His eyes flash blood-red.

'It won't be anyone at this rate, will it?'

I move forward and level my face with his.

'*I will find her,*' I say.

I'm so close to him I can feel the warmth of his breath and just as I'm wondering if he will spit at me we are called for our first Theory class of the day.

Since then I've spent the entire day trying to look like Dominic's words didn't bother me. But they did. They bothered me so much I haven't been able to think of anything else. The horrifying fact is; he's right. I haven't manifested. I'm no closer to finding Kelci and I'm not out there night and day, like I should be. What am I even doing any more? It has been nine days since she was taken. *Nine days!*

I've locked myself in a cubicle in the girl's toilets, the only place I can find away from prying eyes. Now I'm in here I can't hold back the tears. He's right and he's only saying what everyone else is thinking. I'm letting *everyone* down. As I heave a sob I hear a soft tap on the door of my cubicle, then Lucy's voice, quiet.

'Nina, are you ok?'

How did she get in here? I didn't hear a thing.

'Lucy, leave me alone,' I say, unravelling a wad of toilet paper. 'I'm fine.'

'Don't be ridiculous,' she says. 'You're sobbing in the toilets. Even I know that's not a good sign.'

I blow my nose.

'I just want to be left alone.'

'Come on,' she says. 'I promise I'll just listen and I won't judge.'

I sigh heavily. I suppose it won't do any harm to talk… And if someone could listen to me, without judging, wouldn't that be a first? I unlatch the door and step out, the toilet paper still in my hand, covered in mascara. She smiles at me softly, then perches herself on the side of one of the washbasins.

'I'm listening.'

I perch myself on another washbasin. Then I let it all out. Kelci. My parents. Terence. Even Mason. She just nods, and listens, as she promised. At the end of it all I feel better, lighter. Then she helps me to look less like a panda. As she dabs away at my cheeks with a wet tissue, she tells me that she wants to help me, she really does and she is not just some silly girl and that Alisdair has never let her do anything because he's so afraid that something might happen to her but it just means she never gets to *live*.

She talks earnestly and sweetly, in a way, and I can't help but wonder if I should just let her join me. But then there's Alisdair and he has a point. She seems so young and small and way too innocent to know what she's getting herself into. She didn't see those men like I did … she thinks it's all a game. But for one so young and small and innocent she will simply *not give up*. And after a while I find myself being told that I need a team and that *she is it* and that she will wake me tonight and together we will see what we can find out.

It is 2am and I feel an insistent tap on my arm. It's Lucy of course, and she's breathless. She's all ready to go and so am I, dressed in preparation under the bed sheets. I try to ignore the weight of foreboding that bears down on me. What happens if we get caught? I would *not* like to meet an Apprentice up there in the dead of night.

What if there's a Snake lurking? Lucy holds her finger over her mouth, as if I was ever going to make any noise. I lead the way, creeping out with her close behind. We dash through the labyrinth of corridors in the Trainee quarters and up the stony stairs until we reach the Theory corridor, which looks very different now – dark and spooky with moonlight streaming onto the floor through the round windows. The outlines of the animals on the ceiling look eerie in this light. I lead us through the shadows until we reach a staircase at the end of the corridor, which we promptly ascend.

On the next floor there's a square space with doors on all four sides and we begin to methodically nudge each door open, peeping through to see what lies inside. The first few reveal nothing but empty rooms with fancy wooden desks and chairs. It's almost impossible to tell what we are looking for. Then suddenly my heart leaps. There's someone here. We scramble into the nearest doorway pushing ourselves back into it, desperate to stay hidden. All we can do is hold our breaths and watch as a girl walks briskly out of the room, a file tucked under her arm. We wait until she disappears down the staircase.

'Let's go in *there*,' hisses Lucy.

'What if there's someone else inside?' I say.

'Let's just see.'

Before I know what's happening Lucy is at the door and sneaking a peek inside. She turns to me, beckoning.

'It's empty. Come on.'

I take a massive breath and run towards her, finding myself in a room with flickering computer screens and electronic maps lit up on glass screens.

'Let's check the computers,' she says, beside herself.

And so I find myself in front of a bright screen with my trembling hands over the keyboard. I click onto one of the many folders then search through the documents – finding pages of writing that mean nothing to me. Bang, bang, bang, goes my heart. *Hurry up, hurry up, hurry up.* My eyes flick to the door. Lucy stares at her screen as she taps fervently on the keyboard. I open a document and see a symbol. A purple flower… Surrounded by green leaves… Suddenly I realise, I know that symbol! *It was on the jackets of Kelci's kidnappers.* I begin frantically scrambling through the document. There are co-ordinates, for a building of some kind. Lucy stands close to an electronic map on the wall.

'I've found something,' I hiss.

She almost jumps out of her skin.

'What is it?'

'Check these co-ordinates on that map, behind you.'

'Ok, ok,' she says, jumping over to the screen.

As I whisper the numbers of the co-ordinates she finds the location on the map, touching it as it moves under her fingers. She zooms in. Europe.

'Switzerland,' she says.

She's so excited she jumps up and down, but just as I am about to run over I hear a noise behind me – the door, it's opening! All I have time to do is dive under the nearest desk and curl up with my knees jammed under my chin. I look out and see Lucy is still there, scared stiff.

'Someone's coming,' I spit out. 'Hide!'

Can she hear me? It's too late. She has nowhere to go, she's completely exposed, and whoever is coming through that door will either be in the room in less than a second or is there already. All I can do is watch her lean against the map as the sounds of voices begin to fill the room. I squeeze onto my legs, waiting for trouble to hit but as I keep my eyes on Lucy I see her twist around, and then disappear, right in front of my eyes. Just like that, she is gone. I stop breathing.

What just happened?

The voices get louder – one male, one female and I have no choice but stay curled up under this desk. *Did she just manifest? She's gone.* I stay as quiet as I can, as they talk in hushed voices and sit at their desks. Time passes, I can hardly tell how much but eventually they leave the room and I hear the door shut once again.

'Lucy! Where are you? Let's go!'

She suddenly re-appears in the same place she disappeared, looking shell-shocked, confused and wildly delighted all at the same time.

'Did I just, did I just – disappear?'

'Yes!'

'I vanished. Into thin air – they couldn't see me. Right?'

'Yes!'

Her eyes shine. Her irises are turning slowly from green to purple, and her hair is morphing into burnt orange.

'Your eyes are changing colour,' I say. 'And your hair.'

'I'm a Chameleon!' she says. 'I'm a Chameleon!'

'You are,' I say, smiling.

'I got the co-ordinates,' she says, still looking dazed. 'I memorised them.'

'Good. Now let's get the hell out of here.'

It doesn't take long for us to get back to the dorm where we whisper and communicate mostly in gestures. We sit on Lucy's bed, side by side, too energised to sleep. Suddenly there's a thud from somewhere in the room and we snap our heads round to see what it is. Over there, in the darkness Heather Jackson is staring at us, makeup-less, curls tumbling around her shoulders. *How much did she hear? Does she know what we just did?* I exchange a look with Lucy and after that, nobody says a word until morning.

20. Nostrils Flare

Ten days since Kelci was taken, Trainee Quarters

Heather knows what we did last night. I have a feeling she heard us too, talking in the room before we left. She's been keeping those foxy eyes of hers on Lucy and me all day, giving us sidelong looks, wearing an expression I just can't seem to read. Is she suspicious? Judging us? It doesn't seem so. It's more like curiosity, like she wants to talk to us, to say something. The whole thing makes me jumpy but I just keep telling myself: *we found a clue to where Kelci might be.* A real life clue and it came to us because I remembered something, about the night she was taken. The purple flower… It came back to me. It must be a valid clue, surely… I've never seen that symbol anywhere else before. Perhaps I *can* be of some use. And now I have my partner in crime, Lucy. She might not be what you would call stable, or trained, or in any way predictable but her heart is definitely in the right place. She showed that last night, risking herself to help me.

She's spent the entire day revelling in her newfound status as a Chameleon, showing off and disappearing but she's not quite used to it yet so she tends to bang into things and sometimes she ends up to walking into walls rather than vanishing into them. She and James lark about together, making for a bizarre but amusing pair, what with Lucy's eyes and hair changing colour every few seconds and James bounding around. Even Alisdair wears the hint of a smile today. He must be relieved. To know that his sister is an Anitar too, to know that they can stay together and she has strengths now that she can train and protect herself with.

All in all, I would say this is the most light-hearted day of the program so far. Things are going so well I don't even notice that there has been no sign of Lady Muldoon all day. It doesn't occur to me once, until we are all assembled in the Training Hall for what I expect will be a one-on-one combat session. I'm bracing myself for another fight, wondering who I will be paired with and secretly hoping it will be Linda because I managed to beat her last time, a small victory that I have clung to ever since. We are sat on the benches as usual, waiting to be told when the combat will start. There are giggles as Lucy makes her hair change colour every time James touches it: eggshell-beige to pond-green to candy-pink. But the tittering stops when a loud bang resounds across the length of the hall. All heads turn towards the door. A slight tremor travels along the floor, which feels familiar to me, it can only be

173

one thing – a Rabbit's thump. Sure enough, swooping through the door is Lady Muldoon, flanked by two Apprentices either side, each of whom are clearly Rabbits with their snowy-white locks and cherubic faces.

Lady Muldoon wears a thick, wine-coloured cloak with her hair swept back and a look on her face that I can only describe as *formidable*. She carries a wooden staff in her right hand, which I remember being told is the only weapon a Deer ever uses, a weapon used solely for defense. I'm not quite sure why Lady Muldoon is holding hers but I have a sinking feeling the reason is not good. Silence descends. I get a nervous, spinny feeling in my stomach. What does she want? Why is she here like this? She hasn't said a word but it is obvious that everyone is wondering the same thing. Lucy's hair turns slate grey.

She stops in front of us and stands there, grim faced, with the Rabbits either side, all of them looking equally stern. Shadow appears by Lady Muldoon's side and even he projects an air of disdain. The whole entourage stands there for some moments, not saying a word. All eyes are on Lady Muldoon whose expression is now, without a doubt, furious. Her nostrils flare, she grips the staff tightly, looking down on us with her cheekbones held high. The feeling in my stomach spreads, my heart flutters and my knees begin to go weak. I give a sidelong look at Lucy whose face is, for once, grave. Another slight but no less worrying tremor runs along the ground and Lady Muldoon starts to speak.

'In all my years as Principle of Muldoon Academy,' she begins. 'I have never encountered such *insolence* from a group of Trainees.'

Her eyes scan the benches, from one end to the other. I gulp. Lucy gulps.

'It has come to my attention, that one of you has committed violations that simply can not be tolerated within these walls.'

By now my body on the inside is a jangling ball of confusion – my heart, my stomach, my knees. *She knows.*

'It has come to my attention that certain off limits parts of Muldoon Academy were entered last night and highly sensitive, classified documents were tampered with.'

She glares at us. My eyes flick to Heather. *She must have told them what she saw in the dorm last night. No one else knew.*

'Two of my Rabbits on their nightly rounds found evidence of violation. We already know that it wasn't one of our own Apprentices. This act was perpetrated by someone in this room.'

It wasn't Heather. And Lady Muldoon doesn't know who did it. Yet.

'It is with great regret that I come to you in this way. However, such treachery from individuals who are invited into this Academy and trusted to be in this space simply can not be tolerated.'

Treachery? No, it wasn't that bad, but somehow I don't think she would agree with me right now.

'Someone in this room knows who did this.'

My throat tightens. With Lady Muldoon against me, what chance do I have? If I am expelled now, my chances of finding Kelci are excruciatingly slim. I will be sent away, with my memories erased, just like Dominic said. I'll be dropped back into my old life again, whether I like it or not, a million miles from finding Kelci. I'll be clueless, and what if I'm made to forget the co-ordinates? I'll have lost the clue, the one clue I have. What about Lucy? She can't be punished for this… It's my problem, she wouldn't have gone in search of secrets if it weren't for me.

'I only want to punish those who perpetrated the crime. But unless someone here tells me who did this, every one of you will be punished.'

Dominic gives me a sly look. It is glaringly obvious that I was the one who went up there to find the information. And he knows it. And now he gets to watch me thrown out in disgrace. I'm the only one who has gone on about needing to find my sister. James shuffles in his seat and Ben looks anxious.

'I am not afraid to make you all pay. The security of the Academy has to come above all.'

I look around the group, frantic. Heather will tell them it was me … Lady Muldoon glares at us, eyes flashing.

'You have one more chance.'

I've got no choice. If Lucy stands up, she'll be punished, I'll have to face the consequences myself. I begin to rise from the bench, slowly.

'It was…' I begin.

Lucy pops up.

'…me,' she finishes.

Before I have a chance to react another voice pipes up and a figure rises.

'It was me.'

Heather.

'Me too,' say James and Ben, in unison, rising together.

'And me,' says Alisdair, rising.

I don't know what to do, what to say. *What is going on?* James… Ben… *Alisdair… Heather…* Standing up… for me…? There's a long, awkward silence as we stand there. Lady Muldoon glares at us.

'*Six of you?*' she says. 'I don't believe it.'

A commotion starts up. Dominic glares at us, incredulous.

'They didn't all go,' he says. 'They're just trying to help their *useless* friend – it was obviously Nina who did it. She's the only one stupid and selfish enough. You should punish her. Just her.'

His eyes glow like two rubies.

'*Be quiet, young man,*' says Lady Muldoon, giving him a withering look. 'If I am ever in a situation *desperate* enough to ask for your counsel, you will be the first to know. Meanwhile, hold your tongue.'

Dominic looks appalled and so angry he looks set to burst but he doesn't say another word.

'If these six are admitting guilt,' she says. 'Then they shall be the ones to face the consequences.'

21. Clenched Jaw

Ten days since Kelci was taken, Lady Muldoon's Study

The six of us stand here in Lady Muldoon's office, staring at each other in total silence. After a few more seconds, I can stand it no longer.

'*What are you guys doing?*' I say, my voice hushed even though Lady Muldoon and her Rabbits just stormed out, locking us in here to await our fate.

Everyone begins talking at once.

'It's obvious Nina, they want to help you, *help us*, we can go find your sister, follow the co-ordinates…' says Lucy.

'I thought it would… Make things easier…' says James, who looks like he isn't totally sure what's going on.

'I'm not letting Lucy take the wrap for this alone… If she's involved, then so am I,' growls Alisdair.

Ben says something in Swedish. Heather just stands there, arms folded, one eyebrow lifted, looking at the rest of us.

'You!' I say, to Heather, squinting at her suspiciously. 'What are *you* doing here?'

She shrugs her shoulders and pouts a little.

'Let's just say it didn't seem right.'

'What do you care what's right?'

'I heard you guys last night in the dorm, saw that it was Lucy who dragged you along and it didn't seem right – for you to lose your place here.'

She cares about my place on the program? Since when? She twists a strand of hair around her finger, watching it slide from her grip.

'Why do you think I have such bad intentions?' she says.

'I don't know, because *you do*?'

I swear a glimmer of hurt passes across her face, but I can't be sure. Her plump lips squeeze together.

'Look,' she says, smoothly. 'I don't blame you for not liking me. And believe me, I've felt the same since I met you, and with good reason.'

I roll my eyes.

'However, we've all heard so much about this sister of yours, it's time for us to put an end to it. Things have been getting a little boring around here anyway.'

'What do you mean?'

'I mean, we go. We bring her back.'

I look at her open-mouthed. Ben and James are murmuring in agreement.

'Yes! Finally!' cries Lucy, who promptly goes on to tell them about what we saw last night and the co-ordinates we found.

Alisdair stays stonily silent but the rest of them begin feverishly making plans, as though we are all about to embark on a really exciting field trip. Heather confidently claims that she will be able to 'convince' Kenny Collins to take us anywhere we want in his plane so long as we get moving fast, it doesn't seem to bother her that the co-ordinates are

179

thousands of miles away. The glint in her eye gives me the distinct feeling that this is not the first time she has broken the rules. *Can she be trusted?*

Lucy urges us to go tonight, and the rest of them - aside from Alisdair - seem to agree, nodding their heads in earnest. They start listing the things we should bring, what we should wear. What choice do I have here? The plan is flimsy to say the least: disastrous at worst, foolish at best. But what was I expecting? A team of fully trained Anitars to fly me out there? I look around at this unlikely band of Trainees. An effervescent, loyal young girl and her moody older brother. A pair of guys who have shown me nothing but kindness since we met: one a literal jumping bean and the other an enormous, mild-mannered Swede. And to top it off, a girl who *redefines* the word foxy, who has given me absolutely no reason to trust her any further than I could throw her (which is not very far). *But this is my chance to find Kelci.* And provided Lady Muldoon doesn't physically restrain us for the entire night, or have us removed from the island right this second, I give my agreement when Heather announces that we will meet, at midnight exactly, on the airstrip just next to the lake.

———

I listen to the growl of the engine. We arrived, at midnight, backpacks strapped over our shoulders just as Heather told us to and now we're inside a plane, similar to the one we had to jump out of in the first

———

challenge, and it feels like we've ended up in the belly of a hungry dragon. It's too loud for conversation despite the fact that we're facing each other, girls on one side strapped in by seatbelts clamped over our shoulders, and boys opposite. For the first time, I am thankful for the terrifying nature of the training. Without it, fear would melt me, I'm sure of it. I place my hands on my knees to stop them from shaking. I look at Alisdair, directly opposite me. If his hands are shaking, I don't see it. All I see is a clenched jaw and frozen ocean eyes.

My mind swims with the events of the day. I still can't believe these guys are willing to do this. I'm not quite sure if they are incredibly supportive or incredibly stupid. Alisdair is neither. He's here for Lucy, that much is blatantly apparent, and the fact that he blames me for leading her into this, is also blatantly apparent. Heather, well, so far she looks like she is plain old having a good time, like she was built for 'clandestine missions' such as this. I think of the grilling we received from Lady Muldoon when she came back into her office this afternoon. It would probably have been more comfortable to stand in front of a burning furnace for half an hour. For all the apparent gentleness of the Deer, Lady Muldoon firmly retains a fiery side.

Initially I thought we were all done for. It seemed like her telling off was leading up to a grande finale of memory erasure and immediate removal. But instead she listed a series of gruelling punishments, and set an excruciating schedule for us that would have been nearly impossible for us to keep up with, if we had any intention of staying to do it. I feel a pang of guilt knowing that her leniency is going to be rewarded with finding us all gone in the morning.

We've been flying for several hours before the plane eventually begins to nose downwards, curving through the air. Lucy grabs my hand and I squeeze back. A clattering starts up and I turn to see that James is bouncing up and down in his seat. Ben tries to give him an encouraging look but he looks worried. He rattles about as much as his seatbelt will let him. At that moment the plane drops, bashing us from side to side. At first I think it has something to do with James but it was the plane itself jolting. I hold onto my seatbelt with both hands. There's another massive bump. My heart sprints so fast I wonder if it might explode. The plane jostles all the way, but we nose down enough to eventually land with a thud. Soon after, the back of the plane opens up like the mouth of a whale and Kenny Collins stands in the darkness, one arm on the door, hair flapping in the wind. He has a distinctly glazed look about him, like he doesn't quite know what he's doing here. I feel another pang of guilt.

'Bit of a bumpy ride there,' he says. 'Weather's terrible.'

Heather sidles over to him, somehow already on her feet as the rest of us grapple with our restraints. She steps out of the plane, smiles, then whispers something in his ear. He nods in agreement. What is she saying? I take a deep breath. Kenny takes hold of my hand and helps me to the ground. As the others pile out behind me I feel a chill wind on my face. I look up to the nighttime sky gurgling above us like boiling soup. It's starless, with clouds churning along lit by an eerie glow that is both lime-green and violet. I make out the mountains and sense that there is space, lots of it. It smells different here, like flowers mixed with smoke.

For one moment I think of myself at home, tucked under Mason's arm, strolling through Central Park on a Saturday afternoon, warm and safe. It is such an inviting thought, but so at odds with my current situation, I have to shake my head to get rid of it. I turn my eyes to the sky once again and wonder if out there, somewhere close by, is my sister. Alisdair hands us earpieces that he found on the plane. They have little microphones on them and he explains that this is how we'll stay in communication with each other. I am relieved to see that he's getting involved, I was beginning to wonder if he was planning to sabotage the whole thing. As I fiddle with the earpiece, which feels cold and hard in my ear, Heather speaks up.

'We're about six miles from the compound.'

Her face is shadowed but her eyes shine through the dark.

'It should be 43 degrees North East.'

Heather will be able to use her Fox's sense of direction to get us there. Alisdair can do the same. James, as a Frog, ought to be able to but I have a feeling he just isn't there yet. Ever since he manifested he's been unable to control his body, which makes me feel a tad sorry for him, despite the fact that it's entertaining to watch. He's got better, that's for sure. He is able to keep his feet on the ground the majority of the time now. Ben looks out for him of course.

'Just come right back here when you're done,' blurts out Kenny Collins.

'We will,' I say. 'We'll come right back.'

Heather whispers again in Kenny's ear and he walks back to the cockpit of the plane. With that, we set off into the darkness. We trek over fields, through valleys, across streams, along dirt tracks. We hike through a forest, emerging from it to finally arrive at the exact location of the co-ordinates. The first light of dawn is just beginning to appear and I can hardly breathe with anticipation. Could this be where Kelci is? The six of us come to a standstill, looking at what stands before us. Immediately, my heart sinks. There's nothing but a few hills, a smattering of trees and that's about it.

'There's nothing here!' I say, feeling tears prick at my eyes.

After all this, escaping Muldoon, commandeering a plane, jeopardising everyone's future – there's nothing here!

'Wait,' says Alisdair, frowning and holding his hand out to quieten me.

He moves closer to the edge of the forest and crouches down and for some reason we all follow suit. No one says a word. What is he doing? He places his hands on the ground and stares out at what lies in front of us. His eyes narrow and suddenly he whispers:

'There. See that? *In* the side of the hill. There's an opening…'

'There is?' I say, squinting.

'I don't see anything,' says James.

Heather crouches next to Alisdair, peering out.

'That's right,' she says. 'I see it too.'

She turns to Alisdair and smiles.

'Nice work, Snow Leopard.'

Neither I, nor James, nor Lucy, nor Ben can see the opening, but both Heather and Alisdair insist that it is there.

'I'm going in, to get a closer look,' says Alisdair.

Before any of us get the chance to reply he's already disappeared, lightening fast, leaving us looking at each other in astonishment.

'He shouldn't just go off like that!' says James. 'Are we a team? Or are we not?'

'Let him do his thing,' purrs Heather. 'That's how he works.'

Minutes later Alisdair comes back and tells us that he's found three openings, each one manned by a few guards and a camera.

'A few guards?' says James, looking anxious.

Heather pays no heed to that.

'So here's what we do,' she says. 'Three entrances. Three groups of two.'

'We split?' says James. 'What, no? That's a terrible idea. Didn't anyone ever tell you that you should always stick together when you're doing stuff like this?'

'We have the radios,' she says. 'We can stay in touch. We have only one person to find in there and we don't know how big the place is. We need to cover as much ground as possible and if six of us go in together, we could all be caught and that's mission over. We need to split up.'

James looks dismayed.

'Lucy and James,' she goes on. 'You two need to get us in there. There are cameras, right? So Lucy you need to sneak in and get to the control room, disable their systems. There will be a computer server room, where all the systems are controlled – surveillance, doors, everything. I'll talk you through it but you need to take down the camera servers first. Then the doors. And each team, make sure you take a security card or whatever they have from one of the guards. That will help you to get into other areas of the building. There will only be a few minutes before their back-up computers take over, so we must move fast once Lucy is done.'

Alisdair looks horrified whilst Lucy looks a mixture of panicked and thrilled.

'She can't go in there first,' says Alisdair.

'She can get us in, she's a Chameleon,' says Heather. 'That's what Chameleons do.'

'She's never done anything like that in her life,' snarls Alisdair.

'Yes I have!' says Lucy. 'I helped get the co-ordinates in the first place. Chameleons can get in and out of anywhere. They are masters of disguise, experts in lock-picking *and* safe-breaking. A well-trained Chameleon relishes the challenge of getting into the most well guarded places undetected. That's what Artemiz said. I remember.'

She looks pleased with herself.

'But you're not well-trained. You're not trained at all,' he replies.

'Alisdair, you'll team up with Nina, she's the most vulnerable of us all,' says Heather.

My eyes widen. Me and Alisdair?

'I'll go with Ben,' she says. 'Foxes work well with Bears, the perfect combination of guile and strength.'

'A match made out of heaven,' nods Ben, crossing his arms over his chest.

'That's exactly right,' replies Heather.

'No, no,' says James. 'It's a match made *in* heaven. *In* heaven.'

'I should go with Lucy,' cuts in Alisdair.

'Lucy's going to be just fine with me,' says James.

The expression on Alisdair's face shows all too clearly that he does not agree.

'We are a team,' says Lucy. 'And all team members are equal. Nina needs your help. Go with Nina.'

Alisdair remains tight-lipped. I look around us, as the bickering continues. I look over to the hill where Kelci could be, right this moment.

'Guys!' I say. 'Can we please just do this? We're here now. *Let's just get in.*'

———

Alisdair and I crouch behind a bushy strip of shrubbery, which is nestled on the ground some fifty meters from the opening, which I can just about see now. We're so close I feel his arm touching mine. This is it then. We're actually about to do this. I hear him breathing, sense his chest rising and falling. We wait and watch, wait and watch. I see three figures in dark outfits, roaming in front of the opening. Outrage chokes my throat. Was it one of them who took my sister?

We receive hushed updates from Lucy through our earpieces. I try to glean something from the tone of her voice, strain to hear any noises in the background, wanting to know what she sees but I know that she can't afford to talk any more than is necessary. Meanwhile, we watch the camera, which glides back and forth above the door. Alisdair gives me a look, the blue of his eyes radiating in the dim morning light. Then I see the camera stop moving.

'Cameras deactivated,' hisses Lucy, in our ears.

She's done it! The doors swing open. Then they close, then they open again. There's a loud shuffling sound through the earpiece.

'Go, go, go!' she says.

Alisdair turns to me and nods sternly. I do exactly what he has told me to do. I stay behind him, moving as quickly as I can, trying my best to keep up. He's fast, obviously. And he would be much, much faster if I weren't here. But I run as quickly as I can, and it doesn't take long until we're right by the entrance. I hold back, as he told me to, hovering over to the right to stay out of their line of vision, whilst he slinks towards them. He's twenty meters away, ten meters.

He pounces on one of the guards and hurls him to the floor. My heart pulses like a train at full speed. He picks up the guard's weapon and throws it towards me, before turning to the next guard. It hits me in the chest and I awkwardly catch it in the crook of my arms. It is black and heavy and I have no idea how to use it. But there's no time to contemplate that because Alisdair has both guards on him, and one is releasing an electric ray into his chest, just as those guys did to Kelci. When I see that, fury takes over and I run straight into the back of the guard and smack him hard over the head with the weapon. Astonishingly, he drops to the ground right away. Alisdair gives me a look then dispatches the other guard, throwing him to the ground where he lands with a thud.

Remembering what Heather said about the security card, I frisk the nearest guard until I come up with one. I try not to gasp as I see that Alisdair's face has a gash along his cheek and there's blood, running down his face. I follow him to the door, which continues to open and close. As we dive through a feeling of dread consumes me. My hands are shaking so hard I have to clasp them together. Inside, it is deserted. A corridor: long and perfectly white. The first thing that hits me is the smell: sterile, pharmaceutical. There are no windows, no natural light. What is this place?

22. Fine Specimens

We dart along the corridor and eventually reach a turning. I slip behind Alisdair, staying close as he peers around the corner. He beckons me to follow him and I try to keep pace as we move along another passage, running perpendicular to the first and almost identical save that this one has the occasional door, each locked, solid and impossible to see beyond. As we reach another junction I hear sounds, murmurs, coming from beyond the corner. Together we crouch down and hold our breath, hands on our weapons, tensed and ready.

We peek round the corner. I see a massive domed atrium. There are a handful of people marching around industriously, gripping some kind of electronic device, which they tap away at furiously. They are not dressed in the dark combat clothing of the guards but in silvery grey tunics. The whole thing gives me the creeps. *What are they doing?* We lean against the wall, out of sight, looking at each other, sideways. Then, Heather's voice pipes up in our ears.

'Nina, Alisdair. Are you in?' she whispers.

'Yes,' I say. 'We're in.'

'Good,' she replies. 'Us too. There's nothing much here, but will keep you informed.'

I describe the atrium to her, briefly, and we agree to report back when we have made our next moves.

'Did you read the signs?' whispers Alisdair.

I shake my head then glimpse back. Suspended from the ceiling, in the middle of the space, is a sheet of glass with glowing electronic words and arrows on it.

'RESEARCH'

'TRAINING'

'ARRIVALS'

'SPECIMENS'

'SPECIAL OPERATIONS'

'TRIALS'

'LABORATORY'

None of it sounds good.

'What is this place?' I mutter.

He shrugs his shoulders. I can't help notice that his face looks more real to me in this moment than it ever has before. I see every pore, every hair, every contour.

'Where would Kelci be?' I whisper.

'It's too late for Arrivals. I hate to say it, but how about Specimens?'

My stomach leaps and falls sideways at the thought of what *that* could possibly mean. I nod anyway. To follow the arrow for Specimens we need to go through the atrium to another hallway opposite. We watch and wait until the area is clear. I am all too aware that someone could reappear at any moment and I pray that the cameras are still out of commission. There's little else to do other than follow Alisdair as swiftly as possible. We reach the corridor leading to 'Specimens' safely … but as we enter it we see that - just inside - there are two more heavily armed guards guarding a door.

There's no time to pause. Alisdair leaping and kicking one, then the other, in an impressive double move. The moment they are down I push through the 'Specimens' door and Alisdair follows. We are immediately met with another corridor, wider this time and lined regularly with doors all facing each other. The first one is unlocked and I burst in. The room is small, white, windowless and almost empty except for a thin bed, more like a slab than a bed – with a boy laid on it, his eyes closed and unmoving.

'Oh no.'

The boy is strapped down with metallic strips across his arms, legs, stomach and chest. A glass screen hovers at the end of the bed with luminous blue words and letters shining from its surface.

Number: 374

Animal: Fox

Powers: intelligence, night vision, hearing, stealth

There are more words but I don't stop to read them. He's a Fox. Just like Heather, just like the other Foxes at Muldoon. Yet here he lies, seemingly lifeless. I see bruises where his arms are bound to the bed. I feel fear, hot and suffocating. I look to Alisdair.

'We have to keep going,' he says.

'We can't leave him here like this.'

'We will *all* end up like this if we don't keep moving – fast.'

'Kelci,' I say. 'She could be here.'

He gives a grim nod.

'We'll search the rooms, one by one. Let's stick together.'

I glance back to the Fox as we shoot back out into the corridor and open the next door. A Fish girl, her head shaved and her lips an unnatural shade of lilac. Then a Deer boy, pale and corpse-like. Then the next, and the next, and the next. Each door opens onto a similar scene – the bed, the screen, the 'specimen'. My eyes fill with tears. They are young, our age.

We are half way down the corridor and there's no sign of Kelci. The next door opens to reveal a slightly older guy lying there, but this time his eyes are open and his mouth is covered with a strip. The screen at the end of his bed flashes:

Warning: sedation impossible

A Horse. He looks straight at me, eyes burning. I look to Alisdair who is already moving towards the bed. I follow him and watch his hands remove the strip. The Horse's head begins to move around wildly. He shouts out.

'I can hear them. Can't you hear them?'

My entire body goes still.

I have heard those words before.

Before I can say anything the door of the room swings open and a bundle of uniformed men swarm in waving their weapons. The blood freezes in my veins. The guard at the front, a wide faced man with thick eyebrows, growls:

'Looks like two new specimens.'

Another of the guards, a shorter one to the left of their formation, moves towards Alisdair with his weapon pointing at his chest.

'Hold off,' says the leader. 'He wants them unharmed. To begin with anyway.'

The Horse looks up at us with desperate eyes and cranes his neck upwards as far as the restraints will allow. The small guard gives a vicious flick of the wrist and hits the Horse square in the face with his weapon, then keeps his eyes on Alisdair as he backs away.

'We can't trust these creatures, even for a second,' he says.

A stream of blood runs down the Horse's face, as he goes limp and his eyes close.

'Take their headsets,' says the leader. 'And the weapons.'

The small guard rips the headset from my ear and snatches the weapon from my hands.

'Get off!' I shout.

I watch in dismay as he does the same to Alisdair. *We are alone now.* I lock eyes with him across the bed. *He's urging me to stay calm, I can feel it.* With that the two guards swoop towards us with what looks like a pair of black hoods.

————

My eyes are open but all I see is blackness. All I smell is the mustiness of the hood, all I feel is the harshness of the fibres against my face. I sense Alisdair close by, but I don't know where. We trundle along for some minutes, pulled along and sometimes hit across the back. I try to breath evenly beneath the hood but all I feel is the air sticking as it meets the fear that floods upwards. I try in vain to focus through the material of the hood but I see nothing. I feel a prodding to the side of

————

my head from the sharp end of a weapon. We come to a standstill. It feels warmer here, wherever I am. Everything is silent … then a male voice, deep and oily, slides across the room.

'Well, who do we have here?'

There's a note of amusement in his tone and I begin to wriggle against the hands that grip me, but the grip just clamps on tighter. I feel the jab of a weapon prodding my lower back.

'Get off me!'

'Be still.'

'Let me see our visitors,' says the slippery voice.

The hood is lifted from my face and the brightness of the room hits me. Surrounding me are the three guards. One of them stands in front of me holding a weapon close to my face. I turn my head and see that Alisdair is there, surrounded by the remaining four guards. The small one right in front snarls up at him like a yappy dog, but he's not tall enough to reach any further than Alisdair's chest.

Alisdair's head is held high and he looks as confident as ever, perhaps even more so, showing no hint of apprehension. *How does he do that?* I pull back my own shoulders and copy his pose, even though it means the weapon at my back digs deeper into my skin. The guard in front of me steps aside to reveal a man sat behind a white desk that looks as though it's suspended in the air. He has slicked back hair and wears a crisp, expensive looking suit. His forehead is high and tanned like the rest of his face and his eyes slope above sharp cheekbones. He could be some young Congressman or banker from New York, I see those types stepping out of limos on Wall Street all the time.

Stood at his side, and possibly even more startling, is a tall woman who has black hair that curls itself into a bob. She looks like a silent movie star with her ivory skin and fine features. Her lips shine red and she wears a skirt suit. Behind them a symbol – the purple flower surrounded by green leaves - and the words: 'Lotus Corporation' in bold black letters. The woman's smooth hand rests on the right shoulder of the man, which makes them look like a kind of King and Queen, presiding in their chambers.

'Ah, who do we have here,' says the man. But it's not a question. 'And to think how lucky we are, to meet this time. We're growing so rapidly these days I hardly get the chance to visit the outer compounds. Now *I am glad* we came.'

He gives a smile showing a set of square white teeth.

'Young Nina Gregory,' he says, nodding right at me. 'And Alisdair MacDowell at your side. What a pleasant surprise.'

23. Max & Valerie

Eleven days since Kelci was taken, Lotus Corporation

The man talks as politely as if we were at a dinner party, introducing himself as Max Wilder and the woman next to him as 'Ms.Valerie Redfoot'. Meanwhile, my heart is in my mouth in horror. *How the hell does he know who we are?* Even Alisdair seems to lose his cool, shifting uncomfortably on his feet, brow furrowed.

'How do you know our names?' I say, pulling against the guards.

'I wouldn't be doing my job if I didn't know who you were, sweetie.'

He leans back in his chair.

'What job is that?' I spit out. 'Kidnapper? Torturer?'

I think of the Anitars we just saw, laid there like corpses, the life sucked out of them. He just grins.

'That's not quite how we see it.'

'How *do* you see it?' says Alisdair in a low growl.

'Well, our work here is incredibly important,' he replies.

My head spins. The woman looks at Alisdair with a weird fascination that makes me want to knock her out.

'You have no idea what you've got yourselves into,' says the man, running a finger lightly over his tie. 'I shouldn't be surprised by that. The only one of your esteemed family without powers, the only one who's struggled to manifest. You should have stuck with your pretty little Manhattan life. Much easier than getting involved in all this. A girl like you, an Anitar? You ought to stick to your love affair with fashion.'

My 'love affair with fashion'? How does he know all this? A creepy feeling, like spiders crawling across my skin, ripples all over me. If he knows who we are, he probably knows who we are looking for.

'What have you done with my sister?'

'Don't worry about your sister, Nina. There's just yourself to worry about now. Tell me, were the great Luke and Stella Gregory terribly disappointed when you didn't manifest?'

'My parents love me for who I am,' I say.

And I realise that it's true. My parents *do* love me for who I am.

'What is he?' says the woman, still peering at Alisdair.

Something about the sound of her voice makes my stomach turn.

'Always look to the eyes, Valerie,' he says. 'To know what you're dealing with.'

The woman looks enthralled.

'He is a Snow Leopard. The eyes, the hair, the slight arch of the back. Unmistakable and extremely rare.'

Alisdair glares at them.

'Very good,' says the woman, looking at Alisdair like a hungry cat might look at a bird.

'Useful, *very* useful.'

Useful for what? I scan the room, desperately looking for a means of escape.

'Tell me, how are dear old Luke and Stella? I'll bet they were anxious when their firstborn failed to manifest. God knows they were *desperate* to manifest themselves, all those years ago.'

He knows my parents? I stare at him, appalled.

'I can relate to you, you know Nina. My Mother wasn't at all pleased when *my* efforts came to nothing. She was a Tiger, just like yours. We're not so different, you and I.'

I grimace.

'I'm nothing like you!'

'Of course you're not,' says Alisdair. 'Don't listen to him.'

'Oh,' says the man, keeping his eyes on me. 'So you didn't care when they left you out of everything that was important to them? All those years? All for the "good" of the Anitars. I know how it goes. If you don't manifest, you are nothing to them. They take away everything from you, even your memories.'

Alisdair shoots me a wary look.

'However, *your* mother is still alive, for now at least. Whilst mine is dead.'

My knees turn to jelly.

'See, there's always something they're not telling you. Ugly little truths like the fact that my mother died on a mission – murdered by the killer she was assigned to track. Bet they didn't teach you that kind of thing at Muldoon Academy, did they?'

I am speechless.

'And how is dear old Lady Muldoon?' he says. 'I'm sure she hoodwinked you into hanging on her every word, I'm sure she has you believing her decisions are oh so just and oh so right.'

'More just than you ever could be,' I say.

He laughs.

'There are countless victims of the Anitar life. Collateral damage. But you must know all about that, with your friend Terence Bonfant.'

'Terence?' I gasp.

'He's messing with you,' says Alisdair, pulling towards me as the guards crowd in tighter around him.

'How do you know about Terence?'

He gives a bitter laugh.

'Typical. They didn't tell you, did they?'

He shakes his head, still laughing.

'Typical, typical, typical.'

'*What?*' I say, my heart bursting.

'Whatever it is, don't listen,' says Alisdair.

'Terence Bonfant had begun to *manifest*, but he didn't know what was happening to him. His parents, in their infinite wisdom and desire to put the Anitar way first, never told him what they really were. When he started to hear the voices in his head, is it any wonder he did what he did?'

My mouth hangs open.

'How do you–? Terence wasn't–' I say, my mind in a whirl.

'Oh yes he was,' Max says. 'Another victim of Horse manifestation. Driven mad by the voices.'

I want to scream that it isn't true, that it can't be true. *But the Horse we saw back there. He used the exact same words Terence did that night on the roof.*

'The boy's parents are Anitars — they *chose* not to tell their own son.'

Terence's parents are Anitars?

'You didn't know. What a surprise.'

He gives a smug smile.

'They're your parents best friends. Do you think it was a coincidence that you lived so close to them?'

His voice is mocking.

I'm dizzy with confusion.

'Anitars claim they rid the world of evil,' says Max, turning to Alisdair. 'But who decides who is evil and who is not? Anitars take memories from others. Why? Whenever it isn't convenient for them? Who gave you the right to strip a person's mind?'

I think of Lady Muldoon's threat to remove me from the program, and my memories.

'Why all the secrecy? Why operate in the shadows? Why not out in the open for all to see? Our own mothers wouldn't tell us the truth of their lives.'

'You can stop now,' spits Alisdair.

'Fortunately,' he goes on, '*I* am now in a position to do something about it.'

The bewilderment has me reeling. *Focus, Nina. Try to focus. Remember, we are here to find Kelci.*

'What do you want with us?' I say.

I try to remove the desperation from my voice but it's there, I can hear it. He looks me up and down.

'There's not a great deal we can do with you,' he says, turning to Alisdair. 'But our friend Mr MacDowell here, there's an awful lot we can do with him. More than you could imagine. In fact, you showing up here like this saves us a lot of time and resources.'

'What's that supposed to mean?' says Alisdair.

Max looks up at the woman and lets out a low chuckle. She looks towards me with flashing eyes.

'You're crazy,' I say.

They both shrug.

'Crazy is a relative term,' says Max. 'Especially when you're dealing with what *we're* dealing with. Sometimes a little destruction is necessary … in order to create something wonderful.'

'Wonderful?' I say, scanning the room.

'You couldn't begin to understand, sweetie.'

'She got into your compound, didn't she?' growls Alisdair.

The man sits back in his white chair and rolls his eyes.

'And here she stands with the barrel of a GH77 Electron poking into her back. A weapon I designed myself.'

I feel the 'Electron' dig deeper into my spine. I smell the breath of the guards mingling together and it's disgusting. The woman presses her long fingers into Max's shoulder even harder as he folds his arms across his chest.

'I have a strange feeling of regret each time we deal with one of your kind. But knowing that your gifts will contribute to something greater gives me comfort. Don't you agree, honey?' he says.

'I do,' replies Valerie.

'You're so concerned with your own kind you don't look out into the world,' says Max. 'Can you not see what is wrong with it all?'

What is he talking about?

'Enough now. It's time to take them into holding. Get them prepped.'

'Prepped for what?' I say.

'Don't concern yourself,' says Valerie. 'You two will *love* it down there.'

She winks at Alisdair, her lashes swooping. It's glaringly obvious we will not 'love it' down there. I spin around to face him again, with a pleading look in my eyes. He gives me a nod ... then catapults himself forward with a roar that resounds around the room. I let out a cry from deep in my throat and I do the only thing I can think of – kick the guard in front of me as hard as I possibly can. He lets out a surprised yelp, then the arms of the other guards tighten around me.

Alisdair has knocked two of his guards to their knees. Another one of the men shoots bright, fierce beams at him, while he throws another guard against the wall – so hard a huge dent is revealed as he slides down to the floor. Max and Valerie are motionless, fascinated. After a few moments the great glass doors of the room swing open and another group of guards enter the room. The last thing I see is Alisdair continuing to fight, just before I feel a jolt. A split-second ... and everything turns black.

24. No Windows

Twelve days since Kelci was taken, Lotus Corporation

My eyes feel like they have been sealed shut. I have to rub them to get them open. I look down and see that I am laid on my side as though I've been dropped here. My left leg is twisted at a disconcerting angle, which I use my hands to straighten, and as my eyes dart around all I see is white – blinding, stomach churning white. I see another leg which, alarmingly, isn't mine and I recoil from it but then I see that the leg is attached to a body, a body that I recognise – Alisdair. He lies on the pure white floor like a fallen giant, eyes closed, head resting on his arm. His thick eyelashes rest on the tops of his cheeks and lying there, unmoving, he looks angelic. I lean my face next to his and feel his warm breath on my cheek. He's alive. I gaze at him. But then I get a strange sensation that I should stop, that it's somehow not right to watch him like that.

I didn't know my body could hurt this much all at once. My back, my legs, my neck and it feels like someone has stamped on my bum. *What did those creeps do to us?* The room spins but I can see that it is small, way too small and white. Always with the white. The décor in this place is just terrible. There's nothing in this room, not a single object apart from two white cubes in the middle which I suppose are for sitting on. The whole set up looks like a trendy art gallery in

Manhattan except there's no art and no windows. My mind is a swirling whirlpool of turmoil. Is it true what Max said about Terence? That he was *manifesting*? His parents are Anitars? My parents never told me that! How does he know all that stuff about me? Has he been spying on me? I shudder, creeped out to my very core.

How long have we been holed up in this room? I don't know how to find out. And what about the others? Heather and Ben, Lucy and James – has Max got his hands on them yet? I scan the room, frantic. There's the indent of what looks like a door at the opposite side of the room, so I stagger towards it, searching with my hands. There's no handle just lines where the door is and no possible way of opening it. *We need to get out of here!* The walls sway in on me and I hit the door despite the futility of the gesture. Alisdair makes a grumbly noise behind me. The room keeps on closing in, my heart flip-flops and my throat is getting smaller. *Can I still breathe? I can't breathe.* I keep hitting the door. I see him leap up and move towards me until his hand is on the small of my back. The feeling of his hand halts me. He stands there, still. His eyes rest on me. I stop hitting the door.

'Nina, it's ok,' he says. 'It's ok.'

His other hand takes hold of my wrist. There's dried blood on his face.

'I hate being in rooms with no windows.'

I swallow down the urge to cry. There's compassion in his eyes, for once.

'Me too,' he says.

My throat opens up a little, letting the air pass through again.

'Thank you,' I say, grateful he didn't tell me to stop being so stupid.

My heart slows and I take a few deep breaths.

'Are you hurt?' he says.

'I mean, I hurt all over but I can function.'

'Good.'

'And you?' I say, looking at the blood. 'Are you ok?'

'Yes,' he says. 'I'm all right.'

He moves his hand from my back, then turns away as if searching for a way out.

'These people are mad,' I say.

He frowns.

'We can't trust anything they say,' he replies.

We pace the room, running our hands along the walls and ceiling. We find nothing and after some time there's nothing left to do but sit down on the floor.

'What do we do?' I say, desperate.

'For now, we rest and conserve our energy.'

What he means is there's nothing we *can* do.

'And the others….'

He looks as agonised as I feel when I say this. His jaw sets.

'If they so much as touch Lucy… If they do anything to her, they'll die.'

I shake my head, regretful.

'I should never have let her come here,' I say. 'I just wanted to find Kelci so badly… But I didn't have a clue what this place would be like, these people…'

'Listen,' he says, his voice softer. 'I know I've been blaming you for her involvement, but I know my sister. She fights hard to get what she wants. Besides, she's right. There's no point having these gifts if we can't help anyone with them. And the Anitars in here, they need help…'

'They do,' I say, thinking of the ones we saw.

'All I've been concentrating on is manifesting,' he goes on. 'And getting our places secured at an Academy. My father was a Fox and this is what he wanted for us, my mother wanted it too… I swore to her I would keep Lucy safe. But my sister was born ready for adventure. Only really, she's not ready. She's not trained. She's still naïve.'

'Maybe she's tougher than she seems,' I say. 'She got us in here didn't she? No one else could do that. And she's a Chameleon now, she can disappear, surely that has to count for something in a place like this?'

He nods slowly, thoughtfully.

'Sometimes I feel like little sisters can be seriously underestimated,' I say. 'I know I underestimated Kelci. I was so wrapped up in what *clothes* she was wearing and how she looked and if she cut her own hair, I stopped seeing *her*. You know, seeing her as she is now. Not just as she was as a little girl.'

He looks at me for a second, and I'm pretty sure there is a glimmer of recognition in his eyes.

'That man, Max,' he says. 'He talked about someone called Terence. What did he mean?'

I sigh.

'Terence Bonfant. He was my best friend. He killed himself, and I couldn't save him.'

He raises his eyebrows.

'He killed himself?'

'Yes. From his rooftop. He jumped five storeys, and I was there, trying to talk him down, but he didn't listen. If he was manifesting – it's news to me. I didn't even know his parents were Anitars and I don't think he did either. If I'd known… I could've helped him, at least let him know he wasn't going mad.'

'But you didn't know. You still don't for sure, these people could be lying.'

I nod.

'Before that, I tried to manifest every day. But after that… It's when I gave up. I just wanted to avoid it all. I didn't want to go through anything like that again. So I guess I opted for a normal life.'

Alisdair smiles.

'You're still holding out for that?' he says, looking up at where we are.

I let out a dry laugh. Then I shake my head in disbelief. He laughs too. And I realise this is the first time I've ever heard him laugh. I also can't help noticing the way his hair curls around his ears. Then the door opens and six people in tunics bowl in. Without a word they split down the middle and three reach for Alisdair, clamping restraints onto his arms while the other three come for me. I scream. They pull at my arms and drag me along. Alisdair and I are locked in a desperate gaze.

'Alisdair!'

I reach out for him, but within seconds he is gone.

One of the threesome is a woman who grabs my elbows and begins to drag me out of the room. A burning sensation starts up inside me. I try to punch her but then she raises her Electron to my side and zaps me, releasing a bolt of electricity right into me. I feel the energy spreading its wicked fingers all through my body followed by a horrible feeling of weakness. I try to break free, but I can't. I want to cry out, but I can't. They hook my arms under theirs and drag me along. I'm barely conscious as we travel some distance through the building. We eventually stop at another room. The temperature is lower in here and there's an empty table and two chairs either side. I fight for speech.

'What do you want with me?'

The woman throws me into the chair furthest from the door and I sit there seeped in exhaustion. All three of them file out without looking back and lock the door on their way out. I lay my arms on the table and let my head fall on to them. *What kind of a sick weirdo works in a place like this?* My head rolls onto its side and I sink past disgust, into a deep kind of sleep.

I wake up with a knot in my stomach. The door bursts open and the three of them are back - accompanied by two others. One is a guard – the uniformed and weaponed variety, with a look of outrage on his face. His nose is bulbous with a red tip that looks set to burst.

Alongside him is someone more surprising: a guy who looks a bit younger than me – perhaps Kelci's age. Despite the highly unflattering gown he is wearing, which makes him look like a hospital patient, I see that he is darkly good-looking. His face is bruised, framed by thick brown hair; his arms behind his back. The guard shoves the door shut and grabs the boy and plonks him down in the chair opposite me.

'What the hell is going on?'

The guard takes a few steps back and holds an Electron by his side.

'Quiet, little girl,' he says.

I turn from the guard back to the boy and see the left corner of his mouth curl up ever so slightly. The guard barks like a sick dog.

'Find out what she knows.'

'What's that supposed to mean?' I say.

'*What is she thinking?*'

Silence.

'Answer me.'

The guard moves towards the boy and lifts the Electron to the side of his head.

'I don't know,' says the boy. 'I can't see that yet, it doesn't work that way.'

I frown. The boy is definitely not one of them.

'What are you doing here?' I say to him.

'Quiet!' shrieks the guard.

The boy's eyes flicker from me to the point where the end of the weapon digs sharply into his temple. I watch a trickle of sweat run down his forehead, over his cheeks and onto his neck. His eyes are locked onto mine, brown and wide, so earnest it feels as though he is trying to communicate something.

'How did she get here?'

I stare at the boy, ignoring the pang of the bindings holding my wrists. He's a Horse. He must be. I see the same shades of empathy in his face that Artemiz has and the same luscious quality to his hair. His voice has an accent, Italian I think. A Horse, just like Terence, or so Max said. He nods, vigorously.

'I need to talk to her first,' he says. 'Create a bond before I can help you. My name is Matias…'

'Shut up!'

I glower at the guard.

'You're not capable of finding out anything yourself so you send in one of your captives to do it for you. How courageous.'

'I will use this if I have to,' he says, waving his weapon around.

'Yes but if my mind is frazzled how will you find out what you seem so desperate to know?'

'Enough!'

'Manners clearly are not a priority in this place but if you wouldn't mind butting out for a minute…'

I turn back to Matias, whose lips give away the slightest hint of a smile. The guard gives a low growl.

'Cheeky brat. Now, you boy – tell me what she knows. *Now.*'

With that he lifts the weapon and swipes Matias across the face with it.

'No!'

I shake at my restraints as I watch the blood run from a gash below his right eye.

'I suppose you think you're doing this for the good of mankind or some such rubbish?' I scream.

My eyes rest on Matias who is ever so slightly shaking his head at me from side to side.

'I just sense her fear,' he says.

'I could have told you that. Find out who she's working with.'

Matias keeps on gazing at me and I shift in my seat as fingers of dread creep up my spine. The others. I try to erase the thought of them like chalk on a blackboard. And Kelci... Why I'm here... His eyes flicker.

'Who else is here? Who's with you?' asks Matias.

I meet his eyes.

Matias, tell him the Snow Leopard and I are working alone.

'Nobody else,' he says, turning his head to the guard. 'She and the Snow Leopard are alone.'

'That's not true. Ask her again.'

'That's all I'm getting.'

'Impossible.'

He snaps his head to look at me.

'We need to know *who* you came with. We need to know *now*.'

He hits me in the ribs. Matias frowns, jaw clenched. I feel the stabbing sensation travelling all the way down my body.

'You don't need to hurt her, I'm *telling* you her thoughts.'

'Who are you with?' says the guard.

I keep my mouth closed and I try not to show the pain. This man will get nothing from me, I know that much.

'*Who are you with?*'

Matias looks up at the guard, a defiant look on his face, saying nothing, though he knows, my thoughts racing with images of our team - of Kelci.

'Tell me!' roars the guard, lifting his Electron high in the air and landing it across Matias' neck with a crack.

I scream.

'Stop!'

Matias' head rolls back as a red streak lights up along his neck.

'She came here herself,' he croaks.

'Not true!'

Matias looks at me.

'Your sister is here. I've seen her. She's in the Burrows, with the Rabbits, deep underground… There's a lift, near the atrium…'

The guard whips back his arm again and before there is a chance to say anymore he hits Matias again across the neck with another excruciating crunch. Matias' head lolls forward, bruised and quiet, eyes closed. The guard peers at his face. Then he turns to face me.

'Doesn't matter what he tells you. You're never getting out of here.'

He raises his weapon high in the air and stalks toward me. I steel myself for an almighty blow, but then, through the corner of my eye I see the outline of someone familiar appearing from the whiteness of the wall close to the door. Then, one by one, in lightning quick succession, the three other guards drop to the floor. I begin shouting, wailing … trying to cover the noise of their falls; to keep the attention on me. Meanwhile in the background I sense the figure getting closer … raise its arms and pound down on the back of the guard's head. There is a bewildered look on his face before he too drops to the floor. His Electron spins across the ground.

'Nina!'

Lucy, her face intent. Her eyes flashing scarlet.

'He said Kelci is here!' I say, pointing at Matias. 'He told me where she is…'

'We have to go now,' says Lucy.

She grabs the Electron then makes a lunge towards the door flinging it open to reveal James already moving into the room looking extremely edgy, his eyes landing on me.

'This place is insane!' he shouts. 'It's worse than my uncle Steve's house! And that's really saying something.'

He bounces over to me and grabs hold of me by the shoulders.

'Matias,' I say. 'We have to help him. He's a Horse. He just saved me and told me where Kelci is.'

I lurch across the table. I touch his cheek but there is nothing, his face is smooth against my fingers but there's no animation there, nothing at all.

'Matias! No!'

'We have to go, Nina,' says Lucy. 'Now.'

'But… He's an Anitar…'

I lift my hand to his neck, searching for the beat of life in him. There's nothing. A sob rises up in my throat but before I have the chance to say anything Lucy is lifting me at the elbows. Here's a boy I didn't even know, willing to give his life to protect me, the mission, Muldoon and my sister. All of it. Hot tears well up in my eyes and I place my hand on his face which is still warm and soft.

'We won't let them win,' I whisper to him. 'I promise.'

I look at the guard lying on the floor his face turned upwards with his nose glowing. With that Lucy takes a tight grip on my hand and with James at our side she leads me out into the blank, white corridor.

25. Why, Thank you

Twelve days since Kelci was taken, Lotus Corporation

We race down the corridor but my mind stays with Matias, in the room whose door is slipping away as we hurtle down the hallway. I think of his lips held tight even when that guard was about to end his life. That last blow to his neck. The sickening sound of the crack. The walls whizz by, Lucy swirls ahead and James runs close at my heels. I have no idea where we're going. In my head I hear the sound of Terence's body hitting the street. I see the way he looked moments before he was gone.

'There was nothing I could do,' I say.

My breathing is coming out in pants. Lucy turns to look at me, frowning.

'Of course there wasn't Nina. Their weapons are deadly.'

'No, I mean…'

My voice trails off. Lucy drags us to the corner of the hallway and grabs hold of my shoulders. James' face hovers over her shoulder, looking at me.

'Damn, girl,' he says. 'You did what you could for that guy. That ugly guard killed him. Not you. He wanted to help you, he told you where your sister is. I say let him help you and let's *get out of here.*'

'Nina,' says Lucy, eyes searching. 'Next we have to find Alisdair.'

The sound of his name is like a slap in the face. Alisdair. His face swims into my head and it's like seeing a shadowy apparition rise up out of the gloom. He's not here, with us. He's… god knows where.

'Alisdair…'

'Yes,' replies Lucy. 'And Kelci.'

I wince. I see Kelci's face swirling up to replace Alisdair's. I reach for the glasses case tucked in my trouser pocket.

'I just wish I could've…'

Lucy's frown melts and she curls a strand of my hair around my right ear as her eyes glow violet.

'I know you do,' she says. 'But don't let his death be in vain.'

'Yes sir, I could not agree more,' says James, nodding his head.

I frown, then nod.

'Ok, ok.'

I rub my eyes and shake my head from side to side.

'Now where did they take that big wild cat friend of ours?' says James.

'I don't know,' I reply.

Did they wheel in another Horse to interrogate him? They won't make Alisdair talk that way, but how far will things go? They *killed* someone in an effort to get answers from me. How many of those Electron blasts until a person ends up in the 'Specimens' section? A new wave of panic rises up.

'Let's try the East part,' says Lucy, pointing to the nearest door. 'We haven't been there yet.'

'Ok, yes,' I say, hardly recognising the croaky tones of my own voice.

I feel Lucy's hand holding mine, freezing and delicate.

'The only way to the East side is through there,' she says, pointing to the nearest door.

We nod. Lucy whips out a security card and swipes it through the entry system. The door glides open with a hiss and we walk through, finding ourselves in a cramped passageway which is set high up near the ceiling of a cavernous room covered in screens. I gasp. Far below there are people hovering by banks of workstations, some huddled in little groups, talking.

'Look at all those glum-faced freaks,' hisses James.

'Shhhh!' says Lucy. 'You've got to shut up some of the time.'

James glares at her but he does shut up. We shuffle along and no one looks up towards the balcony, they're too intent on whatever it is they're doing down there. Regardless, the three of us crouch down below the barrier. I glimpse a map of the world flashing on the largest screen but there's no time to take in the details. We scrabble along the passageway picking up the pace as we go. Eventually all three of us slip out the door to the other side.

We head for the east side of the building, hiding around corners, slipping into doorways and ducking inside rooms for cover. It doesn't take much longer to reach the 'Research' area and without a pause Lucy begins to check each of the rooms.

'Alisdair,' she says eventually, her voice grave. 'In there.'

My stomach lurches. Lucy has turned pale and her hair is snow-white. I try to calm my breathing. There are four people in there, she tells us. Three guards fully kitted up with Electrons and a woman hovering around Alisdair, 'doing things to him'. I try not to choke at the thought of him in there. *Doing what things to him?* We line up – Lucy nearest the door, me next, then James. My muscles tense in preparation.

We blast into the room. Alisdair is as Lucy said – laid out on a bed, strapped down, with a band across his mouth. The three guards hover in the corners of the room and the women hangs around Alisdair next to some grim, pristine looking machines. I sense Lucy and James behind me. Immediately, one of the guards shoots me with a bolt of electricity, sending me flying across the room, smashing into a wall. A shock of pain travels from my neck to my legs. I touch my head and feel a wetness there. Blood, sticking to my hair.

'Nina!' cries Lucy.

I manage to open my eyes for a second, in time to see her dodge another shock of electricity. She races towards the wall and disappears from sight. James dives towards Alisdair on the bed but before he can get there one of the guards hits him with his Electron across the back and the other guard zaps him with a jolt of electricity, making him judder and fall to the floor. The unarmed woman, by the bed, stares open mouthed at him writhing around beneath her. I'm weak, so weak I can barely move. All three guards pull James up, hitting him and kicking him, as Alisdair lies motionless on the bed. *We're all going to be caught.*

Just as I'm trying to lift myself back up, out of the corner of my eye I see Lucy's little body whipping through the air so fast I can barely make her out – I just see the guards dropping James to the floor and then themselves, dropping to the floor as they try to fend her off. She's so quick … and now she has one of their Electrons, which she turns on them, letting out a wild cry as she hovers over them, shooting wildly. She pivots to the unarmed woman too and turns the Electron on to her. The guards and the woman are quiet now, laid out on the floor. James picks himself up. I feel my head once more, feeling woozy from the sight of more blood on my hand, but I manage to pull myself up, sensing some strength coming back to me. I drag myself over to them and turn to Lucy.

'That was *seriously* badass,' I say.

'Why thank you, Nina,' she says, in a sweet voice, grinning.

The three of us move over to Alisdair. His shirt hangs open with lots of wired up monitor things clinging to his chest, all of which I remove in one disgusted motion.

'What were they doing to you?' I whisper.

His eyes open.

James rips the band from across his mouth and works his way downwards removing all of the restraints.

'Nina.'

Relief washes over me.

'We're here.'

He gives me a weary smile. I touch his brow. It feels unnaturally cold.

'Are you ok?'

He nods, looks me over.

'What about you? What did they do to you?'

I shake my head.

'I'm ok.'

He nods again then holds his head and sits up. Lucy runs into his arms.

'You're ok,' she says, looking up at him as he strokes her hair.

He gives her a little smile and looks around, taking us all in. He looks surprised when he sees the groaning bodies below.

'You guys have been busy,' he says, raising his eyebrows.

'It was all Lucy,' I say.

'Lucy?' he says, looking at his sister.

She shrugs her shoulders.

'Oh, you know, it's my job to look out for my brother sometimes.'

He ruffles her hair. Then he edges off the bed, moving stiffly and putting his arm around my neck. I feel the bare skin of his shoulder against my cheek. And I become burningly aware of his bare chest right next to mine. Without my permission my cheeks are getting hot, and I'm praying no one can see.

'Did you find Kelci yet?' he says right into my ear as we stagger towards the door.

'No,' I reply.

He squeezes my shoulders.

'I'd say it's about time we did.'

Together we tumble out the door, Alisdair and I first, followed by Lucy and James. There's no one in sight but I hear voices around the corner. Loud voices. Tense. Familiar.

'Heather,' I say, breathless. 'Ben.'

I hear exclamations around me and we swarm as one around the corner, following the voices. Sure enough there they are – Ben and Heather battling it out with three guards, dodging Electron rays, throwing kicks and punches. The Fox and the Bear. My heart rises. I crane my neck to see if maybe, just maybe, they have Kelci but she is nowhere to be seen. We race towards them and just as Heather delivers a final whip-like blow to the last guard, catapulting him to the ground, she turns to face us, exposing a cut down the side of her face. Heavy breaths fall from her mouth and she frowns, startled, as though ready to keep up the fight.

Without turning to him, her hand reaches for Ben who spins to face us. His hulking frame rises and falls with each hefty breath. Their bodies kind of sag in relief. Up close they look bedraggled with their clothes torn and half of Ben's top is burnt; Heather with blood on her hands, as well as her face, and bright streaky marks across her wrists. Ben has a dark swollen bruise on the right side of his neck and it looks as though some of his hair and a bit of his right eyebrow have been burnt off.

'Right on cue, people,' says Heather, pulling herself together then placing a hand on her hip.

She checks over her shoulder, as does Ben.

'Did they capture you?' I say.

222

'Briefly.'

'I know where they're keeping Kelci,' I say.

'You do?' she says, echoed by Alisdair and Ben too.

But before I get the chance to go on, she raises an eyebrow. Then she cocks her head to the side.

'Do you hear that?' she says.

We fall silent. There's a rhythmic kind of rumbling sound.

'Footsteps,' says Lucy.

James curses loudly. A ripple of apprehension works it's way through the group. We stare at each other for a moment as the sound grows. Before we have a chance to move I spot them. A thick swarm of guards, all armed and all headed in our direction.

26. Deathly Quiet

Twelve days since Kelci was taken, Lotus Corporation

The first thing I am aware of is Heather grabbing me by the arm, putting a weapon into my hands and willing me forwards at top speed.

'We know a place with more room, we'll have to take them on there. We'll be destroyed in this corridor.'

We all run, side by side. I turn to see the uniformed mass behind us, bearing down with pulsing footsteps. We run towards the huge atrium, the same one Alisdair and I came through when we first arrived and I see the doors for the lift that Matias described. *The way to*

Kelci! But there's no way I can get to it now. We arrive in the atrium and see that there are stairways running across the walls, held in by long, curved balconies. We catapult into the space with such force the people who have been wandering around dressed in their tunics scatter immediately. Heather yells instructions – Alisdair and Ben to remain on the ground, James and Lucy up to the lowest set of stairs and Heather and I up to a higher level. And so I stand here on the white steps looking down as the bodies pour into the space below. My fingers shake as my right hand touches the balcony. All of the guards are heavily armed.

They trample in, stony faced, determined. *Where have they all come from? We can't fend all of them off.* I wipe the sweat from my brow – almost too tense to notice the heaviness of my aching limbs. The guards are moments away from Alisdair, who stands tall as they come towards him. I can just see Lucy on the other balcony, her hair flashing rainbow-like. James is hopping madly and I hope he doesn't bounce over the edge. Ben runs a hand through his hair, pushing it back from his face, and lets out a low growl. At least fifty of these guards must have entered the space before one of them, slightly taller, slightly broader than the rest raises his voice.

'We are giving you *one* chance to step down and come with us.'

His eyes flicker from left to right beneath heavy brows. A long pause follows until I catch a look from Heather who is clearly urging me to respond.

'We will do no such thing,' I say, trying to sound authoritative.

Their leader locates me with his glare, craning his neck up to see me.

'You are trespassing. It will be better for you all to come forward peacefully. Otherwise, my men will be forced to use all means available to them.'

His neck looks like that of a rooster, crinkled and flapping.

'We will not surrender.'

He turns to his men. I see Lucy out of the corner of my eye. She discreetly points from herself to the guards as if asking my permission to move. I turn to her and nod. She rushes to the wall then disappears. The front guards spring forward, followed immediately by those behind them. They hold out their weapons, charging towards Ben and Alisdair. I see that already, at the front of the throng, that guards are falling to the ground, as if tripped by invisible wires, which I can only presume is Lucy working her way through the crowd. Bodies circle Alisdair and Ben as they begin to lunge and kick. I see Alisdair take a hit across his face, which is so painful to watch, it may as well have been me. James catapults himself into the fray and disappears into the sea of grey. I feel the weapon in my hands and prepare myself to go down there and fight. Then I hear Heather, beside me, shouting over the din.

'You have to go get Kelci.'

'I can't do that now!' I shout, gesturing towards the ground. 'They've sent an army. I have to help. None of us will find her if we're dead...'

She grabs me by both arms.

'No, and that's why you need to go, right now, to get her. Most of the guards will be here. We'll keep them occupied. I'll help you get out of here but you must go, now!'

'Alone?'

I feel the blood drain from my face.

'The rest of us will have to stay here.'

I search her sculpted face, those foxy eyes. Now I need to trust this girl with my life? With my sister's life? As though she knows what I am thinking, she says:

'I've come this far with you, Nina. I want us to complete this mission and return to Muldoon alive. This is the best plan we have now.'

I look down at the fighting. I don't see James, I don't see Lucy.

'I can't do it alone, I don't have any powers! It's just me,' I say. 'I just can't.'

What if I get there and I can't help her? What if there's nothing I can do? What if I don't even get to her? Heather grabs hold of my wrist.

'You have to try,' says Heather, squeezing my wrists.

I look at the commotion below and can't imagine how all of us would ever get to this underground place unseen. It dawns on me… it's like chess: I can't afford to get caught up in the distractions, I just can't. I have to go for the piece that wins the game. Kelci. Heather knows that and I hate to admit it, but I do too. I nod quietly. There's just no avoiding what needs to be done. Heather nods back at me and squeezes a security card into my hand.

'Use this. It's access all areas. Now let's go.'

With that we run down the stairs and stick to the very edges of the room, skirting around the battle. Heather punches and kicks as we go, knocking guards aside so I can get through. We finally reach the exit and I give her one last look as she enters the fray. I gulp down the sense that I'm saying some kind of final goodbye and run off, heading for the lift.

It's deathly quiet out here as I face the doors. And empty. Eerily so. I press the large green button to the side of the lift door and see it light up under my touch. The door is small, too small – anyone taller than me couldn't get through it without bending down. There's a low hum before it slides open. I step inside and am immediately and acutely aware that it is a tiny, cramped space made entirely of shiny metal. The door clamps shut and I find myself encased inside the box as it begins the descent. My stomach lurches. Down, down, down I go. There don't seem to be any other stops along the way – it takes me to one place and one place only. I feel the creeping sensation of being trapped spreading over me like ice forming on a freezing lake. I try to calm my shallow breathing. I mustn't pass out or anything stupid – not with the others fighting to stay alive above me, and god knows what below me. The lift continues its never-ending descent. I wipe the sweat from my forehead and cling to the side to steady myself.

I suddenly see a picture in my mind, my first ever memory, the first time I saw Kelci as a newborn baby in the hospital as my Mum cradled the crumpled ball with its spindly arms and legs. I leaned in and she looked right back at me, with enormous blue eyes. I touched the impressive tuft of blonde hair at the front of her head and in that moment I was completely in love. I remember the softness of her skin under my lips as I kissed her for the first time.

Without warning the lift comes to an abrupt stop and my heart stops with it. I press the only button there is in here but nothing happens. Have we arrived? I press the button again but there's no response. The door stays shut. It's hot, much hotter than it was. I must be way, way under the Earth now. *Far enough for a Rabbit's thump not to bring the whole compound down.* My throat is closing up. There's a wiggling motion and suddenly for no apparent reason the lift begins to go again. Relief. I *must* be nearly there now.

As the lift moves I feel deep tremors rumbling in the ground like a hundred dragons turning in their dungeons. I remember the last time I saw Kelci. Looking at me with those terrified eyes, screaming at me to run. Held tight in dark arms. Why hadn't I listened to her at the party? *Because I thought I knew best.* The lift gives a violent bang as it stops. I smash the button and this time it lights up and when I press it again the door slips open and a wave of hot air washes in as I step out.

I move carefully and find myself in a tunnel with huge silver tubes running along the walls. There's a strange, metallic smell, which makes me feel nauseous, and I see how rocky and crumbly the walls are where the bare earth has been carved out. As the lift door closes behind me I instantly feel like I will never get out. I take a deep breath. I tell myself to keep my bearings, remember where this lift is. The floor trembles beneath my feet. I begin with a light run down this tunnel, taking note of the nooks and crannies where I can hide if I see anyone. I turn a corner and pick up speed as I pass along another tunnel. I run past something embedded in one of the walls but I'm moving too fast to see what it is so I slow down and step backwards to get a glimpse.

It seems to be a small cave that has been holed out of the wall with white bars covering the entrance. I creep nearer and there, inside, I see a pair of eyes staring out at me. I gasp, then put a hand over my mouth to stop myself from making a noise. It's a young boy with white-blond hair and angelic features. A Rabbit beyond a doubt and yet at the same time his face is all sunken in and weird. He looks at me with outright terror. Moments later he leans back into the shadows of the cave and I don't see him anymore. There's a lump in my throat so big I can't swallow it down. I run right up to the bars and look in only to see the dark outline of him crouching alone at the back of his tiny cave.

'Do something Nina. Do something now,' I murmur to myself.

I jog along the tunnel and see more barred up holes in the walls – one Rabbit after another, all blindly panicked, some crouching away from me, some grabbing onto the bars as if they are holding on for dear life. There's more rumbling, muffled somehow and I can only guess that they have put something into the floors and walls to prevent their captives from taking the place down. Why are they here? These forgotten creatures? They look out at me with pitiful eyes. I can stand it no longer.

Finally I see a pair of eyes looking out at me so familiar, it makes my heart crumble. Those eyes, blinking at me in all their fullness and all their blueness. But their brightness is gone. I look back at those eyes and I feel everything coming upon me all at once – terror, hope, relief, despair. For there she is, one hand on the bar staring out at me, blinking and confused. Can she see who I am? I run straight towards her, holding my breath, and take out the card Heather gave me with trembling hands. The bars disappear into the ceiling and there is nothing between us, nothing but hot, subterranean air. I reach out my hand, but by now she has backed up into the far corner where she watches me, wary.

'Kelci,' I say, softly.

With that she bends forwards ever so slightly to look closer. She could bolt at any moment, straight out of this cell. She'd be too fast for me to catch her. I lower my voice to a whisper.

'It's Nina. Your sister.'

She pokes her head out of the shadow a little more.

'I'm here to take you home.'

I reach into my pocket, take out the case then remove the glasses. She stares at me as I hold them out to her.

'Here. Your glasses. Put them on.'

At first she just stares at me, then looks at my hand. I nod gently, then slowly, slowly she reaches out for them, then takes them from my hand and shakily puts them on her face. *Why isn't she talking? What did they do to her?* I reach out my hand.

'Just take hold of my hand and we can leave here, together.'

She lets out a murmur. I feel my hand hanging there in the air. There's a noise from outside the hole. I'm aware of the bars. If they were to come down… She wears the same frown she had the day she manifested. I hear another knock from outside and she jolts nervously.

'Please, take my hand.'

Another noise, louder. She doesn't move.

'Please.'

I look into her eyes.

'Let me help you.'

She frowns, scrunching her nose, and closes her eyes. I take a step forward. *Please, please, please let me help you...* I reach my hand out a little further. Half of me expects her to cower away, or run off... But as I look at her with pleading eyes, she reaches for my hand and immediately I clasp it, and pull her towards me.

'Let's go.'

I take her arm and place it over my shoulders, sensing the thinness of her limbs, feeling her laddery ribcage next to mine. We step out. An almighty alarm begins to clang. I look around at the other cages, seeing those helpless faces once again. *I can't just leave them here.* But the alarm gets louder, deafening, and the front of every cave closes up into a series of blanks. No more Rabbits to be seen. I hear shouts from behind and turn to see a group of guards, seven in total, headed our way. *Here we go.*

'Run!' I shout.

And that's exactly what we do. The alarm pulsates. The ground shakes harder. We speed back down the tunnels and I'm surprised that I'm keeping up with Kelci. *How did I get so fast?* We reach the lift and I slam her in. She holds tightly on to my arm with both hands. I hit the button and it lights up. The lift begins its vibrating ascent. I lean back against the metal and let out an enormous breath. The echo of the alarm floats around the tiny box and I look at her. We keep moving upwards and I hold on to her tightly. *We'll be with the others soon.* We remain in silence, just the sounds of our breathing, the alarm getting quieter and quieter, and the groan of the lift as it rises. It feels like we have almost reached the top when, without warning, the lift moves from side to side, just a little. Then it halts. Kelci raises her eyebrows and I feel a pang of panic.

'It will start again.'

I muster up a reassuring smile. We stand there speechless. Still the lift does not move. We remain for what seems like an eternity and still, the lift refuses to move. I hear a rattling sound, far below and it looks as though the walls are beginning to sway in on me. I bang on the sides of the lift as though that may make us move. Kelci stamps her foot and the whole box jerks violently.

'No, Kelci!' I say, before softening my voice. 'No thumping just now.'

Almost too slowly to notice at first, I sense that the lift is moving. Except, the lift is *not* moving upwards, it is moving back *down* the shaft.

27. Your Eyes

The Burrows, Lotus Corporation

Terror grabs hold of my throat and if it weren't for my saucer-eyed sister clinging to my arm, I would be screaming. We are descending and it might as well be straight to hell. Are we going to die? Or worse? Because there is worse, I've seen that now. I take a deep breath. *I don't want to die. I don't want my sister to die.* I look at Kelci, a pale apparition, as the lift trundles on its grim course. I look around and something strange happens. My eyes, they're seeing everything so clearly... I run my hands along the metal. The sides of the lift are smooth and yield nothing. It's not until I reach as high as I can above me that I feel a slight indentation in the ceiling. It's as thin as a thread of linen and I follow it around with my hands – some kind of seam forming an invisible square. *We must get free, we must go UP.* I smash upwards with all my might but nothing happens.

I do it again, this time using more force... More force than I knew I was capable of... There's movement. I lurch upwards again, hitting hard. Then again, falling back to the floor. I hit it again and see that the right side of the join is beginning to come away. The lift keeps on descending. I waste no time smashing upwards and the outline finally peels open like a tuna can. Through it, I see gaping, rumbling darkness. I look at my hands, clenched into fists, and I can't understand how I just did that. Kelci looks up at the opening, then looks at me and immediately, her eyes turn to big blue moons.

'Nina…' she says.

'What?' I say. 'What is it?'

'Your eyes…' she says.

'What about them?'

'Your eyes are golden.'

I put my hands to my eyes and rub them. I shake my head and turn to her.

'Golden,' she says.

I hear the alarm below us getting louder. My sight is zooming in, then out, then in again. I see everything in the most excruciating detail. *What is happening to me?* Then I remember the tour, at Muldoon. *They are able to see things hundreds of miles away,* said Artemiz. Could it be? There's no time to contemplate. I look up at the hole in the roof of the lift.

'You have to jump up there, ok?' I say to Kelci. 'Then pull me up.'

Rabbits are good leapers, but I wonder if she will still be able to jump.

'Can you do that?'

She nods. She stares upwards for a few seconds, nudges her glasses up her nose then without another word and leaps up and disappears through the opening. It panics me to not be able to see her.

'Kelci?' I shout.

Her face appears.

'Pull me up!'

Is the lift moving faster? I reach out both my arms towards her as she leans through the opening. I grab hold of her arms and she pulls me up. I push myself up using my feet against the side of the lift. Kelci drags me through and I find myself lying on the top of the blackened lift, looking up to see a long, narrow shaft, dirty and black, filled with metal bars and cables. I gulp. What do we do now? All I know is that every single fibre of my being is saying UP, UP, UP!

'Get on,' I say, turning my back towards her.

She climbs on, grasping my shoulders just like the times we would piggyback when we were kids. I secure her and focus my eyes as far up the shaft as I can. The lift *is* descending faster and the alarm is getting louder. There are shouts and bangs echoing all around. I hear Lady Muldoon's words in my mind. *All you need to do, is believe.* I look up the shaft once again. I lift my chin upwards. I close my eyes. Then, my feet rise up from the metal. First my heels, then my toes, until I am no longer touching the surface of the lift. Kelci gasps. I gasp. Then I fall back down, my feet hitting the metal. *I don't know what I'm doing. How do I do it?* The lift must almost be at the bottom…

'Nina,' says Kelci, almost screaming. 'Please. We can't go back there.'

I stare upwards again, trying not to think. Thinking isn't helping! I let my feet, somehow, rise again, higher this time. But then there's a thud as the lift reaches the ground and then another thud as my feet hit the metal once again. *Come on, come on, come on.* The alarm is deafening and there's scrambling and noises coming from the lift. They're inside it. Kelci is screaming now.

'Please! No! Please!'

I grab onto Kelci's hands as they claw around my shoulders. At the opening two gloved hands appear, one holding an Electron. *They can't get us, I won't let them get us.* I squeeze my eyes shut and hold Kelci tight. Somehow, I don't even know how, my feet come off the metal and we begin to ascend.

I'm flying.

But it is narrow, so narrow and I don't know what I'm doing. There are great bunches of cables travelling the whole length of the shaft. I feel a sharp pain in my calf as the Electron ray hits me. I let out a scream, and so does Kelci. We hit the side of the shaft. I don't look down, I can't look down but I hear curses and hollering. My leg sears with pain. I stare upwards, willing myself not to stop, not to fall, not to let go of Kelci. I see a slit of light, at the top of the shaft. *If we can just get to that.* I feel Kelci's hands slip a little on my shoulders and I shout at her to hang on. Her terrified breath rings in my ear.

'I'm slipping!' she shrieks.

Her grip loosens a little more and I try to pull her arms around me, tighter. We're both slick with sweat. We start to spin in the air and smash against the cables. The side of my face gets covered in oil as we hit them. I push against them with my foot, to keep us away, trying to steady us. There's so little room, it's dark, and it's hot, *so hot.* I can barely breathe. If I were to stop flying now… If we were to fall… It's becoming a long way down… Kelci feels so heavy on my back. I stare at the light, sweat pouring down my face. There's an almighty creaking sound that resounds from below and my heart stops beating. The cables begin to grind against each other, moving. I sense Kelci looking down, frantic.

'They're coming!'

I glance down for a second and see that the lift is beginning to ascend. I look to the shaft of light and fly as fast as I possibly can towards it. It seems like an agonizing age before we finally reach it. I slow to a hover. Kelci feels even heavier when I'm not moving so fast. It's an opening between the doors, but what now? I bang against the metal with my right hand, whilst still holding on to Kelci with my left. *No one is going to hear you. No one is going to open those doors for you.* I let out a cry as I smash the doors again then run my hands along the seam between them.

'Let me kick them! Let me kick them!' screams Kelci.

She's so unsteady on my back, but I have no choice. I turn away from the door and feel a sharp push as Kelci slams her foot into the doors. They vibrate under the force, but it has made her even harder to hold on to. The lift is close now, rattling and churning just below us. How long until we are in the range of an Electron? She thwacks the doors again with her other foot this time, leaving us both reeling in the air. Everything spins, but there's an opening now, between the doors.

'Hold on!' I shout.

Kelci's whole body tightens around me and I lurch towards the opening, grabbing on to what little floor there is exposed between the doors.

'Climb off me!'

It's all we can do. I cling to the floor, with my arms and elbows, my whole body shaking with the effort. Kelci scrambles on my back and lets out a yell as she hauls herself over my shoulders, my head and onto the floor. She turns to me, on her hands and knees, then starts pulling my body through the opening. She heaves and I use what energy I have left to push myself through. We are utterly breathless, covered in sweat, dirt and oil. Kelci's expression is as astonished and battered as I feel. But there's no time, the lift will arrive any second… I grab her by the hand and we run, high-speed all the way to the atrium. I look at her as we dash along and for one moment, despite all the pain, all the exhaustion, all the shock – seeing her beside me makes a sweet wave of relief, and love, crash over me. *We are alive. We are actually alive.*

———

There are uniformed bodies strewn all over the floor, loads of them, some moaning and clutching their limbs, others silent and still. Then there are the ones still standing, too many of them, brandishing their weapons and raising their voices, just as they did before I left. I catch sight of Alisdair, deep in the uproar. He's battered and cut, covered in blood. Then there's James, brandishing two Electrons in each hand, shouting and whooping, bounding from one end of the room to the other, taking swipes at those below. He's bare-chested, with his t-shirt, now covered in blood, wrapped around his leg.

'You didn't know a Frog could be so *bad*,' he shouts to one of the guards. 'Did you? Did you?'

Lucy appears from one of the walls, her hair electric blue, diving into the action. There's Ben too, looking huge with sweat running in streams down his face, his body heaving. Heather is shooting an Electron from one of the balconies and there's another

———

figure next to her, leather-clad and chestnut-haired… Artemiz! She has a bow in her hand, and she's shooting arrows – fast, strong and unrelenting. Then there's another figure, wearing a cardigan, having a fistfight with two guards. Professor Dunedin! And close by him, lifting another guard high above his head is Kenny Collins. *How did they get here?* But there's no chance to answer that because there's a guard, hurtling towards us at full speed.

Kelci stamps her foot, sending shock waves through the ground, then she moves forward to shove the guard in the chest, hard. I run up the steps to the highest balcony and I stand there, looking down on the mayhem. I climb up onto the edge, my feet balancing precariously. I hear James call my name. Then Lucy. Then Heather, Ben, Alisdair, everyone. I place my arms at my sides. I look down and my stomach lurches. *Is this real? Can I do this?* I look down at my toes and hold my breath. There's nothing else for it. I use my feet to push off. My whole body drops down and for a moment I feel out of control. I think of the Eagles I saw at Muldoon, how they let their bodies soar and I let my body relax a little, just a little and it is enough to allow me to swoop across the space. For one short moment, it seems as though everyone in the room stops what they are doing and turns to look at me.

'Man, that girl is *flying*,' says James.

I home in on a guard firing at Ben, flying right over, snatching his Electron, then swooping back to knock him to the ground with it.

'Nina!' hollers Ben, gaping at me as I swoop past.

I smile at him for half a second then Kelci begins stamping her feet, harder and harder and it starts to feel like the floor, the walls, the ceiling, everything is shaking.

'It's time to get out of here,' shouts Artemiz.

There's a crumbling sound and I look up to see that the ceiling is beginning to crack, great slabs of concrete are beginning to fall…

'Quick,' Artemiz again, 'Follow me.'

I land, then grab Kelci and follow her. Alisdair fights his way through and joins us, rubble falling all around. James grabs Lucy, as Ben pounds his way through with Professor Dunedin and Kenny Collins. Artemiz leads, and we all follow, running as fast as we can. Finally, we reach an exit and are catapulted out into the fresh air. The whole scene, dazzlingly bright, looks completely unreal but nobody stops to look around. We run and run and run, then run some more.

We are hungry, exhausted and injured, especially James who struggles to keep up because of a huge gash on his leg. My stomach churns and groans, my skin is tight; my feet light up with pain at every step but still, we scramble through forests, over branches and boulders. There's just one point where we stop, at a stream to drink thirstily from it, relieving the sandy dryness of our throats. Eventually, the tiny image of the plane that brought us here flickers in the distance. I almost cry when I see it. We pick up the pace, knowing that there is an end, pulling ourselves along until we finally reach it.

28. Guys Like Us

Three days later, Infirmary, Muldoon Academy

My eyes fly open and I see the infirmary ceiling above my bed with its ornate swirls. My whole body is covered in sweat, as it seems to be every time I wake up since returning – enough to soak the sheets and make me feel like I've been hosed down in my sleep. I just had another dream, which hangs around in my mind as I lie here, so real I still feel trapped in it. I found myself in 'Specimens', running from room to room, from Anitar to Anitar, frozen like ice statues on their slabs.

When I tried to move them there was nothing. The last one I saw in there wasn't an Anitar at all – it was Mason with his hair swept over his face and all the colour drained from his skin. There's never anything I can do for any of them. I lie in my bed still staring at the ceiling, trying to forget the dream. I roll onto my side and see the sun streaming through the windows. I see the glorious mountains with their patches of purple, all the way down to the lake which shimmers, as though nothing ever happened.

I've been recovering here for a few days now. There's only one thing I remember about arriving here. Lady Muldoon's face, as we piled up outside the Academy, a bedraggled mess of bodies. She looked so furious I thought, for one moment, that she might refuse us entry. She didn't, thankfully. But since then I haven't seen her, I can only presume she is letting me recover, and I'm not totally sure I want to see her at all. We were all in here to begin with, all six of us, and Kelci, passing in and out of consciousness. Now there are three of us left – me, James and Kelci. Every time I wake I check to see if she's still there. Right now she's tucked up in the bed closest to mine, wisps of hair lying across the pillow with the cover right up to her face. Every time I look at her I continue to get bursts of relief in my heart.

There's colour in her face now, replacing the pastiness, the pinkness of her cheeks blossoming again. She sleeps for hours at a time and with every sleep she recovers a little more strength. I continue to stare at the ceiling tracing the outlines of the patterns. I turn my head as the door swoops open and Heather, Lucy, Ben and Alisdair enter the room. I pull myself up in my bed.

'Hello, you guys,' says Lucy, turning to me. 'Hello *Eagle girl*.'

Her hair is pink and her eyes are green. She dances towards my bed and gives me a kiss on the cheek before darting off to James who sits there propped up on a mountain of cushions, his leg all bandaged up. Kelci sits up too, clearing her throat. Heather perches herself on a wooden chair, her hair rolled up onto her head. She wears a red jumper with a furry collar that runs right up to her chin, with a pair of citrine earrings, orange-yellow and sparkling – the gemstone of the Fox. Alisdair stands next to her, close, his hands in his pockets, dressings on his face and arms. I can't stop wondering exactly *how* close until Kelci begins to speak.

'I'm glad you're all here,' she says before turning to me. 'I asked them to come. Well, Ben did on my behalf.'

Even though days have passed, it still feels weird to see Kelci with everyone. I vaguely remember introductions taking place, whilst we were on the plane. And a stern telling off from Artemiz and Professor Dunedin, who it seems came over at Kenny Collins' request – when Heather was no longer around and her charms had worn off.

'I wanted to say something to you all,' says Kelci, looking awkward.

She inhales and exhales deeply.

'Thank you. For enduring my sister for as long as you have.'

She keeps her face straight.

'Kidding. No really. I just wanted to say thank you, for getting me out of that hellhole.'

She tucks her hair behind her ears.

'If it were me, I wouldn't have been so keen to get in.'

'A place like that is no problem for guys like us,' says James, picking out a grape from the bunch at the side of his bed and popping it into his mouth. 'I tell you, you got to watch out for guys like us, we're fearsome, formidable… fun-loving too.'

Everyone smiles.

'So,' I say, 'How much trouble are we in?'

I toss the covers away and sit up cross-legged on the bed.

'Lady Muldoon is coming to see you, after us,' says Lucy.

My heart drops. I can't even imagine what kind of trouble we are in.

'What did she say to you guys?' I say, looking at Lucy who shifts uncomfortably at the side of James' bed.

'You'd better speak to her yourself,' she replies.

243

I glance around and see that, clearly, no one wants to talk about this.

'The whole place is on high alert,' says Heather. 'Extra security measures are in place. The Eagles are on twenty-four hour watch, circling the skies.'

The Eagles.

'The Tigers, Snow Leopards and Rabbits are on the ground. The Foxes are planning. Lessons have been suspended for now and no more Trainees are allowed in – no more Manifestation Program.'

I raise my eyebrows at that.

'There's been no sign that the Lotus Corporation traced us back here. That was the first worry, that they somehow followed our plane and found our location.'

'And you guys? What are you doing?'

'We told them all we could about what we saw at the compound and now we're training with the rest of them, helping our Houses.'

She breaks out into a grin.

'I spend all day with my fellow Foxes.'

My heart leaps at that. They are in their Houses… Training. Amongst it all, everything we saw on the tour.

'And the other trainees?'

'They are too.'

I feel a stab in my chest as I realise that it can't last. That this is one of the final times we will be in the same room together, for a very long time, if ever. We've blown any chance we had of staying at

Muldoon, that's for sure. Will we even be permitted to be Apprentices at *any* Anitar Academy now?

'Everyone is talking about you,' says Lucy, pointing at me.

'Me?'

'Yes. You. Silly. You've become a legend, the Trainee Eagle who got her sister back, against all odds. Mythical proportions, apparently.'

I raise my eyebrows.

'I've always dreamt of mythical proportions.'

'You should see Dominic though. He's fuming. He doesn't actually believe you're an Eagle. He thinks it's all a lie, that none of it actually happened.'

Alisdair puts his hands in his pockets.

'Don't eagles eat snakes?' he says.

I raise my eyebrows at that and as we share a look, smiling wicked smiles, a moment passes between us.

'Kelci and I need to leave soon, to see our parents,' I say.

Alisdair clears his throat.

'I'll be coming with you, for a few days,' he says.

'Huh?'

'Your parents and Lady Muldoon – they asked me to chaperone you guys home.'

Wait. Woah. My eyes nearly fall out of their sockets.

'You're coming back to New York with us?'

He nods. *My city, my home, my parents.* But wait… *Alisdair and Mason cannot be in the same place at the same time…* They just can't! I feel my cheeks getting hot.

'Me too,' says Ben.

'Oh right, ok. Yes. That will be great,' I say, desperately fiddling with the bedcovers.

Stay cool Nina, stay cool. Lucy looks at her watch.

'We'd better be off. Next duty starts in five minutes.'

They nod at her and she reaches down to embrace me, quickly tucking the hair behind my ear and whispering into it.

'Lady Muldoon asked all of us who would like to chaperone. It was Ben – and *Alisdair* – that insisted the hardest. I wanted to come! But he *insisted*.'

She gives me a wink as I look at her, open mouthed. Before I get a chance to say another word they dart out the door, leaving the room quiet once again.

Not long after, Lady Muldoon shows up by my bedside with Shadow trotting alongside. She looks particularly dramatic today, in a sweeping purple gown with silver trim. She frowns down at me, pursing her shiny lips. I reach to pat Shadow's head as he looks up at me with moonlight eyes.

'Hello Lady Muldoon,' I say nervously, pushing myself up in the bed again.

'Hello Nina.'

There's an awkward silence, then:

'My Deer tell me you are recovering well?'

I nod, touching the cut on my head that is beginning to settle.

'Of course,' she goes on. 'You wouldn't need to be recovering from anything, had you stuck to the rules and not gone gallivanting across Europe on an unsanctioned mission.'

'I wouldn't have my sister back if I hadn't gone,' I say, trying my best not to sound too surly.

She won't like it if I'm proud or sulky, I know that, but it's true, isn't it? She nods slowly.

'I do wish Nina, that you had come to me. This mission has accelerated the process of rescuing the captives to a rate I'm not sure we can handle.'

But we have to handle it.

'We saw Anitars in that place, dying and abused,' I say. 'It was unbelievable.'

She nods again.

'I have been informed of those things. And believe me when I tell you that nothing is of greater importance than those who have been captured. Our future depends on it. I believe you met Max Wilder whilst you were there?'

'Yes,' I say. 'He knows who I am, he knows my parents, he knows everything about my life.'

'He has eyes and ears all over the world. He is building his empire at a formidable rate.'

'I know. I saw.'

'Max was a Trainee of mine, once.'

'He was?'

'Yes, and he had lots of promise too. I've rarely seen anyone as utterly determined to excel as Max Wilder. Extremely ambitious. He wanted to manifest, wanted a place at Muldoon; that young man wanted it all. But he was so very intent to prove himself, so competitive, so *eager...* He was always the one at the front, pushing himself, but as others began to manifest around him, he found it harder to compete. I tried to coach him through it, but it wasn't to be. I was sad for him - I knew how *very much* he wanted it.'

I can't help thinking that I almost ended up down the same route, the 'never happened' route. How many others have found themselves at the end of the same path? I wonder if Max ever found out that I manifested, under his roof, in his compound. I'm certain he hated it, if he ever did find out. The thought almost makes me smile.

'He was on the same Manifestation Program as your mother and father,' says Lady Muldoon. 'They were all on the program together. Your parents, the Bonfants and Max. He had his Memory Erased but somehow… it appears there are residual memories.'

'So that explains how he knows them. And it's true that Terence Bonfant's parents are Anitars too?'

'Yes,' she says, with a regretful look.

'Did you know about Terence? That he was manifesting as a Horse?'

It's bad enough that my parents knew and never told me… Lady Muldoon looks thoughtful for a moment.

'You ought to have been informed.'

She's not apologising. *I ought to have been informed.* I trace the edge of my pillow with the tip of my finger.

'Why didn't the Bonfants tell Terence they're Anitars?'

'Some parents simply choose not to …'

I shake my head, slowly, thinking of Terence. I could never tell him the whole truth of my family, and he never knew the whole truth of his. But he's still with me, he's always with me.

'Max said a lot of things,' I go on. 'About the way Anitars operate, all the secrecy. He thinks we should be open about what goes on.'

Lady Muldoon's face hardens.

'You have seen that Max Wilder is not a man to be trusted. Being open is not an option. Not at this time. There may come a point in the future where those of us who have gifts can come forward but right now, it is a lengthy road to reach that point.'

I sigh. Before I came here, I probably would have agreed with Max. That telling everyone, putting it all out in the open, was the best option. Make it so I don't have to hide the truth from my own boyfriend anymore. But something about the memory of the captured Anitars in that compound makes me think that the world is not ready for the truth. Lady Muldoon leans forward, and sits down on the edge of my bed.

'Nina,' she says. 'Quite frankly, what you did was stupid.'

Here it comes.

'Extremely stupid. Leaving the Academy, taking other Trainees with you. Risking their futures, their lives… Risking your own life. Deliberately manipulating Kenny Collins, and in such an *unseemly manner*. I gather that was Miss Jackson's idea which is no surprise but you were just as much a part of it all the same. Not to mention the fact that Max Wilder and his 'friends' had an opportunity to escape.'

My heart sinks into my stomach. What if more Anitars die because of me? Matias wouldn't have died…

'What happens to us now?' I say, my voice small.

I watch as she strokes Shadow's head as he nuzzles his big nose next to her leg. She turns to me, catching my gaze in hers.

'Now, Nina,' she says. 'You take your sister home. And you see your family once again.'

There's enough finality in her voice to make me feel gloomy. I can't help wondering if this is the last conversation I will ever have with Lady Muldoon.

29. Food Stalls & Hot Dogs

The next day, Muldoon Academy

It doesn't take me long to pack. Just that one small bag I was allowed. A little while later, alongside Ben and Alisdair, we say our goodbyes to Lucy, James and Heather, all of us promising that we will be together again soon. But honestly, I don't know how that will happen. It feels like this is the last time I will ever see Muldoon Island. I'm on the outside now, I've done something Lady Muldoon can never forgive. And I can't even blame her. I knew what I was doing, we all did. But to leave Lucy, James and Heather behind makes me want to sob, after everything we've been through.

I think of Lucy, the first time we met, huddled together at the induction talk, how even then she was saving me from myself when she didn't let me say something stupid in front of everyone. I think of James who has been my friend, unquestioning, since that first day too. I'm so glad that he doesn't have to go back to his uncle Steve's, that he will find a place as an Apprentice, somewhere, even if it is thousands of miles away from me. And then there's Heather. The girl I never dreamed would risk her life to help me. But in the end, that's exactly what she did. There's still Ben, and Alisdair, for the next few days, and I am grateful for that.

It doesn't seem to take long to fly back over the ocean, much less than it took to get here and soon enough I am standing on American soil, looking at the exact same car that brought me to the plane just a few short weeks ago. Ben, Alisdair and Kelci bundle out and Kenny Collins pokes his head out of the cabin window.

'Welcome home.'

He winks at me.

'Thanks, Kenny.'

He seems to have forgiven us. I don't think I would take it so well, but Kenny seems just fine. I watch as Alisdair strides out to the water's edge that separates us from Manhattan. I watch him taking in the skyline, wearing a battered leather jacket and dark jeans. *A Snow Leopard in New York.* I can't tell from his expression if he is impressed. Kenny bangs down the steps of the plane and swings open the baggage compartment whilst Alisdair wanders back to join us. We gather round and look at the mountain of bags, the majority of which are mine, the big flowery ones. It looks like they've been breeding whilst we've been apart.

'You brought these to the program?' says Alisdair.

He looks amused.

'Yes, I did.'

'Did you bring your actual wardrobe?' says Kelci.

'Thank you, Kelci,' I say. 'But we're not all light travellers.'

Images of boiler suits, fire suits and all-in-one rubber suits flash through my mind. What had I been expecting? But I shrug my shoulders. *It's not like I'm going to give up everything in those bags just because I manifested, nowhere does it say an Anitar has to give up all their worldly goods.*

252

Meanwhile Ben, Alisdair and Kenny grab the luggage whilst I think about how, with my strength returned, I could probably carry them all in one go. There's quite a bit of pushing and pulling to manoeuvre everything into the back of the car and it needs all three of them, bums shoving down on the boot to get the lid to close. We pile into the car and I find myself in the right seat at the back, in the exact same place I was on the outwards journey. I could never have dreamt then, that I would return like this. Kelci is perched in the middle with Ben to her left and Alisdair sits in the front. Soon we're speeding over the Brooklyn Bridge, my favourite, and as we arrive on the island and the bustle of the city lights up around us, Ben bursts into song.

'New York! New York! I want to be a part of it…'

He sounds even more Swedish than usual. I laugh.

'Come on everybody. Sing along!' he bellows.

Kelci looks at him, horrified. But he tries to get her swaying in time with him.

'Oh come on,' he says. 'Don't you ever let your hairs go free?'

She wrinkles up her nose.

'I think you mean… let my *hair down. Don't I ever let my hair down.*'

'It is much better to let your hairs go free, Kelci.'

I giggle and glance towards Alisdair whose head is turned towards the window. The people, the flashing signs, the shops that sell everything you could ever need, the food stalls, the hot dog stalls, the endless stream of yellow taxis. A whir of movement. Avenues stretching on for miles, buildings reaching up, up, up. *I want to know what he thinks of it all.* Has he ever been somewhere like this before?

How does a Snow Leopard feel, surrounded by this many people? The streets become more familiar as we get closer to home – we pass the dog park with the big dogs running up and down in one part, and the little dogs tottering about in the other. We're nearly there and I feel a ripple of nerves when I think of seeing my parents again. I feel another ripple, which turns into more of a lurch, when I think of seeing Mason. Finally we arrive in front of the house and jump out. Alisdair and Ben look up and down the palatial street.

'Wow,' says Ben.

I turn to the rooftop where I last saw Terence. It looks completely different now with the walls painted white and bunches of white and purple flowers overflowing the rim of the garden. The bags are gathered and the five of us position ourselves on the top step in front of the door. Home sweet home… at last. It feels weird to be knocking on my own front door. Kelci and I hold our breaths. The door opens and there stand Mum and Dad, with looks of love and relief on their faces. They open up their arms and hug us so tightly we can't move.

———

For the last 24 hours, Mum and Dad have barely left our sides. All four of us Gregorys have been sort of clinging together like one of us might be ripped away at any moment, with Ben and Alisdair hovering at the sides. Mum and Dad keep staring at me, inspecting my eyes and my face, unable to get over the fact that I am now an Anitar. It calms me to see them begin to look more like their old selves again, the dark circles falling away, their mouths upturning. They tell us how they can eat again, breathe again – the relief at not searching, searching, searching every moment of every day. They broach the subject of my manifesting as though walking on eggshells – presumably because they think I may explode when they ask me about it, as I always used to.

Yet when I tell them about manifesting as an Eagle they can hardly stop themselves from bursting. Mum goes on and on about the House of Eagles and how 'in her day' it was the most incredible school (second to the Tigers of course) and how she used to go and watch them practice just for the sheer beauty of it. We haven't discussed the dark side yet, the realities of where Kelci has been all this time, the nitty-gritty of how we got her out of there. For this first day it seems ok for us to simply be here.

Ben and Alisdair have been welcomed into the fold with open arms. My parents already knew that 'these two boys' were part of the mission that recovered Kelci and that automatically makes them heroes. Mum keeps looking at them with great interest and mouthing to Kelci and I how gorgeous they are, which is deeply mortifying. She brings them tea and biscuits at every opportunity and neither of them are impolite enough to say no so they constantly sit there holding onto various types of biscuits and sipping from steaming mugs. Mum looks long and hard at us sometimes, as though she is working it all out in her head. She looks at Alisdair too.

'A real Snow Leopard if ever I saw one,' she says, at one point.

This makes me almost melt into the carpet with humiliation and all I can do is pray he didn't hear. She is sensitive enough to give him the bedroom right at the top of the house, away from everyone else, where he can stay undisturbed. He has already disappeared up there quite a few times. Right now, we are in the games room, which is on the first floor of the house. It's just the four of us for the first time – Kelci, Ben, Alisdair and me. I decorated this room a couple of years ago and it has a distinctly feminine air about it. We sit in plush little armchairs, covered in flowery pink material, but they are too small for Ben and Alisdair. I insist we play Cluedo, my personal favourite. I keep winning which I can tell silently maddens Alisdair. We play and laugh. As we chat, Kelci nudges me.

'What?' I say.

She clears her throat.

'Mason is here,' she says. 'I can hear him. He's chatting to Dad in the kitchen.'

Everyone turns to look at me.

'Who's Mason?' says Ben, innocently.

I cross my hands on my lap and sit up.

'Mason… Mason is my… he's my… my… friend.'

'He's Nina's boyfriend,' says Kelci, offhand.

She doesn't seem to have noticed my obvious discomfort. Eyebrows shoot up, including Alisdair's, ever so slightly.

'Oh,' says Ben. 'I didn't know you had a boyfriend.'

'Yes,' I say. 'He's very nice. I had better go and say hello.'

Very nice? He's very nice? I jump out of my seat, dash towards the door and dive out of the room.

30. In My Heart

Gregory Residence, New York

I approach the door to the kitchen. I can hear him. The sound of his voice reminds me of warm honey sinking into hot buttered toast – familiar and exciting, all at the same time. But to hear it again, after all that has happened, makes me nervous. He thinks I've spent the last few weeks by my sick aunt's bedside. The fact that I lied to him makes my stomach churn. Mason has always been sweet to me, he looked out for me in my dark days, he didn't judge me, he understood. *I will never forget that.*

I take a deep breath and walk through the door, into the kitchen. Mason and Dad turn to me and a moment of silence descends. Dad raises his eyebrows, takes a last sip from his BEST DAD EVER mug, then gets up from his stool. Mason sits on a stool too, with a hand on an expensive looking box on the table next to him. He turns to look at me, beaming. I forgot how bright his eyes are. His hair is slightly longer, and even more swished over to the side. He flicks it back then jumps up from his stool, whilst Dad shifts his eyes between the two of us.

'I'll just be in my study,' Dad says, moving towards the door.

He gives me a kiss on the forehead as he goes.

'Baby girl,' says Mason, reaching his hand towards my chin tenderly. 'You're home.'

The touch of his hand is soft and light and it sends a shiver along my neck.

'Hi, Mason.'

His smile is warm, open, like sunlight streaming through the window on a bright morning. He sidles up to me and slips his hand around my waist, then leans in towards me. I want to kiss him, to melt against his soft lips, to let myself be held in his arms. *Wouldn't that be a sweet reward after everything that has happened? To let myself forget it all for a second?* But as his hand slips along the back of my neck, underneath my hair, I step back, before he has a chance to plant the kiss on my lips. He scrunches his eyes and peers into my face.

'Wow,' he says. 'You look *different*.'

He moves back as if to get a better look.

'I am,' I reply, quietly. 'Different, I mean.'

He looks me up and down.

'I can't put my finger on it...'

I can only hope my eyes aren't flashing; I still can't control that fully.

'Your hair,' he says. 'Did you colour it? And your eyes? Are you wearing contacts?'

He comes in close, so close I feel his breath on my face.

'Damn, honestly, you look hot. What have they been feeding you in London?'

I give a self-conscious smile.

'The food was not that great, actually,' I say, thinking of the Trainee canteen.

'Don't worry, I'll take you for some real New York food soon. There's this amazing new sushi bar on East 77th. Oh, and I found you a great new tea place too. You'll love it.'

He's like a puppy that just wants to play.

'Sounds good,' I say.

He pushes the box towards me.

'Hey, I took a trip to the shop where we got those peach shoes for you. Did you wear them whilst you were away?'

I clear my throat.

'Yes,' I say. 'I wore them.'

Until they got covered in mud and thrown into the bottom of my bag. I unwrap the hot pink bow on the box and it feels seductively smooth underneath my fingers. I open the lid and inside lies a dress, which I pull out and hold up in front of me. It's silky, dusty pink, floating like magic in the air. I place it down on the table, and thank him.

'Do you like it?' he says.

'It's gorgeous.'

'You can wear it, when we go for sushi…'

Once upon a time, this is all I ever wanted: a silk dress, a beautiful boy and a promise of sushi. But now I can't even begin to comprehend how I feel. Everything has changed. I can't tell him the truth, or at least I don't think I can. Lucy said that her mother wasn't an Anitar and her Dad was so maybe it can be done… Perhaps I could have both worlds, somehow. But then there's Muldoon… My new friends… A pang of guilt rises. Suddenly the vague sound of laughter travels into the kitchen. Mason tilts his head, with an inquisitive smile.

'Who's that?' he says.

My cheeks begin to colour.

'That's Kelci,' I say, too quickly.

'Sounds like a guy to me,' he says. 'Or a few guys even?'

'Oh yes, guys?' I say. 'Kelci's friends.'

'Kelci has friends?' he says, raising his eyebrows. 'I have to see this. Kelci has guy friends?'

He starts pulling me by the arm.

'Come on,' he says. 'You have to introduce me.'

I feel panicked at the prospect of Mason going up there.

'Oh no, we should leave them alone. You know Kelci. She's touchy about that kind of thing.'

'That's exactly why we should say hi, it'll be fun,' he says, 'maybe I know them.'

He tugs my arm and leads me out of the kitchen.

'You definitely don't know these guys,' I say, reluctantly following him upstairs.

He drags me along to the games room, following the laughter. We walk in together and immediately the laughter stops. Ben and Alisdair are perched on the flowery chairs and Kelci sits cross-legged on the floor.

'Hey, guys,' I say, my face beet red by now. 'This is... This is Mason.'

'Hi,' says Mason, looking at everyone.

'This is Ben,' I say.

Ben nods, smiles and introduces himself. For a minute I worry that he will stand up and show his full size but he stays sat down and puts his hair behind his ears instead. He's wearing a red and blue knitted jumper covered in snowflake patterns and it does nothing to slim him down. Babs lounges on his knee, purring. Despite a lifetime of indifference, Babs adores him more than anyone ever, even Mum; she just can't get enough of his Swedish baby talk.

'And this is Alisdair,' I say, my stomach in knots.

Alisdair doesn't speak, he nods instead and looks at Mason through what appear to be mildly suspicious eyes.

'Into Cluedo, huh?' says Mason, nodding at the board game in front of Alisdair. 'That's cool. I like video games myself but you know, each man to his own.'

Alisdair frowns slightly. My mind scrambles for a reason to leave.

'We'd better hit the road,' I say, turning to Mason.

Ben looks puzzled and turns to Kelci.

'Why would they hit a road?'

Kelci rolls her eyes and begins to explain, whilst I drag Mason back out of the door.

'Bye!' he says, on the way out.

I pull him through the hallway, down the stairs and out of the house. As far away as I can.

'The blonde guy is massive and what, he's Swedish? Where did she pick him up from? And the other guy... *Damn,* he's frosty.'

I don't even know where to walk, so long as it's away from the house. Mason drops into an easy stroll and puts his arm around my shoulders. I need time to *think* about it all. I can't hurt him. I cannot hurt the guy that stuck up for me and bought me frozen yoghurt that Sunday in *Charlotte's*. But every time I lie to him like this, I feel like I am hurting him already. Maybe I should just tell him the truth, then deal with whatever comes… It all spins around in my mind and I barely even notice where we end up.

It's nighttime now. Calm and dark. And I'm alone, thankfully. I sit on the ledge of the open window of the games room gazing out at New York in all her magnificence. Candles in the room, almost burnt out, continue to flicker. The TV keeps shining, the images of a soundless movie. Kelci announced to us, after I came home, that we were going to have one of our lounge nights. I wasn't really in any mood for this particular tradition of ours, which has taken place since we were old enough to set up the games room with mountains of cushions and blankets. But I went along with it, because Kelci hasn't insisted on a lounge night in a long time.

Alisdair sat there, wedged in between two enormous pink cushions and Ben munched on marshmallows, gazing at the screen. It was kind of fun but I couldn't shake off a growing sense of unease. When I look at Kelci's face, I see it in her too, and it's definitely there in Alisdair and Ben. It lurks in the background in all of us like a shadow, a reminder of what we went through. We all saw what is going on. And now as I sit here in the darkness whilst everyone sleeps, I can't help wonder what will become of us. What will become of the captured Anitars? The thought of them tugs at my heart. What will happen when Ben and Alisdair leave New York the day after tomorrow? What is going on at Muldoon right now? I look back out the window – back out at New York. The wind caresses my face. I sense the drop below and know that there's nothing left to do but rise up and stand on the windowsill. I've wanted to do this since I came home. *It's time to fly.*

It doesn't take long to get up here, above everything, the whole of Manhattan below me. It's a cloudless, moonless night – nothing like the mountain-lined, star-filled nights of Muldoon Island – the darkness I soar through has a yellow glow from the ocean of lights below. The wind rushes along my bare arms, against my stomach, my hair flies free and my lungs fill with air so fast it makes me gasp. I head first to Central Park swooping far above it, making out the trees like dots and the winding paths and rows of skyscrapers all around. It's all mine: every twinkling window, every road, every building. I fly down over Midtown, right along Park Avenue, until I reach the Empire State Building, glistening like a candle-filled birthday cake, allowing the energy of the city to flow right through me.

I get to the bottom of Manhattan and see her there – standing majestically, holding her torch high with that noble look on her face. The Statue of Liberty. I keep on flying, right across the water and I don't stop until I get right up and land like a fly on her crown. I sit down, dangling my legs over the side. I really am like a fly resting on her, but somehow, I'm comfortable. I settle into the quiet and gaze out at the great bundle of skyscrapers that is Manhattan sitting across the water.

The thought of the Lotus Corporation people, their belief that they're actually doing something good gnaws away at me. I may not know how my future will play out right now – where I will train, *if* I will train, or who with - but the one thing I do know is that I *need* to fight them. I just can't live with myself if I don't do *something*. As I stare out at the scene I long to see my friends again and I wonder what Lucy is doing right this second, what colour combination she has going on, what she would think of New York. I think of Lady Muldoon swooping about the Academy. I think of Shadow, and of Artemiz. James, Heather… I really don't know what my future holds but I know that the shape of it has changed.

I watch my legs, swinging from side to side, and see the murky waters below. Terence and I came here a few times, to take one of those cheesy boat rides around the statue. I remember it fondly. We must have been 14 the last time, giggling and crunching on M&Ms. It is strange, and sad, to think that he and I could have been Anitars together and I am sorry, so sorry, that I didn't know he was manifesting. I didn't know and he didn't know, and in the end, there was little I could do to stop him from taking his own life that night. I still miss him … and I always will but I will make sure he stays with me for whatever lies ahead. I will take him with me, wherever I go, *in my heart.* He would never have wanted me to hide away from life, from what I could become, because of what happened that night, not the Terence I knew. He loved me for who I was. I smile to myself, knowing that he would love the drama of me being up here, at night, and if he knew I could fly… Well… I think he would love that too. With that thought in my mind, I stand up and balance myself on the outer most edge and look across the sea. I speak out clearly, into the darkness.

'This one is for you, Terence Bonfant, my sweetest friend.'

With that, I shoot high into the sky, from the edge of Lady Liberty's crown, curving over the waters.

31. Jammy Dodgers

Gregory Residence, New York

Later that evening, Alisdair sits next to me on our rooftop, holding a steaming mug of strawberry tea to his lips. I found him here when I landed, prowling around alone. His elbow and shoulder are right next to mine. We sit here next to each other on the same bench I tried so hard to lift, just after Kelci had been taken. The same one Artemiz had rescued me from that day in the rain. It was wet then, and cold, but now the air is balmy and there is a faint smell of doughnuts on a gentle breeze.

'Thank you,' I blurt out. 'I mean, for helping to rescue Kelci. You risked a lot, to do that. And I appreciate it.'

'I'm glad I did,' he says. 'Now I know what we're up against.'

'It's bad, isn't it?' I say. 'What we saw.'

His eyes scan the endless rooftops. No words are necessary. He places his mug on the garden table and takes a jammy dodger from the flowery plate. He leans back, snug against my arm and takes a bite out of the jam filled biscuit. There's a long pause as I look at him, trying to read his face. As he works his way through it, I can't help wondering how one guy can look so good whilst eating a jammy dodger, but then I stop myself for thinking such a thing.

'So, what's next for us all?' I say.

He turns to me and I notice that, up close, somehow he still smells of fresh air and forest.

'You mean the six of us? I guess we go on to become Apprentices, somewhere. I doubt Lady Muldoon will take us, after what we did. The best we can hope for is entrance to one of the other Academies.'

Does he feel the same dull ache at the thought of not being part of it all at Muldoon? At being separated?

'It's not right, us all going our different ways. We're a good team,' I say.

'I'll probably end up in the Asian Academy,' he goes on. 'It's supposed to be the best for Snow Leopards. Apart from Muldoon of course.'

The ache grows. To not see him. I almost feel tears pricking my eyes, but embarrassment stops them from coming.

'The six of us... Split apart... After all we went through...' I say.

'We'll find each other again.'

The side of his foot touches mine. He turns and looks at me and I look back at him. Does he want to say more? Does it bother him that within days we could be on separate continents? His expression has softened, that's for sure. A familiar rattling noise starts up and I immediately look towards the door of the roof garden. It wobbles a bit more, then crashes open and Kelci stands there in her dressing gown. She pushes her glasses up her nose, then announces:

'There's news from Muldoon.'

We race downstairs, Kelci first then Alisdair and me close behind, all the way to the kitchen. We find Mum and Dad in silk kimonos standing there and Ben in a big black furry dressing gown with matching slippers. Where did he get them from? Mum eyes up Alisdair and me as we roll in, fully dressed.

'Where were you two?'

'On the roof. Having a cup of tea.'

'What were you doing on the roof?'

She peers at us.

'Having a cup of tea,' I say. 'Mum, please. Not now.'

'At this time of night?'

All eyes are on me.

'I was out flying, and Alisdair was on the roof when I came back.'

Kelci clears her throat loudly and gives an insistent look towards the expensive looking envelope in Dad's hand.

'I can explain later, guys. *Please*, tell us what's going on.'

Dad puts his free hand on Mum's shoulder and whispers something in her ear. She nods reluctantly.

'Shall we get down to business?' he says, clearing his throat and tightening the belt around his dressing gown.

'Yes!' we all say.

'This has just arrived by special courier. A young Frog delivered it... all the way from Muldoon.'

'A Frog? What? From Muldoon? Oh my God.'

268

My voice has risen to a high pitch. The others are murmuring and shuffling.

'He said specifically that we *all* needed to be here when it is read out.'

I hold my breath and stare at Dad's face. He opens the envelope and begins to read.

'Dear Nina, Alisdair and Ben,

As I have already expressed to each of you individually, I am extremely disappointed by your blatant disregard for the Academy's rules. Your unsanctioned mission was both irresponsible and selfish. We can only take heart that one of you is not seriously injured, captured or dead.'

I gulp. I can almost hear Lady Muldoon saying the words, hear the scorn in her voice. Nervous looks pass between us.

You may have only had a small amount of training, but you all know what is expected from you. As Anitars we must work as a united whole. Without that, there is no trust. Without that, we are all at great risk. Your actions, and those of your fellow Trainees James, Heather and Lucy simply cannot be condoned. And for that there must be a punishment.'

A sense of despondency pervades. She wants us all punished. Dad looks up at us, his face grave, then looks back down at the letter and continues to read.

'However, as Principal of Muldoon it is not only my duty to enforce rules. It is also my duty to recognise the qualities in our Trainees and Apprentices that deserve acclaim. Despite the methods resorted to, you have shown that you can act as a highly effective team, under high levels of pressure. You have displayed perseverance, skill and determination. You have all displayed strength of will and

courage. At this moment in our history, this is exactly what is needed. We are experiencing an even greater emergency than we anticipated and these are extraordinary circumstances. Thus, we would request that the four of you return to Muldoon Island to complete the Manifestation Program.

Yours Sincerely
Lady Muldoon

There's a long pause as Dad stops reading and folds the letter back up, carefully. Nobody says a word as it sinks in. *We're going back. We're all going back.* Lucy. James. Heather. We will be together again. All of us. Grins begin to form on the faces of Kelci, Ben and Alisdair. I'm smiling too… I want us to stick together… Muldoon Academy… The Eagles… But then I catch sight of the box Mason gave to me, still there on the table, the pink ribbons lying on top and there's a pang in my heart as it dawns on me that this means he and I will be apart again… Meanwhile Ben has his arms wrapped around Kelci who is beaming the biggest smile I've seen on her face in a long time. Even Alisdair is *almost* laughing and I giggle as Ben starts waltzing Kelci around, chiming:

'We're going back, we're going back.'

After a few more moments I notice that there's a distinct lack of excitement emanating from Mum and Dad's side of the room. They are looking at each other with frowns on their faces, so I step toward them. They turn to look at me with concern in their eyes. They don't even need to tell me how they feel, I already know. They don't want to lose us. And I don't want to lose them either.

'This is our chance to help,' I say to them, gently.

'*Even greater emergency than we anticipated,*' says my Mum, who has taken the letter and is reading from it.

'We are Anitars now,' I say.

'I know,' she says, earnest. 'And that's the most incredible thing… You know it's all I ever wanted. It's just, after what we've all just been through. The situation, the danger…'

'I know,' I say. 'I *really* know.'

They both nod, torn looks on their faces. Mum takes a deep breath, raises her chin and looks me right in the eyes.

'You know, Nina. I used to think that you were just like me. But now I know I was wrong. *You are just like you.*'

She wraps her arms around me.

'On the day we brought you into the world,' she says, into my ear. 'We knew then what could happen. Same with Kelci. We knew exactly what our sweet, gurgling little babies could be destined for.'

'And now the time is here,' says Dad. 'It's scary for us, but we're proud.'

Mum nods, wipes a tear from her eye and smiles, then touches Dad's hand on her shoulder.

'Part of me will always think of you as our precious babies, but then the other part of me knows that you are *not* babies, anything but. We have always tried to bring you up in a way that prepares you. It's just now that it's here well… Wow.'

Dad strokes the hair back from her shoulder.

'But we won't hold you back. We always knew that times like these could come and now that they are here, well, I am astonished at how wonderful you both are.'

I feel Kelci at my side. Together we drop into their arms and I close my eyes, feeling the soft fur of Babs as she circles around our ankles.

- THE END -

Author's Note

I would like to take this opportunity to say a big thank you for choosing to read ANIMAL. The writing of this book has been a huge labour of love and I am excited to finally have it out there and in the hands of readers like you!

If you would like more stories from me please sign up for my newsletter where you will be the first to hear about new releases:

www.gsbanks.com

Acknowledgements

I would like to say thank you to my mum who has believed in me as a writer since I was a little girl. Also to my dad who was the first to bring stories alive when he read them out so vividly to us as children. I love you both so much.

Thank you to my auntie Kathleen who has been an avid reader of my stories for a long time and has always given me such love and encouragement. Thank you to everyone who has supported me on Wattpad, especially those very early followers such as Charles Moonstone, Bernadett David and Lotti Gosar. You guys have been cheering me on for years!

Thank you to Wayne Clingman and Catherine Hardy for being so lovely and helpful. I also greatly appreciate those people who were beta readers for ANIMAL, your feedback has been invaluable: Madara Liepa, Kayleigh Paley, Darby Laurvick, Sara Kemper, Rebecca Garrett, Holly Dunbar, Nairi Simonyan, Allyson Brink, Emma Ortiz and Kaylinn Manuel.

Last of all I would like to say an enormous heart-shaped thank you to my best friend and husband Matt Brown who has been here, by my side throughout this entire journey, giving encouragement and feedback and love at all the right moments. Also to my son Arran who inspires me to be the best I can be. This book was possible because of you guys.

Printed in Great Britain
by Amazon